Mapton Wedding Daze

Sam Maxfield

Published by On the Wing Press
'Mapton Wedding Daze' copyright © 2022.
Samantha Maxfield

Samantha Maxfield asserts the right to be identified as the author of this work in accordance with the Copyright Designs and Patents Act 1988. All rights reserved.

This book is a work of fiction. Any references to historical events, real people, or real locales are used fictitiously. Other names, characters, places and incidents are products of the author's imagination, and any resemblance to actual events or locales or persons, living or dead, is entirely coincidental.

For Gail Burns and her wonderful Alys (singer extraordinaire)

Readers can download a FREE Mapton Starter Bundle by subscribing to my newsletter at sammaxfieldbooks.com

Wedding Plans

'I thought you'd set the date for May 27th, and booked the registry office.'

'I changed me mind,' Gina said. 'I want a June wedding in the church.'

'But you're not religious,' Stella said.

'I am,' Gina said.

'Since when?'

Gina wriggled round in her seat to glare at Stella, who was buckled into the Rover's immaculate back seat.

'I might not be a church-goer, Stella, but I'll have you know I'm a very spiritual person.'

Stella laughed. 'Since when?' she repeated.

'Always,' Gina said, with dignity. 'I don't talk about it; it's private and personal.'

'Rubbish,' said Stella. 'You just want a big traditional wedding in a church.'

'Well, why shouldn't I?' Gina burst out. 'It's the only bleedin' wedding I'll ever have. Why shouldn't I get to do it proper? I don't want no poxy register office, and neither does George. Do yer, George?' she said, poking him in the ribs.

'Don't do that, love,' George said mildly.' Not when I'm driving.'

George drove between forty to forty five miles an hour at all times, except in a thirty mile zone where he dropped down to twenty just to be on the safe side. They were doing twenty now.

'I've always been C of E, Stella,' George said, smiling at her in the rear view mirror. 'I admit it's been a few years since I last went to church, but I used to go every year at Easter and Christmas. I'd much prefer a church wedding too.'

'See,' Gina was triumphant. 'It ain't just about me.'

'Fine,' Stella relented. 'But why am I here?'

They drew up to a pretty stone church set in a little green just on the edge of Mapton.

'I thought you'd like to see it,' Gina replied.

'I've seen it loads of times,' Stella said.

'Yeah, to drive past,' Gina said. 'But I'll bet you've never been inside it.'

Stella had to admit she hadn't but she still found it hard to believe Gina had invited her along just to admire the inside of a church. Sharing the aesthetic delights of religious architecture wasn't something she'd associate with Gina. She knew her grandmother well enough to suspect there had to be another motive for asking her along.

Still, she decided to hold her tongue.

St Bartholomew (or St Bart's as everyone called it) had served Mapton and Siltby for hundreds of years. It wasn't the only church in town but it was the place to go for a picturesque wedding. It also boasted the nearest thing to a hillock in the Parish, which, aside from the flood embankment that led up to the sea-promenade, was flat for miles around.

No one knew how the grassy knoll got there, or why it had been created, but it rose out of the church yard like a gift to wedding photographers, with its scattering of daffodils in the spring and daisies in the summer, not to mention its lack of the gravestones that crammed the rest of the grounds. It was the perfect place for wedding-party shots, with just enough space for the various groupings of clan members to line up with the bride and groom.

It was a beautiful, old church, Stella thought as she stepped out of the car, but other than the big moments – christenings, weddings, funerals – and the mother of them all, Christmas, she wondered how many people filled its regular services.

She and husband Rick were atheists. Gerta, their three year old, naturally hadn't been christened and Gina had never brought it up. As far as she knew neither herself nor her mother had been christened, and in all the years she'd known her grandmother, Gina had not stepped into a church.

'Have you ever been in a church?' Stella asked, as Gina came round the car, leaving George still fussing in the driver's seat. He liked to check the handbrake was on a few times before getting out.

'O' course I have!'

'When?'

'I'm always having to do things as mayor, yer know that. I've done three church events already.' It was true, against all odds Gina Pontin had become mayor of Mapton.

'But before you became mayor? You never went when I was a kid.'

Gina looked uncomfortable. 'I had to go when I were in school – Christmas carols and the like. Harvest festival.'

She made 'harvest festival' sound like a dirty word.

'Anyway,' she said, catching hold of Stella's arm. 'I'm doing this church wedding thing for George. Don't make a fuss about it.'

Stella squeezed her hand. 'All right, I won't.'

George joined them and they wove their way along the path to the church.

After the September sunshine the interior of the church appeared gloomy.

Stella said in a low voice. 'I'll look round while you see the vicar.'

'No, come with us.' Gina grabbed her arm.

'Why?'

'I might need a witness,' Gina said.

Stella looked alarmed. 'A witness? Why, what are you going to do?'

'Nothing,' said Gina.

'Let her look around,' George said in a church whisper. 'This is about us, love.'

'No, I want Stella with me,' Gina insisted. She hadn't dropped into a church whisper.

Stella eyed Gina suspiciously. George looked bewildered.

'Ahem.' A man cleared his throat loudly and they all jumped.

The vicar, who'd appeared out of his office at the end of the aisle, started towards them.

He'd only been in place for two months. The old vicar, who'd been rather ancient, had passed away the previous year leaving the church, and its dwindling flock, in the hands of visiting priests until a permanent replacement was found.

Stella had heard about the new vicar but never seen him until now. He was as handsome as the gossips said, with startling blue eyes ringed by dark lashes and the thick hair of an American soap star.

'I told you he don't look like a vicar,' Gina whispered, still far too loudly in Stella's opinion.

Stella gave her a sharp nudge.

'Ah, Mayor Pontin and Mr Wentworth, my assistant noted your appointment.'

He looked at Stella, smiling. 'And this is?'

'Stella, me granddaughter. Although people always think she's me daughter because I look so young. I brought her up after her parents died in a car crash.'

Stella stood abashed, feeling a little embarrassed; Gina had never introduced her in that way before. She felt the vicar's gaze on her.

'I'm sorry to hear that. It was very good of you,' the vicar said.

Gina nodded sadly. 'You do what you can, don't you? Your Christian duty.'

At this, Stella almost fell over. Since when had Gina been interested in any 'duty' never mind Christian?

She tried to catch Gina's eye but Gina was too busy looking saintly. Then Stella understood. Gina assumed that to get married in a church she had to impress the vicar. She stifled back a laugh.

'Well, I'm very pleased to meet you, Stella,' the vicar said, holding her with his blue eyes. 'Are you a church goer?'

Before Stella could answer, Gina jumped in. 'We used to be, didn't we, duck? We used to go a lot when we lived in Nottingham. St Mary's, remember in the Lace Market?'

What Stella remembered about St Mary's was that it was a beautiful church set in the tranquil old churchyard that she used to use as a cut through on her way to her Saturday job in the Broadmarsh shopping centre. That was as close as she got to going to church, and she certainly didn't remember Gina stepping foot in it.

Now Gina linked her arm through hers in a seemingly affectionate way, but the tension of her muscle was iron.

Suppressing a giggle, Stella forced her face into a serious expression. 'Every Sunday, Grandma,' she said. 'Just like you said we should.'

Gina gripped her a little tighter.

The vicar was still gazing at her with those stunning eyes. 'But you don't now? I haven't seen you in here before – any of you.'

'Oh, we always come at Christmas,' Gina lied. 'And I do a lot of church things in my capacity as mayor.'

'Of course,' the vicar said. 'Easter and Christmas are extremely important but it's the regular services that show true commitment don't you think?'

'Which is exactly what Gina – I mean Grandma – was saying to me just last night,' Stella said, squeezing back on Gina's arm. 'In order to get married in St Bart's she feels it's only right to attend every Sunday to show her commitment. Too many people just want the pomp of a church wedding but forget about the real meaning. Isn't that right ...' She turned to Gina. 'Grandma?'

'Excellent idea,' said the vicar. 'That would be wonderful. I need to boost the numbers attending Sunday service and the mayor's attendance would set a great example. And we are in complete agreement, Stella. Too many hypocrites want the romance of a church wedding but not the commitment to Christ's work.'

'That's not true of Gina and George,' Stella said piously.

Gina and George looked slightly stunned but neither protested.

'When are you thinking of the wedding?' the vicar asked.

'June,' George said, clearing his throat.

'Oh, we're booked up,' the vicar said. 'How about July?'

'I want a June wedding,' Gina insisted. 'Traditional like.'

'June weddings are always popular,' the vicar said. 'They book up a long time ahead.'

Gina set her jaw mutinously, but the vicar forestalled her by holding his hand out in a peaceable gesture.

'But I do my utmost to make sure our regulars get what they want. Let's say you'll be attending this Sunday. And by June …' He counted up the months on his fingers. 'In nine months you'll be at the heart of the congregation, yes?'

'Yes,' Gina agreed, digging her fingernails painfully into Stella's arm. 'Of course we will. If we get a June wedding.'

'Let's step into my office and see what we can do,' the vicar smiled.

As they turned towards the office, a woman poked her head out of the door.

'Mrs Faraday on the phone, vicar,' she called.

'Thank you, Pauline. Tell her I'll ring her back in half an hour,' the vicar called back.

'Pious Pauline!' Gina looked horrified. 'What's she doing here? I thought she was one of them evangelist-culters.'

'Miss Watkins – Pauline – is my new assistant,' the vicar said. 'She's proving very helpful.' He stopped and eyed Gina. 'I hope 'Pious' isn't meant as an uncharitable nickname, Mayor Pontin?'

Stella waited for Gina to tell the vicar what she really thought of 'Pious Pauline' but Gina looked as contrite as she could manage.

'Of course not,' she said. 'People call her that cuz she's so good. It's meant affectionately.'

'Hmm,' said the vicar. 'Well. In future I'm sure just Pauline will suffice.'

Stella stayed behind as they walked towards the office, but the vicar noticed and looked back.

'Not coming?' He smiled at her.

'I'll wait outside,' Stella said. 'You don't need me for this.'

'But I'll see you on Sunday for the service?'

'Actually,' Stella admitted. 'I'm afraid I'm a non-believer.'

'Stella!' Gina gasped, but the vicar only smiled wider. He seemed almost delighted.

'Well, we'll have to see what we can do about that,' he said.

Something about his smile made Stella blush.

#

'So is the vicar as hot as the ladies say?' Rick asked Stella later.

'He's very striking,' Stella admitted, thinking of those blue eyes. 'Tall, dark and handsome.'

'Wow,' Rick said. 'And single so I hear. Gay, do you think?'

Stella didn't think so; not the way he'd looked at her. It had made her pulse shoot up.

'I didn't get that vibe,' she said to Rick.

'Really?' Rick raised his eyebrows. 'So if you suddenly start going to church I should be worried?'

Stella laughed, maybe a bit too loudly. 'That's not going to happen,' she said. 'Not for me, but it is for Gina.'

She told him about the morning.

'You're a cruel woman,' Rick said, laughing. 'Gina in church. It's hard to imagine.'

'She's dead set on a June wedding, and you know what she's like once she gets an idea into her head. I don't know why she's so fixated on it. A wedding's a wedding, whatever the month.'

Rick shrugged. 'The heart wants what the heart wants.' He took her hand across the kitchen island where they'd perched on high stools for their coffee.

Stella nodded. 'That's true. Gina's ruled by her emotions not logic.'

'Aren't we all?' Rick smiled at her, stroking her palm with his thumb.

'Some more than others,' Stella said, abruptly getting up to take her cup to the sink. For some reason, Rick's affectionate touches had begun to irritate her lately. She had no idea why; she'd always loved his little gestures.

'I wonder who got bumped to make room for Gina's June wedding?' Rick said, lightly. If he'd noticed her recent irritability he hadn't shown it.

'What?'

'Well if June was really booked up – and I bet that it was – the vicar will have to cancel some couple's wedding to make room for Gina.'

'I hadn't thought of that,' Stella said. 'No, surely not. He must've been exaggerating to get Gina to come to church.'

'Maybe.' Rick rose, picking up their empty mugs. 'Either way, it seems a bit Machiavellian for a vicar.'

Stella had to agree. Then the memory of the vicar's intense smile popped into her head again.

Fancy Dresses

'That's the dress I want,' Gina said, pointing at the TV. 'But I can't find no one to make it for me.'

Grazja could see why. The dress Gina desired, shimmering on the screen in front of them, was worn by a very young Judy Garland in Meet Me in St Louis. It wasn't a wedding dress in the film, but a white frou frou extravaganza Judy wears to the St Louis World Fair, matched with an enormous bonnet and frilly parasol. It had more ruffles than a meringue has air and was just as saccharine.

Grazja hadn't expected anything subtle from Gina but this was going to be quite something for a woman of Gina's age to pull off. A young Judy Garland, at her slimmest during Meet Me in St Louis, was obviously corseted in so tight her waist looked impossibly tiny in its satin sash.

'You think you can fit in?' Grazja asked. After a stint as Gina's carer following an accident, Grazja had no fear of offending her friend. She had seen Gina at her very worst and at her best, changed her knickers when she'd wet herself, endured Gina's xenophobic insults, and ultimately befriended her despite Gina's best efforts to drive her away.

'Of course I can, if I have it made to my measurements.'

'You won't look like that,' Grazja said, waving her hand at Judy's image. 'She young and slim.'

'Well, I ain't no lardy-arse,' Gina huffed. 'I don't want to look exactly like Judy, but that's the dress I always wanted to get married in ever since I first seen it.'

Grazja turned to her with interest. 'I didn't know you always want to get married.'

Gina pulled a face. 'Not married so much,' she said. 'I wanted a wedding so I could have a dress. All little girls want that. Once I found out what dirty boggers men are, I didn't want one of them, but I still wanted the dress.'

'And the wedding?'

'The wedding day. Not the rest of it. Not the whole thing.'

'You get the whole banana with George,' Grazja pointed out.

'Banana,' Gina shrieked with laughter. 'You mean the whole shebang. Banana! You keep George's banana out of this you dirty mare.' Gina's cackle woke up Ginger Rogers, her fat Corgi, who'd been napping on the sofa next to her.

Grazja started laughing too. 'I mean you not just marrying George for wedding day are you? For the dress?'

'Don't be daft.' Gina said. 'You know I love George. I waited all me life for him to come along.'

'With his banana,' Grazja added.

'Well, I don't hold that against him.' Gina said.

'That a shame for him,' Grazja said.

That dissolved them into laughter again. Ginger Rogers, giving a little disgusted snort, jumped down from the sofa and waddled out of the room.

'She don't like dirty talk,' Gina said, wiping her eyes. 'Hates it when me 'n' George have a cuddle on the sofa. Right little prissy miss.'

'She doesn't know what we say,' Grazja disagreed.

'You'd be surprised what they understand,' Gina sniffed. 'Not like cats who only look at you like you're gone out. That's cuz there's nothing in their brains.'

'Who you try to make the dress?' Grazja asked.

Gina scowled. 'Mel's Bridal in Lawton, but they don't make 'em, just buy 'em off the peg. Lilacs & Lace, the same. Something Borrowed – they're just for hire. I need someone who can make it 'specially for me. I called a couple of bespoke designers – one in Lincoln and one in Nottingham but they said they were all booked up and you needed to order about a year ahead which is just bloody ridiculous.

'And,' she added, getting worked up, 'It's not like they even have to bleedin' design it. I know exactly what I want. They just have to copy it, is all. Oh, and make the hat and the parasol.'

'Dressmakers don't make hats,' Grazja said. 'Milliners make hats. Not easy, I think. You probably have to find one off peg for hat and parasol.'

'They have to be exactly like Judy's,' Gina said. 'Exactly. Anyway, I don't want to travel far for fittings and whatever, so I need to find someone nearby.'

'Oh well then,' Grazja said. 'You make life easy for yourself. All you have to do is find a person who is excellent dressmaker who can also make hats and parasols and live nearby even though we live in one of least populated counties in England at edge of countryside in very small seaside resort. Hmm, I see no problem.'

'Very funny,' Gina said sourly. 'Just cuz I live in a small town don't mean I can't dream big.'

She patted her hair. 'I am mayor after all.'

Grazja laughed. 'Are you? You never mention it.'

Grazja felt stupid calling Frank her boyfriend. She was a forty year old widow, while he was an ex-Catholic priest and both had a considerable weight of personal baggage they each lugged around in their psyche.

To Grazja 'boyfriend' was what teens and carefree twenty-somethings called their lovers, and girlfriend was a term so light it could flutter away like a butterfly.

She was no girl and Frank no boy but their relationship was still very new and it was only recently Grazja had allowed herself the painful pleasure of falling in love again. And she had Frank to thank for that – not just the actual falling in love part but also because it was Frank who had freed her from the crushing guilt imprisoning her heart. As a nurse in Poland, Grazja thought she had accidently killed a comatose patient through a mistake she made in an exhausted state following the death of her beloved husband from cancer. Frank had travelled to Poland and finally discovered the truth.

Grazja was still trying to get used to the feeling of lightness the lifting of such a burden produced. It was actually scary to feel so buoyant and carefree.

Today, she and Frank were taking a trip to Skegness to deliver some Halloween props to a shop called Whatever You Fancy. Technically, the things they were delivering weren't designed specifically for Halloween but were actually spare props from Frank's ghost train ride which he ran in Mapton's small fairground, dressed as a spooky, hooded monk. Hence he was known locally as Brother Frank.

Recently, Grazja had been working hard, retraining to be a veterinary nurse and volunteering at Eleanor

Branwin's animal sanctuary, so it was good to be getting out of Mapton on a little trip with Frank.

He looked across at her, smiling and she couldn't help but smile back, experiencing a little rush of love chemicals. Ah, it had been a long, long time since she'd felt that thrill.

'So, why this man want your ghost train props?' she asked. 'For shop window?'

'Apparently not,' Frank grinned at her. 'It's a bit more interesting than that. He does a drag act and wants some dramatic stuff for Halloween.'

'Drag act?' Grazja said. 'Men who dress as women?'

'Drag queens,' Frank nodded. 'It's popular, apparently, these drag shows. They get lots of hen parties.'

'Women going to see men dress up as women?'

'Apparently. Yes. And gay men.'

'Hmm,' Grazja said. 'I find it hard to understand why British like this stuff so much. Pantomimes. Prince Charming is girl playing a boy in sexy fishnets tights, and Dame is man playing silly old woman. I don't know why.'

Frank laughed. 'I've never understood pantomime myself either but it's fun. You have to accept it and join in to enjoy it.'

Grazja clicked her tongue. 'I been to one once.' She said. 'I found it confusing. Everyone shouting back and such bad acting.'

'It's meant to be bad,' Frank explained. 'It's very exaggerated. There's nothing subtle about pantomime. It's very over the top.'

'I want lack of subtlety and over the top I spend time with Gina,' Grazja said. 'Every day like a pantomime with her.'

'True,' Frank agreed.

'I tell you about the wedding dress she wants,' Grazja said. 'Will make you laugh.'

They laughed and talked all the way to Skegness, finally drawing up in front of a row of shops, the end one of which was Whatever You Fancy, spelled out in a swirling cursive against a cerise background. The window displayed mannequins, bewigged and dressed in various outfits; a sexy nurse, a princess, Wonder Woman, a pouting Marilyn, a seductive vamp, a cheerleader and one mannequin decked out in hen night paraphernalia. Elvis jutted his pelvis as a token male.

Frank peered at the parking restrictions sign. 'He said I could park round the back to unpack but I'd need to let him know I'm here so he can unchain the entrance. Could you just nip in and tell him we're here?'

Grazja clambered out of the van and pushed open the shop door, setting off a tinkle of chimes. The interior smelled surprisingly fresh, with some undertone of citrus zest, and, she thought, sandalwood. She realised she'd unconsciously braced for a musty, sweaty smell, expecting this from clothes repeatedly hired out to excitable party people.

The shop brimmed with hats, rhinestone jewels, feathered masks, bright wigs, and racks and racks of costumes all arranged precisely. One section was dedicated wholly to hen party fever. There were bride-to-be banners, pink hats, and headbands, fairy wands, emblazoned tee-shirts, and some chocolate penises, to name but a few things Grazja had time to note, before a handsome middle aged man, emerged from behind the deep pink velvet curtain that marked the back of the shop.

He had the silver-fox hair of George Clooney, with dark eyes and an elegant face.

'Hello,' he said, sweeping Grazja's jeans and tee with a swift assessing glance. 'Do you need any help?'

'We here to deliver the ghost train props,' Grazja said. 'Can you undo chain so Frank can park in your back way?'

Amusement seemed to flash in the man's eyes, but he said. 'Oh yes, of course. I didn't expect you to arrive on time. Most people are late.'

He hurried forward, out of the shop, leaving Grazja inside. She saw him wave to Frank and disappear to the side. Satisfied that all was in hand, she took the opportunity to look around.

She had never worn fancy dress, at least not since childhood. The chance to shed normal life and dress up as someone else intrigued her.

Grazja was attractive in a neat, well-turned out, practical way. She was blessed with good bone-structure, and her hair, light-brown, straight and tied back shone with good health. Grazja mostly avoided the Mapton diet of sugar and lard and was naturally active and slim.

Gina had once looked her up and down and sniffed: 'Can tell you're not English, you got no waist and hips. Men prefer women with a bit o' shape to 'em.'

'Thanks,' Grazja had replied. 'I go get bustle and corset to give me more shape. Then maybe I catch me a man.'

Really though, Grazja was happy with how she looked. She had perfected her subtle make-up years ago and had no desire to 'stand out' in the way Gina did, or even the way Stella did with her boho artist look and wild curly hair.

But now, looking at all the costumes available, all the different personas to choose from, Grazja suddenly felt excited.

How fun it must be to play dress-up and become someone else for an evening.

What really drew her were the wigs. Most were zany, nylon creations in garish colours of shimmering pink, blues and purples. Or sleek, straight, shiny black wigs for vampires and witches. Or cheap bobs made of tinsel. But the two that made Grazja itch to try them on were much more realistic with lustrous curls; one in Marilyn-style platinum blonde and the other in gorgeous auburn. They were arranged on blank mannequin heads, the auburn tresses tumbling over the shelf edge. Next to them a sign said. 'DO NOT TRY ON THE WIGS WITHOUT ASKING'

Grazja could hear voices coming faintly from somewhere at the back of the shop.

She did want to try on the wigs. It was such an urge, as strong as the one she used to have at six, standing in front of her mother's jewellery box, dying to slip on the diamond ring that was her mother's one valuable possession, materially and emotionally.

Little Grazja had been forbidden to wear the ring without her mother being present, and even then she was only allowed to slip it on for a moment to admire the sparkle.

One day she had been very daring, and, sneaking into the empty bedroom, had tried the ring on alone. It was loose of course on her six- year-old fingers, so she put it on her thumb and turned it this way and that to catch the shafts of sunlight. This wasn't enough. She wanted very much to take it outside and see it sparkle in the full sun.

Grazja could still feel the guilty thrill of tiptoeing through the house, her mother busy in the kitchen, the ring stuffed in the pocket of her dress. It was simultaneously horrible and delicious, knowing she was doing something naughty. She would only take it outside for just a little while, and then sneak it back up to the jewellery box before her mother knew it had gone.

Outside, the diamonds didn't disappoint, the sun bouncing off their facets in brilliant flashes, igniting Grazja's imagination. She was a princess; only a princess would wear such a ring. To make her dress twirl she spun in circles in the long grass, arms stretched like wings, watching the ring glitter on her thumb.

And then the ring flew off her thumb, arcing through the air, a white spark against the blue sky.

Grazja's heart stopped.

She raced towards the spot where the ring plopped into the grass, but she hadn't been the only one to see the ring fly. A magpie had seen it too – this wonderful piece of glittering magic – and wanted it with all his greedy magpie heart. He swooped down on swift wings into the long grass, and almost immediately launched upwards again, the ring dangling from his beak.

Grazja cried out as she watched the ring being born aloft into the sky. It was gone forever.

She'd been roundly punished when her mother found the ring gone and a confession wrung out of her.

Since then Grazja had never really allowed herself to give in to vanity or frivolity. She knew that trying on the alluring wig without permission wouldn't be likely to result in the kind of retribution and shame that losing the ring had caused, yet the fear still wormed in her stomach.

And what was it about the wigs, with their flowing locks that she found so stupidly alluring?

Maybe I want to feel like a princess again, Grazja thought, amazed at herself. I want to see if I look different in them, just like I did with the ring.

But she didn't want to ask to try one on, because she felt it was just too silly. Plus she would be embarrassed in front of Frank, even though Frank spent much of his time in the costume of a creepy monk.

She was so lost in these surprising thoughts that she didn't realise the shop owner had come through the velvet curtain, until she heard his voice.

She jumped like a cat.

'Sorry?' she said, feeling absurdly guilty, even though she hadn't touched the wigs.

The silver-haired fox smiled. 'Would you like to try one on?' he asked, nodding to the hair pieces. 'You seem to be entranced.'

Grazja blushed, looking behind him for Frank.

'Your guy's unloading the goods into the storage garage. I wanted to check I wasn't neglecting any customers or being robbed blind.'

'Oh, I not shoplifter,' Grazja said. She pointed to the sign. 'And I didn't try one on without permission.'

'Well, aren't you good,' Silver Fox said. 'I don't mind people trying them on – after all it's a fancy dress shop and everyone wants to – it's just that I ask customers if they'd mind wearing a little shower cap before they try the wigs on. For hygiene you realise. Some people look like they haven't washed their hair for weeks, while most of 'em have so much gel, hairspray, wax or mousse I could open a hair product salon with the 'residue'.' (He pulled his face and mimed the inverted commas sign with his fingers). 'Hence the shower caps.'

'I not need to try them on,' Grazja said.

'Maybe you don't need to,' Silver Fox said, 'But the way you were gazing at them tells me you want to. And why not? They are two of my best – not really fancy dress wigs at all. Much better quality. Normally I keep these two with their sisters in the other part of the shop.' He waved an elegant hand towards the velvet curtains. 'With the bespoke collection.'

Grazja hesitated. Silver Fox crossed to the till area and plucked something out of a glass bowl on the counter. 'Here,' he said, handing her a small piece of fronded elastic that looked like a strange translucent sea creature. 'Pop this on first. I'll go out back to check on your gentleman friend.'

He turned and slipped through the curtain again, leaving Grazja looking at the sea creature and realising it was an unused disposable shower cap, the sort you get in hotels. She unfolded it and placed it carefully over her hair, then, checking no one was about to enter the shop, reached for the auburn wig.

She felt absurdly excited.

Soft waves of hair tumbled over her shoulders and down her back but when Grazja turned to the mirror, she felt disappointed. The auburn didn't do as much for her as she'd imagined. She simply looked like herself in a wig, and slightly ridiculous.

Of course she did! Grazja clicked her tongue, ruefully.

Still, she might as well try on the blonde Marilyn now she'd taken the plunge and get this uncharacteristic urge out of the way so she could get back to being sensible Grazja.

Easing the wig on, she turned again to the mirror only to be amazed. She looked stunning as a platinum blonde, and the shorter, fuller cut and sensuous waves highlighted her cheekbones.

She did not look like Marilyn Monroe but she did look like a different, rather glamorous Grazja.

She heard footsteps returning from the back of the shop, but before she could pull the wig off, the owner slid through the curtains.

'Oh!' He clapped his hands softly together. 'I thought the blonde would suit you.'

'You think so?' Grazja said shyly, touching the wig.'

'Absolutely,' Silver Fox said. 'But I'm here to warn you that your man has almost done, so if you don't want him to see you in it…'

'Thank you,' Grazja said, easing the wig off. 'It not a secret, I just feel a little embarrassed…'

'Well, no need. You look fabulous. But I understand. Would you like to buy it? That one's not cheap, I have to admit. That's why it looks so good.'

'No,' Grazja said automatically, then stopped. She had to remind herself that she had money now. Her old client, Mrs Alexander, had left Grazja all of her considerable estate in her will – a move that had been designed by pernicious Mrs Alexander to enrage her family and make as much trouble for the people left behind as she had stirred up in life. At first Grazja had not wanted any of the money, but Mrs A had made it a stipulation of the will that she couldn't refuse it without consequences. There had been consequences, at first awful, and eventually liberating, and the money was hers.

She had given a good portion of it to secure the future of a local animal sanctuary, but had plenty left. Mrs A had been a very rich woman with a lot of investments and Grazja had yet to spend anything on herself at all.

'Yes,' she decided. 'I will buy.'

They completed the transaction swiftly but Grazja realised Frank would want to know what was in the bag emblazoned with Whatever You Fancy. She didn't know why she was so embarrassed – she wasn't buying a sex toy – but she cast around for something else to buy.

Her eye settled on the display of hen party goods, particularly a gaudy tiara that spelled out BRIDE with 'To Be' in smaller letters nestling underneath.

'I take this too,' Grazja said, grabbing the tiara off the stand. 'My friend getting married.'

As Silver Fox slipped it in the bag, Frank came through the front door, setting the chimes off.

'All done,' he said cheerfully. He stopped. 'Wow,' he said, looking around. 'This is great.' He spotted Grazja's bag. 'What have you bought?'

Grazja flushed, aware of Silver Fox listening. 'A silly hen night tiara for Gina,' she replied.

'Oh, she'll love that,' Frank laughed. 'You might have heard of her,' he said to Silver Fox. 'Gina Pontin, current mayor of Mapton.'

Silver Fox chuckled. 'Oh my God, really? She's a bit of a legend even in Skeg – always in the Lawton Post. That thing where she saved all those donkeys from slaughter!' He pressed his hands to his heart. 'My heroine.'

Grazja suppressed a snort. Gina's real genius had been in taking credit for the donkeys' rescue. Her part had actually been minor but by the time she'd retold the story a few times, she and her Jack Russell, Bing Crosby, had become the main players. She completely neglected to tell the media that she was in the right place when the opportunity to help arose (and to be fair she took the opportunity and did help) because she'd been squatting behind a hedge relieving her bladder.

'That's her,' Grazja said. 'She do everything dramatically. Her wedding will be big, but she's struggling to find someone to make her wedding dress. She wants an exact replica of the dress Judy Garland wear in Meet Me in St Louis. Plus hat and parasol.'

'Really?' Silver Fox's eyes lit up. 'The one Judy wears to the World Fair? It's not a wedding dress but it does look like one. It's a very frothy creation.'

'That the one,' Grazja nodded. Her eyes travelled over the fancy dress costumes. 'I don't suppose…'

'Not in here,' Silver Fox waved his hand dismissively at the off-the-rack costumes. 'But if you step into my parlour,' he said, gesturing to the velvet curtains, 'I'll show you what I can really do.'

Girls' Night In

'No, no, no, no,' Gina cried. 'I won't have a wedding dress made for a bleeding tranny.'

'Drag Queen,' Grazja corrected her. 'It won't be made for anyone but you. It fit only you.'

'I'll be a laughing stock.'

Grazja exchanged a look with Stella that said 'you're worrying about that now?'

Stella turned away quickly before she burst out laughing, distracting herself by settling a throw over Gerta, her four year old daughter.

It was their monthly Wednesday meet-up, when the four of them enjoyed a girls' night in at Stella's, watching an old movie, eating and drinking, gossiping and arguing. Gerta always fell soundly asleep by eight, curled up on her favourite beanbag so that they could talk about things little ears shouldn't hear.

Rick ran his pop-up restaurant in Lawton on Wednesdays, and Henry the cat, grumpier than ever in old age, had slunk out of the room the moment Gina entered, thus ensuring it was a truly male-free zone.

'You should see his creations? They so beautiful,' Grazja sighed. 'Elliot a very skilled dressmaker.'

Grazja had learnt Silver Fox's name was Elliot Grant when he had handed her his card to give to Gina.

'That's the thing, ain't it?' Gina said. 'A dressmaker shouldn't be a man; a dressmaker should be a woman. Men are tailors. I don't want some man measuring me bits and bobs, even if he is a poofter. 't ain't right.'

'That's offensive,' Stella protested. 'Don't call him that.'

'What? Poofter?' Gina said. 'That's what we always called 'em. Or queer. I heard them say it themselves on TV and that.'

'Yes, but you mean it as an insult.'

'I don't,' Gina said. 'Although I don't like the way they go on. It's not natural, two hairy men kissing and cuddling. And what they do 'down there'...' she dropped her voice and pointed to her bottom. 'Disgusting.'

Stella automatically checked to see Gerta was still asleep.

'Ooh, I need a pee,' Gina said, hurrying out of the room suddenly.

'It's a bad idea,' Stella said to Grazja. 'Gina's too homophobic and she'd just insult him. It would be awful. I'd die of shame.'

Grazja shrugged. 'You forget the names she used to call me when I came here,' she said. 'Polack, dirty foreigner... Gina need her prejudices challenged. Besides, if she really want that exact dress she will have to change her melody.'

'Tune,' Stella corrected her. 'Change her tune.'

'Whichever,' Grazja said. 'I somehow think Elliot can handle Gina.'

'Maybe,' Stella said. 'But I think this wedding business is going to ramp her up to eleven. It means so much to her.'

'Yes,' agreed Grazja. 'Which is why I want her to have dream dress. She has had sad life until last few years. You know that better than anyone.'

Stella sighed. 'Yes, I suppose I do.'

They heard Gina's footsteps approaching.

'Talking about me?' she asked as she re-entered.

'Of course,' said Stella. 'It's always about you.'

'It a shame you won't consider Elliot's offer,' Grazja resumed. 'He's a big fan of yours.'

Gina preened. 'Really? How does he know who I am?' She asked this about as disingenuously as Gerta had when she'd eaten half the icing of a chocolate cake but denied it despite the ring of chocolate smeared around her mouth.

'He'd see you in the Post and on the news,' Grazja replied. 'You're well-known in Skeg too. Elliot says you are heroine for rescuing the donkeys.'

Gina patted her hair, eyelashes fluttering.

'He only offered to make your dress because he admires you. And he knew exactly which dress I meant too. I didn't have to show him picture. In fact, he mentioned he wouldn't make time to make a bespoke dress for anyone else right now as he's too busy. But for you, Mayor Gina he make exception.'

Gina was hooked, Stella could tell. She was visibly primping.

'Also,' Grazja finished. 'Elliot very handsome, very well-dressed. George Clooney, Cary Grant type.'

'I thought he were a queen?' Gina said.

'Not most of the time,' Grazja said. 'That his club act.'

Gina sniffed. 'Maybe I could meet him. See what I think,' she said. 'But if he thinks he can dress me up like a drag queen…'

It was just a token protest now, Stella recognised. The irony was that Gina did sometimes look like a drag queen on 'fancy' occasions.

'Excellent,' Grazja clapped her hands. 'Oh, I got you something from the shop too.' She reached into the plastic bag she'd brought and pulled out the Bride-to-Be tiara.

Gina cackled when she saw it, popping it on her orange head.

'It's for hen parties,' Grazja explained, grinning at Stella.

'A hen night.' Gina exclaimed. 'I hadn't thought of that! I want to have one.'

'Oh dear God, no,' groaned Stella, throwing a cushion at Grazja. 'What have you done?'

Harvest Festival Part 1

Gina found the morning service on Sunday as boring as she'd expected and found it difficult not to fidget. The vicar had a handsome face and a fine voice but he seemed to go on forever about God and Christ and the Bible and how it all related to something that had happened to him at the supermarket that had made him think about neighbours (real ones not the Australian soap) and how Jesus said we must 'love thy neighbour' which was all well and good but he didn't live next door to Pam Stimson with her out-size babydoll pyjamas flapping on the line for all to see. Since Gina had moved across the road from her own bungalow into George's more spacious one she got even more of an eyeful of Pam's saucy nightwear. So did George which Gina didn't like. George was a true gentleman but he was still only a man, and she worried about him getting palpitations at the sight of some of Pam's frilly-knickers.

Yet Gina was unusually reticent to directly confront Pam about it. Pam, loved by Maptonites for her kind nature, had once quietly threatened to kill Gina. The look in her eye, as she'd loomed over her, had told Gina she meant it. Gina had never touched Pam's cat again (a dispute over their respective pets had been the source of the conflict). The most Gina had ever done since was get tipsy on Babycham and heckle Pam on karaoke nights at The Diving Helmet. She'd even, in a very rare repentant mood one day this past summer, apologised to Pam for throwing her cat in the boating lake. Much to Gina's discomfort Pam had hugged her. What briefly looked like the possibility of a new warmth between them lasted about three days until

Gina caught George standing at the window, entranced by a new article of Pam's bedtime clothing.

So, Gina thought, you couldn't always 'love thy neighbour.' Jesus should have said 'put up with thy neighbour if thou can manage it.'

She was jerked out of her reverie when George nudged her with his elbow. She'd have sworn he was asleep.

'What?' she hissed, a bit too loudly.

George nodded to the vicar who was smiling at her. 'I think he wants to introduce you,' he murmured.

Gina drew herself up, assuming her mayoral smile.

'Mayor Pontin and Mr Wentworth, we're so pleased to welcome you to our congregation.'

Gina beamed, looking round. The congregation was small and scrappy to say the least. Gina knew a few of them. Mildred and Alf she knew well, and the ancient Parker twins. Others she recognised. Many of them looked like they were already knocking on Heaven's door. Pious Pauline's face shone with enthusiasm, adoring eyes fixed on the vicar. Gina didn't recognise the white-haired man seated at the organ. Including her and George that made about twenty five of them. She could see why the vicar wanted to expand the congregation and get some new blood. This was a right raggle-taggle bunch.

'We're relying on you, Mayor Pontin, to spread the word and help make St Bart's the heart of the community once again.'

Gina nodded, keeping her smile in place. She wasn't much of a one to spread the Lord's word but if it meant securing her June wedding she would praise St Bart's to its beautiful rafters.

'And we would like to invite you to open our Harvest Festival this year,' the reverend continued. 'We know you'll be busy officiating at the opening of the Siltby Harvest and Pumpkin Festival on the Saturday but we'd be very honoured to have you open our more modest display on Sunday. I've heard wonderful things about past displays at St Bart's.' He smiled around at the congregation. Various people nodded back, murmuring agreement.

'We team up with the primary school,' Mildred piped up. 'The children love it. Everyone brings something to contribute and it all goes to local care homes.'

Everyone had turned to look at Gina, awaiting her response.

'I'd be honoured,' she said. 'Of course.' But inside Gina had turned suddenly cold. The term 'Harvest Festival' didn't recall a celebration of bounty to Gina, it recalled social humiliation and shame. It evoked feelings that she didn't want to revisit.

There had been one particular Harvest Festival many, many moons ago that still occasionally haunted her dreams.

'You all right, love?' George asked her when all the after-service chitchat was over and they were back in the Rover. 'You look a little peaky.'

'I'm fine,' Gina lied. She felt more than a little peaky. She felt sick.

#

By the age of ten Gina Pontin had started to gain a reputation at her junior school as a scrapper you didn't want to mess with. She'd pugnaciously built this reputation for herself until even the boys didn't dare take her on. But she hadn't always been so formidable.

In fact, until the past six months she'd been a target for every bully in the schoolyard and in the local streets they played on. None of the children at Baxter Infant and Junior School was from a well-to-do family but they were shod and fed and cared for, their parents employed in various parts of the lace and hosiery business. The boys wore shorts and knee high socks, their hair cut in brutal short back and sides, neck hair burnt off with a candle by the school barber. The girls wore their hair in long bobs or plaits, tied in ribbons, and knee-length dresses with the occasional Peter Pan collar if they were lucky.

Gina Pontin's dresses were never pretty – always hand-me-downs from jumble sales – her plaits were tied with rags. She was malnourished, with stick legs and knobbly knees. Her father was a drunk who was mostly out of work. Sometimes mysterious boxes were carried into the house in the middle of the night and stored in the back room for a few days. Gina was forbidden to touch these or mention them to anyone. Then men would come again in the night and carry the boxes away.

Gina's mother liked to go out dancing at the Palais and other dance halls. She liked dancing more than anything else, including mothering. She slept in late and Gina had been used to feeding herself whatever she could find in the cupboards since she was very young. It was school dinners and the little bottle of milk the children had in the morning that kept Gina going to school. It was often the only hot meal she would get. Also, the one thing her mother was very keen on was that Gina went to school. It got her out of the house and out from under her mother's feet for whatever it was her mother did in the day.

Neither of her parents physically abused her. It was simply as though she was a child who'd wandered in off the street one day and been allowed to stay as long as she kept pretty much to herself and gave them little trouble.

Once or twice some official – Gina never knew who they were – came on behalf of the school after a teacher raised the issue of Gina's hygiene issues. Her clothes were unwashed and so was she. The other children called her 'smelly pants' and 'stinky Gina' among other names.

Her mother would chastise her and make a half-hearted effort to keep her clean but after a week or so she'd simply lose interest.

As Gina got older she began to do the laundry and keep herself as clean as she could but the names stuck and the bullying continued.

Gina Pontin was different. Being different was bad. Different kids got bullied.

The tipping point came with the Harvest Festival in her ninth year. That was the trigger for the big change in Gina, when she decided she'd had enough. When she discovered she had fists and a gob. When her rage ignited.

Baxter Infant and Junior school was one of a few local schools that celebrated Harvest Festival at the impressive, cathedral-like St Mary's in the centre of Nottingham's Lace Market. On the day of the schools' service children brought in their food donations to display in the church.

These were the post-war years so rationing and a scarcity of food made the options a little limited but even in the city, backyards and tiny front gardens, as well as allotments, still yielded fruit and vegetables. It was a source of pride to send your child to school carrying a small basket of provisions to donate.

Gina had never taken a basket to either infants or junior school. The most she could usually scramble together was a tin of peas or a couple of potatoes.

It was just another thing to set her apart and make her burn with shame.

That morning she saw all the other children turning up with their baskets – some small, most modest, a few larger and brimming – while Gina brought a pilfered tin of Fray Bentos Corned Beef from the pantry.

How she longed to be able to proudly carry in a basket packed by a mother who cared about such things.

There was one little girl – Shirley Wallis – two years younger than Gina, whose father was a foreman at the large Baxter and Holmes factory (the school was named after Horatio Baxter as a local benefactor). Thus the Wallis's considered themselves as a 'cut above' as evidenced by the large, prettily adorned basket that Mrs Wallis packed for Shirley to present for Harvest Festival.

Shirley was better dressed and perhaps a tiny bit spoiled, and so, for opposite reasons to Gina, also sometimes bullied. Her mother's tendency to use her daughter to 'show off' her status as a foreman's wife made Shirley a target for the other kids.

Her basket was a very obvious example of this, thus it was that Gina, gearing up reluctantly to enter the school grounds after most of the children had gone in, spotted Shirley, with her splendid basket, crying next to the railings.

Gina approached her cautiously, never sure of the reception she'd get.

'Wasamatter?' Gina asked.

The little girl squinted up at her, frightened. She took in Gina's scruffy visage. If she recognised her as Stinky Gina she didn't say so. 'It's me basket,' she sniffled. 'I don't want it. Me mam made me bring it but they'll call me posh and laugh at me. I know they will. They always do and steal me toffees.'

Gina eyed the basket. It was so beautiful. It even had a little posy of flowers in it for the teacher.

'Tell yer what,' she said. 'I don't have nuttin' but this tin o' corned beef for my class. Why don't we swap. I'll take yer basket and you take me corned beef. Then they'll feel sorry for yer because you only brought that.'

'Won't you get laughed at?' Shirley asked, wide eyed.

'They laugh at me anyways,' Gina said. 'So don't make no difference.'

Shirley thought about it. 'All right,' she agreed, handing Gina the basket. 'You're not so stinky.'

'Ta,' Gina blinked. 'Here's yer corned beef.'

Thinking their problems were solved, they entered the gate and went their separate ways.

Gina's teacher, Miss Grindwold, eyed her basket suspiciously. She wasn't a woman with a lot of sympathy. She regarded Gina's neglected scruffiness as a fault in the child as much as the parents but didn't generally pick on Gina as much as ignore her. This beautifully presented basket couldn't really be ignored – it outshone even Mavis Pearlman's with its pink bow tied to the handle.

'That's a very fancy basket of goods, Gina Pontin,' Miss Grindwold said. 'I thought your family didn't have ha'pence to rub together.'

The class giggled.

'Me dad 'ad a win on the gee-gees.' Gina lied. 'We're a bit flush this week. Look, me mam made you a posy.'

Miss Grindwold sniffed. 'Hmm,' she said. 'A likely story.' But she took the posy anyway. 'Well, put it on the table with the others,' she dismissed Gina.

Proudly, Gina carried the basket over to the table set up at the side of the classroom and placed her basket next to the other donations.

Mavis Pearlman glared at her and the other children whispered and sniggered. Gina didn't care. It felt so wonderful to be able to bring something she could be proud of, even if it wasn't really from home.

After dinner, the children would troop over to St Mary's, carrying their baskets, and take part in a special Harvest Festival service to celebrate God's bounty. Gina couldn't wait.

The church was where it all unravelled.

Although most parents were at work, including many of the women who were employed by the lace industry either doing piece work at home, or in the factories, some mothers did attend the service, including Mrs Wallis, Shirley's mother.

St Mary's was a huge cathedral-like church and packed today with all the pupils and teachers of local schools, as well as parents and parishioners able to attend. Long trestle tables lined the walls, labelled with the name of each school to receive the tributes. Each school knew the time-slot of their arrival so their baskets could be placed and arranged before the next school arrived, and the pupils seated in their classes. Baxter's Infant and Junior School were the last in, the infants first, followed by the juniors.

Gina placed her basket proudly next to the sign that said: Miss Grindwold, Juniors, before joining her class in the designated pew. As usual the other children left a space on either side of her.

Once all the schools were seated, the parents, parishioners and visitors began to enter, many wandering up and down the aisles to admire the baskets.

Gina noticed the carefully coiffed blonde frowning over the baskets in the infants' section but she didn't recognise her as Mrs Wallis. The woman turned her head, scouring along the trestle until her eyes alighted on the basket placed next to Mrs Grindwold's name. She stiffened, then walked over to Gina's basket and lifted it, carrying it a few paces along the trestle to the infant section where she placed it very obviously at the front.

Gina sat up, suddenly alert to potential trouble. Why had the woman moved her basket?

As the woman fussed over the ribbons, neatening them, Miss Turner, Baxter's infant school teacher, hurried over to her.

Gina got a sudden sick feeling in her stomach as the blonde woman responded to Miss Turner's question by waving her hand at the basket, then gesturing to Mrs Grindwold's sign. Miss Turner frowned, and reached over to a tin of Fray Bentos corned beef that had been placed in another basket.

Gina couldn't hear what they said but she could guess all too well. Her stomach lurched.

The blonde woman looked angry. She raised her voice so that everyone could hear. 'I would never send my daughter to Harvest Festival with a tin of corned beef. I'm telling you this is Shirley's basket.' She scanned the pews until her flinty eyes settled on a little blonde head trying to shrink out of sight on the row in front of Gina.

'Shirley, you come out here and tell your teacher.'

In the meantime Miss Grindwold had joined Miss Turner, and as she listened, her eyes sought out Gina. She beckoned her with a crooked finger, mouth a hard, grim line.

Knees starting to tremble, Gina got to her feet and shuffled past her whispering classmates, almost tripping as Bobby Hutton jerked out his foot to catch her out.

'Gerroff,' she hissed.

'You're in trouble, smelly pants,' he scoffed.

By this time, most attendees had taken their seats, and the reverend had taken his place in the pulpit ready to begin the service. He smiled politely at the little group, waiting for them to realise it was time to start and settle. Everyone else was waiting too, and all eyes went to the small group by the trestle table, and the evident drama that was unfolding there.

'Gina,' Miss Grindwold demanded. 'Did you take this girl's basket?'

Gina stared at Shirley. The younger girl had gone pale, her blue eyes pooling with tears.

'Yes, but...' Gina said.

'You *stole* it?' Miss Grindwold said loudly.

People gasped.

'No I never,' Gina protested. 'She gave it to me. We swapped.' She looked to Shirley for confirmation.

Shirley looked at her neat little strapped shoes saying nothing.

'You *swapped*,' Mrs Wallis repeated scornfully. 'You expect us to believe that my Shirley gave you her beautiful basket so she could bring in your ...' she curled her lip, 'tin of corned beef?'

Gina nodded.

'I'm afraid,' Mrs Wallis declared, her voice ringing clear through the church, 'this girl is a liar as well as a thief.'

'I am not!' Gina cried. 'Tell her Shirley, tell her.'

But Shirley, tears running down her cheeks would not admit that she gave away the basket her mother had been so proud of. She simply shook her head.

Mrs Wallis pressed Shirley against her waist. 'There, there, darling. There there. We'll see this girl is punished. Did she hurt you when she stole it? Did she use force?'

'I didn't take it!' Gina cried again. 'She gave it to me.'

Somewhere to her left she heard a classmate – probably Mavis Pearlman – say 'I tode yer it wasn't hers. Said she must've thieved it.'

Mrs Grindwold roughly grabbed her upper arm to march her out of the church, but Gina tore away, sprinting for the church doors as hot tears began to gush.

Gina ran all the way home. It wasn't as though home was a sanctuary, exactly, but she didn't know where else to go to cry herself out.

Her mam was out, thankfully, hopefully getting some provisions. Her dad, unusually, was in the tiny back yard and he called out 'Whose 'at?' when he heard the clatter of her arrival.

Reluctantly Gina went into the back yard to find him squatting atop the old broken rabbit hutch, drinking a bottle of ale in a patch of early autumn sunshine, with a roll-up in between his nicotine stained fingers.

He was in one of his mellow moods, in the friendly, early stage of inebriation so she stepped further into the yard.

He took in her red eyes and stained cheeks.

'Yer all reet me duck? Wasamatter?'

Gina couldn't help it. She started to blub again.

'Ey, ey, stop yer blortin'' he said, holding out his arm so she could tuck herself under it.

He smelled as always of beer and ciggies but Gina leaned into this rare moment of comfort.

'Tell us what 'appened.'

Gina told him. 'Bastards,' he sighed. 'They do all that they can to break yer. I know, duckie. But you mustn't let 'em. You need to fight back. You need to be hard like yer Dad.'

'Are you hard then, Dad?'

'Me?' he grinned at her through bleary eyes. 'No, I'm too soft duck. World broke me a long time ago. No, I meant hard like yer real dad.'

Gina stiffened. 'Me real dad?' she asked, puzzled.

'Aye,' he said casually. 'Yer real dad was a boxer. Tough as ode boots. Bare knuckle. Fought at Goose Fair. Yer need to be more like him'

Gina, who was never one for self-reflection, never knew if it was the utter humiliation of that day in church or that final revelation that ignited the rage that would rule her for much of her life, or both together, but she returned to school a changed girl.

She went back with her tongue sharpened and her fists loaded. The boys and girls who tried to bully her soon found out they'd been prodding a tiger who'd just escaped its cage. It wasn't really very long before the bullied became the bully, and Gina developed a taste for it.

Harvest Festival Part 2

Gina didn't have long to prepare for St Bart's Harvest Festival. Once George had taken Ginger Rogers for their daily constitutional walk along the seafront, Gina allowed herself a good cry then set to tackling the situation with Gina-esque bullishness.

She decided that this was an opportunity to prove that she, Gina Pontin, was as good as anyone else – maybe even better – and this time her basket was going to be all her own and better than anyone else's.

She rang Stella. 'Where can I get a basket?'

'A basket?' Stella sounded surprised. 'What sort of basket?'

'One of them with a handle,' Gina said. 'Wicker. A good sized one.'

'What for?' Stella said.

'For Harvest Festival at St Bart's.' Gina said. 'They asked me to open it next Sunday.'

'Oh!' Stella said. 'You went to church this morning. I forgot. How was it?' She sounded amused.

'I can see why the vicar wants to attract more people,' Gina said. 'Not many of 'em and half o' them look ready to pop their clogs. They need some young blood.'

'And you're supposed to attract them?' Stella laughed. 'You're not exactly a spring chicken yourself.'

'I'm not ancient,' Gina snapped. 'I look at least ten years younger than I am and I am the mayor. The vicar's right. I set a good example.'

'So did you enjoy the service?' Stella asked.

'No,' Gina admitted. 'It bored me pants off. I'll have to think of some more interesting ideas to give the vicar. He's so handsome, he needs to be seen at more events. That'll get the ladies in.'

'And some of the men,' Stella added.

'Don't think them sort'd be welcome in a church.' Gina said.

'They have gay vicars nowadays,' Stella said.

Gina tutted. 'Well, they put urine in them energy drinks but that don't make it right,' she said.

'I don't think that's true,' Stella said.

''tis,' Gina declared. 'Andy Timmis says it's on the ingredients list in tiny writing. Anyway, where can I get a nice basket?'

'Charity shop maybe?' Stella suggested.

'No! I want a new one,' Gina said, who didn't much like anything second-hand. 'A clean one.'

'Probably more likely to get a wicker basket in Lawton,' Stella suggested. 'Or online. What are you going to put in it?'

'Food,' Gina said. 'Nice stuff – tins o' red salmon and the like. Cakes.'

'Eleanor makes lovely jam,' Stella suggested.

Gina wrinkled her nose. Along with second hand goods, Gina didn't much rate homemade food. If it came out of a tin or a packet it was proper in her eyes. It had been tested and approved. You could trust it. 'Nah,' she said. 'I'll buy some. I'll get George to drive me to Lawton tomorrow, see if I can get a basket.'

'It'd be quicker to take the bus,' Stella said. 'The speed George drives you won't get there 'til Wednesday.'

'I feel safer wi' George than wi' you,' Gina retorted. 'You take them corners like a Formula 1 driver, even with Gerta in the back.'

'I don't. It just feels like that because you're used to George's tortoise speed.'

'It's funny to think the Marauders banned him from the rumbles,' Gina laughed. 'Apparently he were a menace on a mobility scooter. Demon driver.'

Stella laughed too. 'Hard to imagine. But then those rumbles are heady. The one time I did it, I ended up in bed with Rick. That's where it all started.'

'Gi'over,' Gina scrunched up her face. 'No need to talk dirty.'

'Why didn't you ever learn to drive?' Stella asked.

'Why d'yer think?' Gina said. 'I'd be a speed-head like you. Danger to society behind a wheel. Where d'yer think you get it from? Never trusted meself.'

'Oh come on,' Stella said. 'When has caution ever stopped you doing anything?'

'You'd be surprised what you don't know about me, Stella. It would fill a book.'

After their conversation, Gina felt much happier. There had been a time in the not too distant past when her granddaughter wouldn't speak to her, their lives separated by physical miles and old resentments. It had once seemed impossible to believe they'd have the close relationship they did now; impossible to imagine Stella leaving hoity-toity London to live in Mapton on Sea.

Now she knew impossible things could happen, Gina decided with more confidence, she could take on the Harvest Festival. In fact, she wasn't just going to take it on, she was going to win it.

#

Grazja received the panicked call from Gina at six-thirty on Sunday morning. Grazja's first thought was that something terrible had happened.

'It's George,' Gina shrieked. 'I don't think he's going to make it.'

Grazja swung her legs out of bed, already on the move. 'Is it his heart? It's probably angina again but…'

'No,' Gina shouted. 'It's not his heart. He can't make it to the Harvest Festival this morning. He's got a dicky tummy. He's been on the loo most of the night. I tode him not to have that pumpkin curry in Siltby but did he listen?'

'Gina,' Grazja said sharply. 'Why you wake me up to tell me this? What you want me do? Wipe his bottom?'

'It's not about George,' Gina said, sounding offended. 'I got the harvest festival to get to wi' me basket. I got me mayoral duty. With George stuck on the lav I need a lift.'

'Now? You need a lift now at six-thirty in morning?' Grazja growled.

'Well no,' Gina said, sounding taken aback. 'But I want to be there early, for eight at least, so I can check out the competition.'

There was a long pause as Grazja turned to Frank, who was sitting up blearily in bed. She waved him to go back to sleep.

'Why me?' Grazja. 'Why not call Stella? She your family.'

'She'll be busy with Gerta,' Gina said, sounding defensive. 'And Ricky needs a lie in on Sunday mornings so I didn't want to disturb them.'

'It okay to disturb me though?'

'I thought you were my friend,' Gina huffed. 'I thought you could call on a friend in need but obviously…'

45

'Oh shut up, Gina,' Grazja said. 'I pick you up at seven-fifty. Make sure you ready. You owe me big cake.'

'I'll buy you breakfast at the diner after the service,' Gina said swiftly.

'Big breakfast,' Grazja said. 'The works.'

'The whole banana', Gina promised.

#

'I don't think it a competition, Gina,' Grazja said.

'Life's a bleedin' competition,' Gina replied. 'It's a dog eat dog world.'

They were walking down the path to St Bart's.

'I'm not sure you've got hang of Christ's teachings yet,' Grazja shook her head.

'Course I have,' Gina said. 'I'm giving to the poor aren't I? Some lucky bogger's gonna get me basket and be thrilled wi'it.'

Grazja shrugged.

'Anyway, if you're so keen on Jesus, you should come to church on Sundays wi' me, regular like.'

Grazja shook her head. 'I'm lapsed Catholic,' she said.

'What about Frank?'

'Very lapsed Catholic,' Grazja said. 'He no go.'

Pious Pauline met them at the door. 'Mayor Pontin,' she beamed. 'What a magnificent basket.'

Gina shot Grazja a look so smug that Grazja had to grin.

Gina had all the subtlety of a five year old.

Grazja noticed that Pauline looked less dishevelled than was normal. Her skirt, although frumpy, was plain navy and didn't completely clash with the huge orange flowers on the cream jumper stretched over her large bosom. Often, Pauline's skirts were floral too and the pattern on her bottom half usually clashed spectacularly with her top half. Not, Grazja assumed out of any wish to make a statement, just simply because Pauline was blind to sartorial matchmaking.

Pauline led them through the nave up to the area before the altar where a display had been set up for Harvest Festival. Compared to the impressive show that had lined the aisles in St Mary's all those years ago, St Bart's was modest, supplied by limited parishioners and the local primary school, yet it was very pretty. Wooden crates, stacked into a pyramid formation supported the goods. Although Mapton was a tourist resort, it was situated in an agricultural county. This was reflected in the carefully placed produce, including ears of glistening corncobs, bags of flour from the nearby heritage windmill, fat cabbages, golden potatoes, orange pumpkins, green striped marrows and a basket of rosy apples to name a few. These flanked the other wares. Tins of various produce; packets of rice, pasta and noodles; bread; jars of jam, homemade and bought; mayonnaise and ketchup; biscuits and cakes; bars of chocolate. Scattered among these were jars and vases of cut flowers. Atop the apex of the display lightly perched on a thin board bridging two crates, was a beautifully arranged wheatsheaf.

'Oh, this is lovely,' Grazja said. She turned to Pauline. 'Did you do this?'

'I helped,' Pauline blushed. 'It was Pam Stimson who put it together. She's so talented.'

'Pam?' Gina grimaced 'I didn't see her here last week.'

'She's not a regular,' Pauline said. 'But the vicar saw one of the lovely displays she does for the Lifeguard shop and asked her if she would do the Harvest Festival for us. He's ever so persuasive, the vicar'

Pauline went dewy eyed as she said this. Her skin seemed to glow.

'Where can I put my basket?' Gina said, eyeing the display as though she was thinking hard about the solution to this thorny problem.

'Oh, well… it is large,' Pauline said. 'Perhaps it should sit at the side of the display.'

Gina cast her a scurrilous look. 'Don't be daft,' she said. 'I'm yer guest of honour. It looks to me that the only place my basket would fit would be on the top there. It's the only space big enough without that.' She pointed to the wheatsheaf.

Pauline bewildered. 'But that's like the crown, you see; it's a work of art. You can't take that off.'

'Oh, you can,' Gina said. 'That would make a lovely decoration at the bottom there.'

'Gina,' Grazja stepped in. 'I don't think that a good idea. Your basket too heavy for that board. Too wide.'

'It's not,' Gina said. 'It just has to be balanced right. It'll make the display. I'm telling yer.'

'It will break display,' Grazja warned.

'Yes,' Pauline nodded. 'It will break it.'

'It won't,' Gina insisted. She carried her basket to the back of the display, placing it on the floor at her feet, as she reached for the wheatsheaf and lifted it down.

'Don't!' Pauline begged.

'It's all right,' Gina replied, shoulders and head looming above the bridge. 'It will fit.'

She lugged the basket up and into place as Grazja shut her eyes and Pauline let out a little moan.

Grazja braced for disaster. After a moment, Gina said: 'See!' and Grazja opened her eyes to see the basket perched atop the pyramid and Gina grinning triumphantly.

Aesthetically, it actually didn't look as bad as Grazja had feared, but it looked precarious, balanced precisely on the thin piece of plywood supported between the crates. The basket's base was wider than the plywood yet Gina had managed to get it central enough to stay in place. Probably, Grazja thought, by sheer luck than any skill on Gina's part. At least the display was still in one piece.

'Ohhh,' Pauline whimpered. 'Pam's not going to like it.'

'Pam don't have to like it,' Gina retorted. 'She should've done her own basket.'

'I mean the way it looks,' Pauline said.

Gina came round to the front, carrying the wheatsheaf. 'What do you mean? It looks wonderful.' She handed the wheatsheaf to Pauline.

'No one else has their name on their donations,' Grazja pointed out. Gina had attached a large red rosette to the basket with Mayor Gina Pontin printed in the middle.

'That's a shame,' Gina said. 'I'd like to know who's done what.'

'I think it supposed to be communal effort,' Grazja said.

Gina looked unimpressed.

Just then the vicar appeared. He was just as good looking as Stella had said.

'Mayor Pontin,' he smiled. 'So good of you to do this. Are you wearing your chain of office?'

Gina beamed and patted her coat. 'Under here,' she said. 'Bit chilly so I'll leave my coat on 'til we're ready to start. I'm afraid poor George is unwell today, so it's just me.'

'I'm sorry to hear that. I hope it's nothing serious?'

'Nah, just a dicky tummy. It's his own fault; he knows he can't take spicy food but he can't resist.'

'Ah,' the vicar chuckled. 'We all fall to temptation sometimes, but we all pay the price too. Lucky for us Jesus forgives.'

The vicar seemed to notice Grazja for the first time, his blue eyes meeting hers. Grazja felt a palpable charge like a small electric shock.

'Mayor Pontin has changed the display,' Pauline tugged at his sleeve.

'Um?' the vicar said, releasing Grazja from his gaze to turn to Pauline.

'She's taken off the wheatsheaf and put her own basket on top,' Pauline said. 'Is that all right?'

The vicar barely glanced at the display. 'It's fine Pauline, I'm sure.' He swung his eyes back to Grazja who suddenly felt a little hot. Was there heat in his gaze?

'I don't believe I've seen you at St Bart's before,' he said. 'Welcome. Are you here for the Harvest Festival?'

'This is my friend, Grazja,' Gina said. 'She gave me a lift with George being unwell.' She lowered her voice and whispered 'She's Catholic' as though she was blaspheming.

'Lapsed,' Grazja said quickly. She wanted to break this vicar's spell.

'Maybe you were just in the wrong flock,' the vicar said. 'I hope you'll stay for the service today anyway? All faiths and non-believers are welcome.'

He offered Grazja his hand to shake, his grip warm and dry. The wattage of his smile ratcheted up a few more degrees before he released her, and turned back to discuss the order of the service with Gina.

Grazja, rather dazed, sought the solidity of a pew to sit on. Wow, had the handsome, younger vicar just hit on her? She didn't know whether she was flattered or alarmed. It had been a long time since a man had looked at her quite like that, even Frank. It was very disconcerting.

She distracted herself by examining the vaulted ceiling and admiring the stained glass windows. St Bart's really was a beautiful church. Then, as the congregation began to arrive in dribs and drabs, Mildred and Alf came over to say hello, and she forgot about the vicar.

More people arrived, and while the church wasn't full, Grazja guessed that Gina's message-spreading at the Siltby festival yesterday had been effective as there were at least fifty people in attendance.

Gina came over, told Alf and Mildred to 'shove up' so she could remove her coat and take her place on the front pew with them, ready to step up for her star turn when the vicar announced her name.

Grazja, turning to see who else had arrived, spotted Pam Stimson marching up the aisle, trailed by her other half, Ray Watts (who looked thoroughly miserable to be out of his warm bed), heading for the display in front of the altar.

'Uh oh,' Grazja thought. She braced herself to intercede in a bust-up between Gina and Pam over the wheatsheaf basket swap as Pauline hurried to meet Pam, gesticulating towards the display.

Gina hadn't seen Pam yet, her eyes fixed proudly on her basket, but Pauline was pointing to the back of Gina's head, and Grazja could see the icy downturn of Pam's mouth.

'Oh, oh,' she thought again.

But then the vicar had glided up to Pam and Pauline, smiling up at Pam, saying something soothing – Grazja couldn't imagine what – and Pam seemed to melt before her eyes. Her body language changed from stiff and bristling to slightly shy and coquettish. The vicar said something else, and Pam laughed, nodding her head, looking pleased. The vicar moved on to talk to another arrival and Pam dragged Ray into a pew.

The dangerous moment was over, just like that.

Grazja shook her head in disbelief. It almost restored her faith; two miracles in one morning – Gina's basket balancing and no bust-up between Gina and Pam. Three, if she counted being found attractive by a handsome younger man.

Pah! Grazja thought to herself. I must be losing it if I think that.

Ten minutes later she dismissed the idea of miracles when Gina got up to proudly 'open' Harvest Festival and the board that had been slowly bowing under the weight of Gina's basket suddenly gave way. A small avalanche of rolling tins, jars, cabbages and apples tumbled down. Glass broke and water splashed; flowers were crushed in the flow, packets hit the flagged floor and split, throwing up a cloud of flour dust that landed over Gina, the vicar and the front pew.

The congregation gasped, Pauline screamed and Gina stood blinking in shock through the flour dust. Soon the only sound was a tin of beans rolling along an aisle, until Ray Watts stuck out his foot and brought it to an abrupt stop.

The church fell silent.

To Gina's left the one thing still standing at the base of the display was Pam's artfully crafted wheatsheaf.

Grazja hurried forward and drew Gina to the pew to sit her down. Fortunately nothing had hit her except flour.

Everybody waited, as the vicar, cassock liberally dusted with white, mounted the pulpit and looked out at his flock.

'As you can see,' he said, sweeping his hand forward. 'What the good Lord giveth, He can also taketh away.' He grinned.

Suddenly the congregation was laughing.

Grazja looked at Gina who blinked back at her with dazed, somehow hurt eyes.

'It okay,' Grazja whispered. 'It is funny. Let's laugh together.' She prodded Gina and began to laugh, nodding encouragement to her friend.

After a second Gina joined in until tears rolled down her cheeks. No one suspected they weren't tears of laughter.

In the Diner

It was three o' clock on a rainy Thursday afternoon two days after Halloween and The Last Resort Diner was quiet. Two men perched on the stools at the counter, behind which Rick was pouring himself a coffee to join them for a chat. One other man – Peter Moss – sat alone in a booth nursing a long-lasting cup of tea and pouring over his monthly copy of Ferret News, while keeping an ear on the conversation.

Frank had come from his ghost train where he had begun painting the cars ready for next season. With the funfair closed up for the winter now that the school half-term had passed, Frank used his time to do all the maintenance jobs that kept the ride running.

'How are the puppies doing?' Rick asked Frank.

'Great,' Frank said. 'Although Grazja says there's one runt they need to keep an eye on.'

The puppies were the unexpected progeny of a sneaky coupling between Bing Crosby and a Great Dane called Daisy, both of whom lived with Eleanor Branwin at the animal sanctuary Grazja worked at. They'd been born two days ago on Halloween and were much anticipated. What the puppies would look like had been a topic of hot debate in Mapton, with such a disparity in size between the parents. It was too early to tell - at the moment they were just wriggling, blind bundles nosing for their mother's teat – but that didn't stop the conjecture.

'Bing's like Tom Cruise,' Rick said. 'He might be slight in stature but he likes his ladies tall. He's secure in himself.'

'Huh,' grunted Ray Watts, the other man at the counter. 'Like me.' His words were light but his expression was glum.

In an earlier life Ray had worked with Pam as a redcoat at Butlin's, and as part of the evening's entertainments, Pam used to settle the diminutive Ray on her knee as they sang a duet together.

Rick regarded him.

'You okay, Ray? You don't seem yourself.'

Ray sighed, a deep, unhappy exhalation. 'Tell you the truth, Rick, it's Pam.'

'Is she all right?' Rick asked. 'Not ill I hope?'

'Oh, aye, she's dandy. Got a real spring in her step and a glint in her eye. Trouble is, it ain't for me. It's for that vicar.'

Rick raised his eyebrows. 'No! The St Bart's dude? I keep hearing about him but I haven't met him yet. Supposed to be a handsome devil. You don't seriously think Pam and him…'

'…are playing toad in the hole?' Ray grimaced. 'Nah, but I'm not sure Pam wouldn't take him up on it if the offer came up. It's more like she's got a crush on him like a school girl. She's been to church every Sunday morning since Harvest Festival and does the flowers at St Bart's three times a week. She tries to say his name all casual-like but it comes out as a high squeak. Worse thing is…' Ray lowered his voice, 'Sunday mornings was me and Pam's … you know.'

'Toad in the hole time,' Frank said, straight-faced, as Rick tried not to laugh.

'Yeah,' Ray said. 'And now it's bloody church instead, with Pam getting up especially early to do her make-up so she looks good for the vicar.'

'Maybe she's just got religion,' Pete Moss butted in from his booth. 'It happens.'

Ray swivelled on his stool. 'This is a private conversation, Peter.'

'Should have it in private then,' Peter retorted. 'This is a public place if you hadn't noticed. And like I said,' he continued undeterred, 'how do you know Pam ain't just got religion? Happened to my cousin Jim. He was the most godless man you ever met until one day, he was parking on a double yellow line, and bam! He said God just came to him in a flash and told him to mend his ways. Now you can find him in all weathers waving a placard in the Brough rest area on the A46.'

'On the way to Lincoln?' Frank asked. 'With the sign that says 'Sinners Pay to Park in Hell'?

'That's him,' Peter nodded, pleased. 'But when he turns his sign round it says 'Repenters Park for Free in Heaven'.'

'Catchy,' Rick said.

Ray was irritated. 'Well Pam hasn't 'got religion'; she's got the hots for that good looking vicar, it's obvious.'

'She's not the only one,' Rick said. 'Mildred has been gushing about the new vicar. Told me the other day he had the best hair she'd ever seen on a man.'

'Mildred?' Ray shook his head. 'She's about a hundred and one. What's she doing looking at men like that? She's not got a chance.'

Rick smiled to himself, finding it touching that Ray assumed that Pam did have a chance with the vicar because in Ray's eyes Pam was an outstanding beauty and utterly irresistible.

'It's not just the more mature women,' Rick added. 'There were a bunch of teen girls in on Saturday morning. I heard them giggling about how good-looking the vicar was. There's talk of him starting a youth club.'

'Bloody hell,' Ray stamped his fist on the counter. 'He's like a disease they're all catching. It's creepy. He's a vicar not a rock star.' He stood up suddenly. 'I'm going to go home and tell Pam what I think,' he said.

'Easy,' Rick said. 'You need to think it through. Don't do anything stupid.'

'It's all I have been thinking about,' Ray said hotly. 'I've put up with it, even gone along to church every Sunday but not anymore. That man is a threat to all of us. You watch, it'll be Stella and Grazja next.'

He grabbed his coat from where he'd slung it across an empty bench and headed out into the rain.

Peter rose from his booth, slid on his waterproof parka, tucked his Ferret News into his inside pocket and announced, 'That's why I live on me own. Never gone in for that relationship nonsense. Nothing but drama and heartache as far as I can see. I've always preferred ferrets to women. Can't send a woman down a rabbit hole, can you?'

'No,' Rick grinned. 'That's a fact I can't argue with.'

'See you tomorrow,' Peter said, tipping them a salute as he ambled out.

'See you Pete.'

Frank looked thoughtful. 'You know, it's Pauline Watkins that concerns me. She's working as his assistant. She's a very vulnerable young woman. Remember she got involved with that nasty Jim character last year. He was using her for sex. She's easily conned.'

'You really think this vicar might be doing the same?' Rick frowned. 'That's a serious accusation.'

'I'm not accusing him,' Frank said. 'It just makes me a bit suspicious. Grazja thought Pauline seemed besotted with him.'

'What did Grazja make of the handsome vicar?' Rick asked, curious.

Frank pulled a rueful face. 'She seemed a bit cagey about him, if I'm honest. Didn't say much.'

Rick nodded. 'That's the impression I got from Stella too. Interesting. So, do you think we have the Devil in our midst?'

Frank shook his head. 'I stopped believing in the Devil a long time ago. It's human beings that worry me.'

'What's this guy's name, anyway?' Rick asked. 'Everyone just calls him the vicar.'

'It's Michael, 'Frank said. 'Michael Rivers.'

'The Reverend Rivers.' Rick said. 'Slick name, slick operator?'

'Maybe,' Frank nodded. 'Worth keeping a discreet eye on I think. Maybe find out where he's come from.'

'P.I. Frank Manning back in action?' Rick said. 'You should start your own agency.'

Frank laughed. 'I'll get a trilby and a trench coat.'

'Hopefully you'll discover that we're all a bunch of sad guys who can't take a bit of competition from a good-looking vicar,' Rick said.

'Most likely,' Frank agreed.

Judy's Dress

'Ow!' Gina squirmed. 'Mind me bosoms. You'll pop 'em at this rate.'

'Stop wriggling then,' Elliot replied. 'And as for your bosoms you're already suffering a slow puncture in that department.'

'Cheeky bogger,' Gina swiped at him. 'I don't stick on a pair of falsies like you do. I bleed you know?'

It was mid-November, and Elliot's third meeting with Mayor Gina Pontin of Mapton on Sea. Today he was at Gina's house, trying to fit the bodice for her Judy Garland dress if only the damned woman would stay still.

The first time he had met Gina, it was with Grazja who'd driven her over to Skegness to visit his shop. Gina was as vivid and gobby as Elliot had expected from various interviews and news reports. He'd enjoyed following her fortunes and misfortunes, from her emergence in the heady days of the Mapton Knights, campaigning against the possibility of a caravan park for swingers, to reports of her jealously smashing every window in her lover's bungalow, to her unexpected election to town councillor (complete with public marriage proposal), to town mayor, and finally - Ta Dah! - to the spectacular donkey rescue of the summer just gone.

Elliot had been looking forward to meeting her so much; and yes, she was as colourful and sparky as he'd hoped, but she was clearly homophobic. That was something he hadn't expected, based on his belief - naively perhaps - that a shared love of Judy Garland would indicate she was gay-friendly. A friend of a friend of Dorothy, so to speak.

She was not. She hadn't openly said so but Elliot had seen it in her eyes and in the curl of her lip. It was a look he knew all too well. Straight people thought that coming out was something you did just once in your life in some flamboyant or dramatic way. But unlike the debutantes, with whom the term 'coming out' originated, and used to be presented at court to enter 'society' and make suitable marriage matches, LGBT people did not get one big reveal as imagined, but came out again and again throughout life in exhausting increments. Every time you booked as a couple into a B&B, or started a new job, or made a new straight friend, you came out. It didn't just end with your social circle and family (if you could tell them). It began with them and carried on forever.

Outside the gay scene or his own social groups, Elliot always experienced that involuntary brace; waiting for the look, the comment, the subtle slight.

Things had moved on of course, vastly so in many areas, but 'gay' still remained an insult in school playgrounds and homosexuality an offence punishable by death in some cultures and places around the world. It was only a matter of decades since male homosexuality was illegal in Britain. Elliot's own uncle had been imprisoned after a police raid on an underground gay club in the late 50s which became a rarely mentioned skeleton in the family closet. In later life, Uncle Malcolm lived with a partner who everyone in the family politely referred to as his 'lodger'. Growing up, Elliot sensed something else lay beneath the careful use of 'lodger' and it disturbed him in a way he didn't understand until his teens. It gave him both a funny thrill in the pit of his stomach and a vague sense of dread and shame. Coming out to his family in his twenties had not been easy for Elliot. His twenties, in fact, had been a whirl of blissful moments and agonising pain. His parents rejected him while his first serious boyfriend died of AIDs. The papers called it 'the gay disease' and others 'God's punishment'. It was a terrifying, confusing time and Elliot had started to unravel. Then one night a friend had hauled him to a drag night at their local gay bar. It had been a pretty ramshackle show, but it changed Elliot's life. In fact, he thought it had saved his life because he'd been edging towards suicidal despair. Elliot had grown up in a family where showing any kind of strong emotion was seen as tantamount to madness and deviating from the 'norm' as untenable. Outwardly expressing his grief, confusion, anger, and pain, seemed almost impossible to Elliot. Yet his exposure to drag suddenly opened him up to the possibility of a new world, one where he could create an alternative version of himself – a herself – that could say all the things he just couldn't say.

His first alter-ego wasn't Glinda Sparkle, which was his current act, but Vonda Mean. And Vonda *was* mean on stage. So much so, that even by the waspish, acerbity of drag queen standards, she sometimes got booed offstage.

But Elliot didn't care. Vonda was such a release for him. Vonda was all rage – a spitting cat - and she was what he needed at that time in his life.

When he was a child, Elliot's older twin sisters liked to dress him in their clothes and experiment with make-up on him. He had loved it – the pretty clothes, the silky make-up, but more than that, the attention lavished on him. He enjoyed the gentle touch of his sisters' fingers on his skin and the constant chatter between them as they chose a lipstick, added a flowered scarf, took a step back to admire their work, wiped it all off and started again.

Elliot never felt so safe and embraced as he did in the room his sisters - Lucy and Caro – shared. Five years older than him, they seemed to possess a secret feminine knowledge that impressed and beguiled him.

Elliot's father had discovered them one day, coming into the girls' bedroom unexpectedly in a rare display of paternal interest. Lucy and Caro had dressed six year old Elliot in Lucy's pink ballet tutu, Caro's cheesecloth flouncy blouse and silver wedge sandals. They'd slid sparkly hair grips into his 1970's bowl cut (cut by his mum) and diligently made up his face with the requisite blue eyeshadow, circles of rose blusher and cerise lipstick.

His dad had gone ballistic.

'Are you trying to make him queer?' he yelled at the girls. Yanking Elliot out of the room by the arm he dragged his small son into the bathroom, and proceeded to roughly scrub off the make-up with soap and water while Elliot blubbed.

The girls hovered in the doorway, shocked.

'It's only a bit of fun, Dad,' Caro said. 'We just practise our make-up on him. He doesn't mind; he likes it'

Caro had assumed that Dad thought they were hurting Elliot and this must be the reason for his rage. Trying to reassure him – appease him – she unintentionally enraged him further.

'He shouldn't like it,' Dad shouted. 'You shouldn't like it.' He shook his son. A feeling Elliot never forgot.

Mum came running up the stairs, appearing in the doorway behind the girls.

'What's happened?' she cried. 'Is Elliot hurt?'

The girls had started crying now, along with their little brother.

'Look at him,' Dad said, furiously scrubbing still. 'See how they've dressed him, Ellen? He's wearing make-up like a girl.'

'Is that all?' Mum was angry. She pushed her way past the girls. 'Stop it, David. You're hurting him!' She crouched as Elliot threw himself into her arms, sobbing uncontrollably.

'Do you want him to become another Malcolm?' his father demanded.

Elliot remembered the way his mother had stiffened, the tremble of sudden fear in her voice as she said. 'Don't be ridiculous, David. He's a little boy. He has no idea what it means. It was just a silly game.' She swept Elliot out of the room.

At bedtime, when Elliot was tucked in, his father came in to say goodnight, seeming sheepish.

'I might have overreacted a bit today, son,' he said, tussling Elliot's hair. 'But you know, you shouldn't let your sisters push you into things. Girls can be silly like that, thinking about hair and make-up and clothes. It's natural for them but not what boys do.'

Elliot listened silently.

His father laughed nervously. 'You didn't like them dressing you up, did you?'

Elliot had learnt a lot that day. He was wise enough to shake his head. 'No,' he said. 'It was their game. I didn't want to play it but they made me.'

His father smiled with relief. 'I thought so. Well, like I said, don't let the twins make you do things you don't like.'

'Yes, Dad,' Elliot nodded. 'I won't. Girls are silly.'

His dad laughed. 'Yes, they are a bit silly, but that's the way they're made and when you grow up you'll like their silly ways but you won't want to be like them. Understand?'

Elliot didn't really, but he did understand that he needed to say yes. He understood that whatever Uncle Malcolm was, he needed to be careful from now on, or risk being like him and thus rejected. Daddy, in particular, didn't like Uncle Malcolm, even though he was his own brother.

'I'm sorry I overreacted,' Dad said. 'But everything is all right now.'

But it wasn't. And when Elliot came out to his parents in his early twenties his father's reaction was worse. Even his mother, who had denied he would turn out like Uncle Malcolm, turned away for a time, although she came round after a year or so. Caro and Lucy always loved him, although Caro once confessed to him that she harboured a secret guilt that they had 'turned him gay' by dressing him up when they were children.

Elliot reassured her that a person did not 'turn' gay. He never believed that his sexuality had been 'caused' but was an integral and essential part of himself. More importantly, he told Caro, that even if it had been possible, it wouldn't matter because, despite what they'd been raised by their family and a great part of society to believe, being gay wasn't something to be ashamed of.

'But you must feel it is,' he said to Caro,' for you to feel guilty.'

'No!' Caro denied this passionately. 'It's just I don't want to be the cause of all the pain you've had to go through because you are gay. Mum and Dad, AIDs,

Adrian's death.' They were both a bit drunk. She looked at him through teary lashes. 'Did I cause that?'

'Never,' he said fiercely, wrapping her into a protective hug. 'You know, those times with you and Lucy, they were the best part of my childhood. I adored my big sisters. And I felt so damn pretty! I missed our dress-up sessions after Dad stopped us.'

Caro half groaned, half laughed. 'Vonda Mean is not very pretty,' she said.

Elliot was in his early thirties by then, and had just met Tim. He was happy.

'You know,' he replied to his sister. 'I'm thinking of retiring her. I'm ready for a new alter-ego – Glinda Sparkle – much prettier than Vonda.'

'And kinder?' Caro asked.

'More a Dolly Parton than a Joan Rivers,' Elliot said.

'I could do Glinda's make-up,' Caro sniffled.

'Honey,' Elliot smiled, wiping away a black rivulet of mascara from Caro's cheek. 'I should be the one doing your make-up. You haven't changed this look since 1985.'

Elliot was jerked out of his memories by Gina hissing. 'Not so tight.'

He realised he'd tried to pin her into a waist that wasn't really going to pinch into waspish.

'Sorry,' he said, unpinning the seam.

He took a step back to examine Gina critically. 'You know, this would work much better if you wore a corset.'

'I don't want a corset,' Gina said. 'I want to be able to breathe at my wedding.'

'I'd make sure you could breathe,' Elliot said. 'But this dress needs some structure beneath it. You need a waist.'

'I got a waist!' Gina said. 'I got the waist I had at seventeen.'

Elliot raised an eyebrow at her.

'Almost,' Gina said. 'Not far off.'

'You've got a perfectly good waist for those elasticated trousers,' Elliot said archly. 'Which are lovely by the way. But you don't have the waist of a young Judy Garland.'

'Judy Garland didn't have the waist of a young Judy Garland,' Gina snapped. 'They kept her on diet pills and put her in a corset.'

Elliot could see the look of horror in her eyes the moment the words popped out of her mouth and she realised her mistake.

'Exactly!' Elliot crowed. 'Even Judy at her thinnest needed structure under the dress. It's just the way these dresses are made.'

'That don't make it bleedin' right' Gina said. 'Get me outta this. I'm boiling.'

Sighing, Elliot unpinned the bodice grimacing at the sight of Gina's sagging bra.

'You know, if you refuse to wear a corset, then at least get a pair of Spanx and a decent bra that lifts you up,' he said. 'Try Miss Mary of Sweden.'

Gina blazed red. 'That's it,' she shouted. 'I knew this was a mistake. I shouldn'ta let Grazja talk me into it. I don't need a big poofter like you telling me what I should wear. You might like to wear a corset for some perverted reason but I don't. You got no right to comment on my body.'

'Ah, and there we have it,' Elliot said stiffly. 'The real reason for your attitude. You're homophobic.'

'I ain't homo nothing,' Gina. 'I don't like you telling me my body ain't good enough.'

'Oh, I suppose calling me 'poofter' and 'perverted' was just a slip of the tongue?'

'Everyone says 'poofter',' Gina said. 'It's like saying gay, ain't it? It's not an insult.'

'It is when someone like you says it and adds 'perverted' for good measure. It tells me exactly what you think. I'm very disappointed, Mayor Pontin. I had so admired you. I didn't expect you to be such a small-minded bigot or I would never have offered to make the dress. I don't need the money or the extra work; believe me, I'm busy enough. I thought it might be fun to get to know you but it hasn't been any fun at all. You won't be getting your wedding dress from me, and good luck trying to find anyone else to make it in time, or any dress really.' He gathered his things and marched for the door.

'You can't not do the dress,' Gina cried. 'You agreed and I already paid you for materials.'

'Oh, I think I will still make the dress,' Elliot flung back. 'I'll make it for Glinda Sparkle – my perverse other self – she's always happy to wear a corset and her boobs and waist are perfect, darling, No sag or thickening there. As for the money, I'll return that tout suite. You can use it to buy yourself some better upholstery, dear Mayor.'

#

Three days later, Grazja walked into his shop.

'Hello,' Elliot smiled. 'Do you want another wig or is this about your friend Gina?'

'It about Gina,' Grazja admitted. 'She very upset.'

'Upset about calling me a pervert and a poofter, or because she won't get her dress?'

'Ah,' Grazja nodded. 'About the dress. The other part she not tell me but I not surprised. My fault; I should have warned you. Sorry.'

'If you knew Gina was anti-gay and anti-drag why did you ask me, of all people, to make her dress?'

'Because you the best,' Grazja said. 'Gina want Judy Garland dress and you make wonderful bespoke dresses. Gina hate everyone at first. That how she is. She hated me – called me lots of xenophobic names.'

'Really?' Elliot was interested. He liked Grazja and couldn't see her putting up with nonsense. 'Why are you friends with her?'

Grazja laughed. 'I get asked that a lot. Gina like wounded animal. She lash out before you hurt her. It's her automatic response, especially if she feels vulnerable. I think early experiences taught her to do that. But she has been good friend to me. Not best friend; her daughter Stella is my best friend but we are very close. She is fiercely loyal once she likes you and funny.'

'She wasn't very funny with me, just bigoted,' Elliot said.

'She got prejudices many of her generation have,' Grazja said. She hesitated then asked. 'Gina claim you humiliate her. You say she got thick waist and saggy boobs.'

'I just said she'd need a corset under that dress,' Elliot.

'You not say she had 'thick waist and saggy boobs'? Grazja eyed him sternly.

Elliot blushed. 'I may have implied it,' he said. 'If that's the way she took it. But she can't carry that sort of dress off without some structure. It won't look right.'

'It was never going to look right to us,' Grazja said. 'That not point. Point is Gina love that dress and wants to wear it to get married in. She will look at herself in mirror and see beautiful woman. Gina very proud of her figure for her age. Doesn't matter what we see. I want her to be happy. She had a lot of sadness in her life; some things I know and much I don't. I saw it when I first meet her and she awful to me and I still see it now we are friends.'

Elliot wondered if Grazja could see it in him too. He was touched by her speech despite himself. He liked Grazja very much. When she'd come into his shop the first time and been so drawn to the blonde wig, yet so embarrassed to try it on, he'd been intrigued. His shop attracted people looking to dress-up, to step into a fantasy and break-out of the mundane, even if it was just for a party or a night out. Trying on costumes and wigs made them laugh. They wanted to show their friends.

Grazja's wanting to hide her purchase from Frank had made Elliot curious. He'd wondered if Frank was abusive, and Grazja needed a disguise to escape from him but he hoped not as he'd liked Frank too. And he didn't really feel that this was the case. Grazja hadn't seemed afraid of Frank, rather just shy and embarrassed. Instead he got the impression that Grazja felt the wig was something too frivolous, too self-indulgent and vain, to want to admit to desiring, even though she'd been unable to resist it.

'Are you here because you still want me to make Gina's dress?'

Grazja nodded. 'I do. Gina want that. She has heart set on that dress. She's willing to apologise, which Gina never does.'

Elliot sighed, pursing his lips as he thought it through.

'All right,' he said.' But I have two conditions. The first is that Gina must come to my drag show, and my second is that you come with her and wear your blonde wig.'

Rick's Surprise

It was a miserable December morning. Rick's hardier early birds had already been and gone, braving the freezing wind and rain for hot coffee and breakfast to fortify themselves before dealing with whatever the day held in store for them.

By nine-thirty the diner was dead. Rick switched off Golden Coast Radio, the local station which seemed to be playing Slade's *Merry Christmas Everybody* on constant rotation with Wizzard's *I Wish It Could Be Christmas Everyday* and Paul McCartney's *Pipes of Peace*. With the radio off he could hear the waves crashing against the shore and the sleet spattering the windows. He liked the natural sounds and the sense of respite from Christmas jollity. Rick didn't mind the Christmas buzz; having a little kid made Christmas feel fun again – magical in a way it hadn't been since he'd been a kid himself in Iowa. Still, it was good to take a break from it. If he heard Slade one more time he might go berserk and smash his radio. He needed to bring in some other festive tunes to play to keep the customers happy without sending himself insane.

He hoped Sue Mulligan would come in this morning. He'd seen her yesterday when she'd sailed up late afternoon, her Rascal Vision mobility scooter festooned in Christmas lights, blasting Shakin' Stevens from her ancient portable CD player. The season didn't start until Sue rocked up on her festive scooter in the first week of December. Yesterday, Sue had put a brave face on it, as cheery and bantering as ever, yet Rick thought she wasn't okay, and hadn't been okay for a year, not since she'd lost her beloved little dog, Scampi. Tears had filled her eyes when he mentioned it but then Gina had arrived, followed by Stella and Gerta and the brief glimpse Rick had of Sue's pain had disappeared again behind her laughing mask.

Sue would never let Gina glimpse a weakness. There was history between them which involved George, and Gina would pounce if she saw the opportunity to land an emotional blow.

Rick guessed that beneath Sue's jolly surface she was fragile and lonely and he felt for her. Sue had been very kind to him when he'd first come to Mapton and he never forgot it.

If she came in today, he'd make sure they'd have a proper chat as it was unlikely to get too busy and Gina didn't come into the diner very often. It had been surprising to see her yesterday, meeting up with Pious Pauline – Pauline Watkins, Rick corrected himself, remembering Frank's disapproval – as Gina had never indicated anything but contempt for the zealous young woman. But it seemed that Gina hadn't abandoned her hope to secure a June wedding by winning the vicar over. She was meeting Pauline to discuss some madcap scheme they had come up with for the church on Christmas Eve.

Sue had muttered to him: 'I thought the cock-up she made of the harvest festival put paid to that nonsense.'

Rick had laughed. 'Well, you know our beloved mayor. She's determined to have a church wedding and the new vicar's making her jump through hoops to do it.'

Sue had rolled her eyes comically. 'You're a saint putting up with her, Ricky. I dunno how you do it, having her as a mother-in-law.'

Remembering it made Rick smile again but his mood soon dipped.

He poured himself a coffee and sat down at a booth with the notebook he kept for jotting down recipe ideas to serve at his pop-up restaurant in Lawton. This year he'd been thinking more and more about moving to Lawton, which was a metropolis compared to Mapton and nearby Siltby. Mapton had been exactly what he needed when he'd washed up here some years ago, a broken-down Michelin-starred chef wanting a simpler life and somewhere to hide. Running his diner, listening to the waves and the everyday gossip, had been all he wanted for a while. Then Stella had come into his life, bringing with her the tantalising echoes of a more cosmopolitan scene. Stella was an artist, and Rick had been one too in his old life, a culinary artist, lauded for his food. Falling in love with her had reawakened his creative juices he supposed, so he'd dipped his toe back into haute cuisine (or posh nosh as Gina dismissively called it) setting up a once a week pop-up kitchen in Lawton at his friend, Jill's deli. And it was very successful, so much so that Rick thought he could make a real go of it and bumped it up to two nights a week, while his partner in The Last Resort Diner, Angela, took over more of his shifts.

During the summer Rick had suggested to Stella that they think about moving to Lawton but Stella really didn't want to, so they agreed to leave it for another year and then review the situation.

Rick had been okay with that back in August.

Sure, he wished Mapton wasn't such a cultural desert sometimes – it didn't even have a book store, although the local library was great – but there was so much here that he still loved. There was the sea with its ever changing aspects, his friends and his customers.. A move to Lawton would make the sea and his friends only a forty minute drive away. His family would come with him or it was a no go altogether. What he would miss were his regulars at the diner. Mildred and Alf taking a ridiculous amount of time to choose which kind of cake to have with a cuppa; Pete Moss always wanting to sit by himself yet butting in to others' conversations; Andy Timmis promising this was his last burger before his big diet began. And Sue of, of course, his favourite. He'd missed her during the summer months when she'd gone for a prolonged stay with her sister.

Rick enjoyed the banter, the gossip, the occasional surprising revelations that made up the rhyme and rhythm of days in the diner.

The door opened in a blast of sleet and icy wind, setting the bell jangling, as a bundled figure staggered in.

Rick got up, crossing smoothly to slide behind the counter as the man managed to shut the door on the insistent wind. Flicking on the radio Rick heard, miracle of miracles, a classic crooner singing Silver Bells. So Golden Coast Radio did have more than three Christmas songs on its playlist, thank the Lord.

The man unwound his scarf, pulled off his woolly hat, unzipped his heavy anorak, hanging them all on the hat stand beside the door. When he turned, Rick saw his dog-collar and startling blue eyes in a chiselled handsome face, and knew he was finally about to meet the infamous vicar of St Bart's.

'Afternoon,' he said, smiling. 'Reverend Rivers I presume?'

The vicar touched his dog-collar. 'Bit of a give-away isn't it?'

'Sure is,' Rick said, thinking but not saying 'that and your movie star looks.'

'And are you Rick? American owner of the diner I've heard so much about?'

'That's me,' Rick said. 'I hope you've been hearing good things?'

'Only good things,' the vicar nodded, perching himself on a stool at the counter. 'People have been telling me for ages to grab a bite at The Last Resort. To tell you the truth the name put me off at first – made me think you'd only eat here if it was your last resort but I've been assured otherwise. My assistant Pauline spent most of this morning raving about your Christmas cookies.'

'I use my mom's recipe,' Rick said. 'Only me, my mom, and my business partner Ang, knows it. Ang had to sign an oath in blood never to divulge it.'

The vicar laughed. So far he seemed like a regular affable guy to Rick. Handsome, yeah, but not the devilish seducer Rick had been imagining.

'Well, I thought I'd come along today and try them for myself with a coffee. Introduce myself to some more locals...' He looked around.

'Wrong time of day mixed with terrible weather,' Rick explained. 'In summer we'd be packed with tourists so the locals tend to come early morning or towards closing time and they tend to keep those hours in the winter even when it's quieter.'

'Ah, I see,' the vicar said. 'Bad timing.'

'But hey, I'm a local,' Rick said, pouring a coffee for the vicar before turning to the cookie jar. 'You can talk to me. I've been curious to meet you; heard a lot about you and St Bart's lately from my mother-in-law. She's been attending regularly on Sunday mornings.'

The vicar's expression was unreadable. 'Ah, yes, our esteemed mayor,' he said. 'Gina's a key member of my little flock. Really proactive. She and Pauline are planning something very special for Christmas Eve that Gina really thinks will bring people in to St Bart's.'

'Oh?' Rick said. 'What's that?'

'An early Christmas Eve service for animals – a chance to have your pets blessed and share the joy of Christ's birth with them,' the vicar said. 'After all our Lord was born in a stable amongst the lowly beasts.'

Rick tried not to laugh. 'That sounds like a recipe for disaster. A church full of animals and Gina. Didn't her addition to Harvest Festival put you off?'

The vicar's smile was beatific. 'Ah, but that's the wonder of God's mysterious workings. What you call a disaster was a gift for St Bart's. We had more visitors to our church after that than before. And while some came to laugh, a few stayed with us. Slowly but surely our flock is growing, and Gina has much to do with that.'

'There's no such thing as bad publicity,' Rick said.

'It wasn't bad publicity,' the vicar disagreed. 'It was an amusing example of human error and the ability to rise above it.'

'That's a very nice way of saying Gina caused a small avalanche because she wanted to display the biggest basket in the place. To me it looks like hubris and nemesis.'

'Ah, you're an educated man, I see. Well, the Greek gods might agree but our Saviour Christ does not go in for that sort of petty tit for tat. These cookies really are excellent by the way.'

'Thanks,' Rick said. 'But what about the proverb 'Pride comes before a fall'?'

The vicar shook his head. 'Not technically what it says in the bible.'

'Ok, more accurately then: 'Pride goeth before destruction, and a haughty spirit before a fall' Proverbs 16:18.'

The vicar seemed delighted. 'I see you know your bible! I'm impressed.'

As though the man had flicked a headlight switch onto full beam, Rick suddenly found himself riveted by the vicar's piercing blue eyes.

'I was raised American Lutheran,' Rick explained. 'My mom's a great believer but me, nah. Not so much.'

'That's a shame,' the vicar said, still holding him with his intense gaze. 'You really should come to St Bart's sometime. Attend a service or come for a chat with me. I'm sure we can rekindle your faith.'

Rick actually felt himself blush. He was a man very secure in his sexuality. Gay men had sometimes flirted with him, and he'd batted away any advances with grace and good humour without ever once considering an offer tempting. But, Jesus, there was something so charismatically mesmeric in the vicar's gaze.

Again, the entrance bell jangled as the wind pushed another customer through the door.

It broke the spell. Relieved, Rick tore his eyes away from the vicar to see Frank pull the hood back on his parka.

'Hey Frank,' Rick called.

Frank lifted his hand as he unzipped his parka.

The vicar gulped back his coffee, deposited the last crumbs of cookie on one fingertip into his mouth and got out his wallet.

'I'll take a couple of cookies for Pauline,' he said. 'She's such a hard worker.'

Rick reached under the counter for a paper bag to put the cookies in, as Frank drew out a stool next to the vicar.

'Frank, this is Reverend Rivers, you know, from St Bart's.'

'Ah, the new vicar,' Frank said, putting out his hand for the vicar to shake.

'Please, you should call me Michael,' the vicar said to both men. 'I'm only Reverend on Sundays.'

'Nice to meet you, Michael,' Frank replied, as they shook. 'I'm Frank Manning. I run Mapton's ghost train.'

'Aha!' the vicar drew back. 'You wouldn't be, by any chance, the Frank Manning who's been making enquiries about me in my old parish?'

Frank didn't blink. 'Caught out,' he admitted. 'I have been making some enquiries, yes. I've been a bit concerned about Pauline Watkins you see. I know she's assisting you but she's quite an easily influenced young woman. She's been taken advantage of before so I just wanted to make sure she'd be safe working with you.'

The vicar nodded thoughtfully. 'And what did you discover?'

Frank smiled, although Rick didn't think it reached his eyes. 'Nothing bad,' he said. 'In fact, Mrs Beaton had only good things to say about you. They miss you a lot.'

Reverend Rivers smiled back. 'And I them,' he said. 'Bless Mrs Beaton but I feel God has directed me to where I am needed.'

He reached and warmly clasped Frank's arm. 'I appreciate your concern for Pauline. I agree; she is a vulnerable young woman. I get the feeling this town hasn't been very nice to her- take the name Pious Pauline, for example. I know about some of her past experiences too and I would in no way take advantage of such an innocent soul. Pauline is very happy working as my assistant and I couldn't do without her. I'm very glad to know there are others who care about her too.'

Frank said, 'We look out for each other in Mapton.'

'As God wants us to,' the vicar smiled. 'You know,' he said, turning to Frank so that they walked together to the door where the vicar gathered his coat and woollies. 'I sense you are a very spiritual man, Frank. I really hope you pay me a visit at St Bart's.'

Frank merely nodded.

As the vicar disappeared into the gathering winter gloom, and the door swung shut, Frank turned to Rick.

'I wouldn't trust that man as far as I could throw him,' Frank declared. 'I swear he just flirted with me.'

Drag Night

'How was it, love?' George asked, as Gina sank inelegantly onto the sofa.

'It were magic,' Gina sighed. 'Loads of old classics. I tell you, that Glinda Sparkle can sing like 'em all – Judy, Marilyn, Doris Day… She's so talented… He I mean… I think…' she lolled her head towards Stella. 'That was Elliot?' She sounded puzzled.

Stella looked at Grazja. They'd just returned from Elliot's Christmas drag night at Pompadours, a cabaret club in Skegness. As designated driver Stella was sober, Grazja was mildly tipsy and Gina was pretty squiffy having downed a few Babychams.

Stella had never met Elliot so she couldn't compare Glinda's staggering glamorous presence to the man Grazja and Gina knew.

Grazja nodded. 'Yes, that was Elliot. I couldn't believe my eyes when I see him. So beautiful!'

You can talk, Stella thought to herself. Grazja had told her about the wig but when she had put it on at the beginning of the evening she'd stunned them. The blonde wig really suited Grazja and Stella even found herself feeling envious of the transformation, especially after Grazja let her try it on. The wig made Stella look like a washed out milk pudding. Stella was definitely meant to be a brunette.

It was a little disturbing to see Grazja looking more glamorous. She was always attractive, but in a pleasant, pragmatic way. Although Stella didn't like to admit it, she was used to being the prettier one. In Mapton she didn't have much competition in that department which was rather nice.

Until this evening, Stella had never realised she unconsciously thought this way. Experiencing a stab of envy and competitive edge towards her friend made her feel guilty and small. Of course she didn't show it. She adored Grazja and hated herself for her uncharitable reaction, so what she'd said was: 'Oh my God, you look fabulous. That wig really suits you!'

What Gina had said was: 'Bloody hell! You look like a movie star. Haven't I always told yer to make more of yerself?'

Grazja had blushed, pleased but shy. As the evening had gone on she'd become more comfortable, less self-aware, and consequently more beautiful.

'What does Frank think?' Stella asked her before they went out.

Grazja pulled her face. 'I not shown him,' she said. 'He not know I bought it.'

'Why?' Stella cried. 'You look amazing in it.'

'I don't know,' Grazja said. 'I feel embarrassed. What if he doesn't like it?'

'It's only a bleedin' wig,' Gina interjected. 'Not a face transplant. You can take it off. Anyway, who cares what Frank thinks. If you like it you should wear it.'

'What if George didn't like you in something you bought?' Grazja asked.

'George likes everything I wear,' Gina said. 'He likes everything about me.'

'Lucky you,' Stella said wryly, thinking that George was just too wise to say anything to the contrary. 'Rick would hate me to change my hair. He loves it. I've talked about having it cut sometimes and he's like 'no, no, no!' He likes it long and curly.'

Gina sniffed. 'You get your hair from your father's side,' she said disapprovingly. She'd told Stella many times that she had 'too much hair'. It was a bit too wild and natural for Gina's taste, who also liked plants to stay neat within their borders with a good show of soil between each of them, or, as she had in her old house in Bobbin Street, plastic plants that never needed pruning or outgrew their welcome. Gina didn't really do 'natural'.

They'd all been trepidatious about their trip to the drag show, Stella more because of how Gina might act if she was offended, although Gina had become as equally fixated on having her 'Judy' wedding dress as she had on a June church wedding. The amount of bargains Gina was making to secure her perfect wedding was mounting up, from attending Sunday service, to organising church events, to attending a drag night. Whatever next, Stella wondered?

In the end, it turned out that Elliot had invited them to a Christmas drag night aimed at a family-friendly audience, not, as he told Grazja, the 'full-on filth' of a hen-night extravaganza or queens disco-ball. His aim, apparently, was to break them in gently.

In the end it had turned out to be a great success for Gina, an enjoyable night out for Grazja, and not the sort of thing Stella would go back for.

'What was it like?' Rick asked later in bed.

'Like Saturday night TV,' Stella sighed. 'Loud, brash mix of comedy, dance and songs but done by men dressed up as women.'

'What were the drag queens like?'

Stella propped herself up on her elbow. 'Mixed bunch. There were three drag acts: Knickerbocker Gloria, whose wig did look like pink whipped cream and make up like Divine. She did a bit of stand-up and some singing. She'd sing really high and then drop really low, and act embarrassed and say stuff like 'Oh my God, you'd think I was a man."'

'That was the joke?' Rick grinned.

'Yep, pretty much the one joke repeated in different ways. But the crowd loved it. Made 'em laugh every time.'

'What about Elliot? What did he do?'

'Elliot was by far the best,' Stella said. 'Glinda Sparkle is rather gorgeous in an old-time movie star way. I couldn't quite work out how he'd done it. His waist, hips and breasts were spectacular – really hourglass, in a red sequin body-hugging dress. Glinda MC'd between acts and performed most of the songs – all Christmas classics that Gina loves.'

'Did Gina enjoy it?'

'She loved it,' Stella said. 'Absolutely loved it. It's right up her street; she's always loved that vaudeville, panto-style entertainment.'

'She's okay with drag now? She was definitely iffy about it.'

Stella rolled her eyes. 'I don't think it's drag so much as an underlying homophobia. She adored the camp entertainment of it, as well as the glitter and tinsel - especially Glinda Sparkle channelling old Hollywood musicals' glamour. You know, I bet quite a few of audiences love drag as entertainment but are still homophobic in real life, or wouldn't want a trans person living next to them.'

Stella sat up against the pillows. 'The weird thing is I think of myself as open-minded…'

'Middle class liberal,' Rick said, stroking her arm.

'Yeah,' Stella laughed. 'I am. We are.'

'Don't spread that around,' Rick said.

'I think people already suspect,' Stella said.

'Go on, you think of yourself as open-minded but...' Rick prompted.

'But I didn't feel comfortable with the drag acts,' Stella admitted. 'I mean, it's not my sort of thing anyway. I hate that kind of Saturday night variety show stuff. I accept that's just a difference in taste. But when I was watching the show I couldn't help feeling drag is a parody of being female – taking the clichéd stereotypes of women – bitchy put downs, gossipy, too much make-up, heels we can't walk in – and makes them something to be laughed at and a bit grotesque.'

Rick sat up too. 'Interesting. I hadn't thought about it like that before.'

'I hadn't either until tonight. Maybe it's my hormones making me grumpy. My boobs are so swollen and sore at the moment, I can't stand my bra. Glinda Sparkle can go home and take her perfect boobs off. They don't go up and down in size every month, have never leaked milk, and don't have to be checked regularly for cancerous lumps.

'Men think boobs are just decorative playthings,' Stella finished grumpily. 'Not working mammaries'

Rick grinned. 'I have to admit, I do like to play with your mammaries.'

Stella laughed. 'Well, not tonight,' she said. 'My mammaries are off limits. I hope my period starts soon. They'll feel better after that.'

'You're usually dead-on each month,' Rick said.

'Most months,' Stella agreed. 'But occasionally I'm later – especially if I'm stressed. Which I am a bit. There's so much to do before Christmas and Gerta won't shut up about wanting a puppy.'

'I know,' Rick agreed. 'She's going to be disappointed. She's got her heart set on it.'

'Are you changing your mind?' Stella asked, sliding down the pillow into bed.

'Nope,' Rick declared. 'Dogs take a lot of time and attention and between the diner and the pop-up, your work, and taking care of Gerta it's not practical. Plus, I can't face scooping the poop.'

'We're cat people,' Stella agreed. Turning on her side, she winced. 'God, I'm going to have to sleep on my back. My boobs are so sore.'

They settled down to sleep, Stella on her back, Rick curled on his side facing her. Their breathing started to slow into the rhythm of sleep, when Rick, only half-awake, murmured. 'Remember how painful your boobs were when you were pregnant?'

Suddenly Stella was wide awake.

Pauline Watkins

Pauline Watkins was feeling buoyant as she ordered her favourite Christmas cookies and a hot chocolate with marshmallows.

'I'll bring them over,' Ang told her as she handed over her money.

'Bless you,' Pauline said. She crossed to a booth next to the window, slipping out of her quilted anorak and piling her gloves, scarf and hat on the table.

With Christmas snow possible according to the forecast, and her chance to play Mary on Christmas Eve at St Bart's only two days away, Pauline could hardly contain her excitement.

This year had brought so many blessings, all because of the vicar.

Michael, Pauline reminded herself with a thrill. Yesterday he had asked her to call him Michael, rather than constantly vicar or reverend.

What did it mean?

She'd asked Gina when they'd met at the church this morning.

'Mean? It don't mean nothin',' Gina had scoffed. 'Not that he's going to marry yer, if that's what yer thinking. It's just the way the vicar is, friendly-like.'

'I wasn't thinking that,' Pauline replied quickly. 'I just mean is it all right, d'you think? Is it respectful?'

Gina shrugged. 'It's up to him, ain't it? Mind, I'd still call him vicar, you working for him. More professional. You should probably call me mayor too, as we're sort of working together at the moment.'

'Yes, right,' Pauline said, nodding slowly. 'But you and the vicar can still call me Pauline?'

'Of course,' Gina said. 'You're our assistant. A sort of underling.'

Pauline preferred 'assistant'. She was proud to be the vicar's assistant. Actually, she would really like to be called 'secretary' which summoned up an image of old-time glamour in Pauline's mind. The indispensable secretary who the boss went on to marry.

Secretly, Pauline did hope that the vicar was in love with her. He was so nice to her, nicer than anyone had ever been, and he trusted her to do a job for him. He made her feel important. No one had ever thought she was important or useful, not since her mother had died.

Pauline was a surprise to her parents, a late baby after years of a childless marriage. By the time she came along her father was fifty, and her mother forty-six. It was a shock indeed.

Still, it was God's will, and they loved their little girl very much. But Pauline's parents were part of a small church community in Mapton called the Grace Home Mission, an evangelist organisation dedicated to preaching to all who would listen (and those who wouldn't). There were a number of denominations represented in the area – St Bart's for C of E, the Methodist church in the centre of Mapton, a Salvation Army hall, as well as Our Lady Catholic church in Siltby. As the years went by congregations dwindled, indicating a lack of organised dedication in the population, if not in belief. The GHM was an offshoot of a larger parent organisation The League Against Immorality, a loose conglomeration of evangelist groups concerned about the religious and moral decline of British society. During the seventies, the LAI identified seaside resorts as a major area of this decline.

They claimed modern resorts encouraged drinking, gambling, sexual promiscuity and indecency, an abandonment of the traditional family values previously embodied by a trip to the seaside. The league, in an attempt to counterbalance what they saw as the shocking sin and sleaze being openly practised in English seaside resorts, decided to set up a string of mission churches in a few resorts. The church building would also serve as residential holiday accommodation for groups of children. Selected upon the basis of poverty and urban deprivation, these were children who never got holidays or saw the seaside, so the Grace Home Missions provided a genuinely charitable service. Who would argue against that? But it also allowed the league to promote their own brand of evangelism in new territories in the hope that their values would spread and stem the tide of Sodom and Gomorrah-like hedonism raging in English seaside resorts. Amusement arcades that encouraged gambling, skimpily clad young women cavorting immodestly on the beach in front of young men looking for easy conquests, 'dirty weekends' away for unmarried couples and adulterers, pubs and discotheques, where alcohol and gyrating rhythms gave free reign to licentiousness.

Grace Home Missions were set up to show holiday makers how to enjoy the seaside in a good, clean wholesome fashion. They set up games on the beach – rounders, badminton, ball-games – for their inner-city children, then handed out leaflets to invite holiday makers to bring along their kids. They put on puppet shows, sing-a-longs and sandcastle competitions.

Pauline's mum and dad ran the residential side of the Grace Home Mission. They'd been deployed to

Mapton from Sheffield, where Louise Watkins worked as a primary school teacher and her husband, Ken, was an electrician who spent most of his free time working with kids as church youth leader.

After years of trying for their own child, they'd given up that hope and accepted it. They gained fulfilment from their church work. It was their pastor who approached them as candidates for a new league scheme to establish the new Grace Homes in seaside resorts. The chance to uproot and move to the seaside felt like the fresh opportunity they needed. When the Lord shut doors he also opened windows.

Louise and Ken successfully established the Mapton Grace Home Mission, recruited a small but dedicated workforce to run both a church and the seasonal holiday home, and ran it for years before Pauline unexpectedly came along.

While the Grace Home evangelists were tolerated by Maptonites, they were also seen as a bit of a joke. The 'mission' in the name was accurate, as a large part of the 'Grace Homers' was missionary in aim – to preach and spread the word of God. Thus they often turned up at events and festivals with leaflets, guitars and tambourines, and a wish to engage individuals with earnest conversation about sin and redemption and finding the 'true way'.

Maptonites didn't want to be told the way they lived their lives was 'wrong' and immoral. Mapton and Siltby depended on the summer season of holidaymakers to spend their money in bars and the 'gambling dens' of penny arcades, and wanted people in flesh-revealing beachwear to enjoy the sands, buy ice-creams and cold drinks, sun hats, buckets and spades and suntan lotions.

Everyone knew that the poor inner-city mites that holidayed at Grace Home were never allowed to enjoy the centre of Mapton, where the enticing arcades would provide too much temptation, or the fairground which pumped out the Devil's pop music.

Still, this didn't stop quite a few Maptonites or holiday makers using Grace Home's organised beach activities as a safe place to dump their own kids for a day. It was really handy for local parents, busy working through peak season. They could pay Grace Home a small fee to enrol their child into the day's activities (including a simple packed lunch) and know they would be happy playing with other children in supervised conditions, either on the beach on good days, and in terrible weather conditions in Grace Home's community hall. If the kids came home singing new hymns, or spouting that 'Dad heading off to the boozer would lead him into hell's fire' it was a small price.

By about eleven years old, children who'd happily gone along with this arrangement the previous summer suddenly turned viciously against Grace Home. In secondary school the 'happy clappy' kids were seen as deeply uncool. Those few adolescents who attended the Grace Home youth club were mocked as 'tragic' and squares.

Pauline Watkins was seen as the epitome of uncool, the queen of tragic. Weird, oddly dressed, and possessing that quality sometimes found in only children of being simultaneously too old yet also immature, the other children were merciless to her.

In terms of fitting in, Pauline grew up with a number of disadvantages. Her parents were older than most of her peer's parents, thus their ideas on raising a girl were already a generation behind the more liberal attitudes of the times. This included a biblical emphasis on the roles of men and women that took the literal form of the man 'wearing the trousers' which meant that Pauline was only dressed in dresses and skirts growing up, often in the frumpy uncoordinated style of her mother. As a teenager, Pauline secretly longed for a pair of jeans.

When she was sixteen her father died of a stroke, so Louise retired from working at Grace Home Mission, moving with Pauline to a bungalow in Mapton. Pauline left school, not being academically inclined, and took a job at Trudi Petz, where she loved to feed the hamsters, gerbils, rabbits and rats, clean out their cages, and try to cure Jolly Roger, the shop's resident parrot of using bad language.

Jolly Roger's favourite word was 'wanker' which he'd picked up from Trudi as it was her chosen insult uttering after an unpleasant customer had exited the shop. Jolly Roger used it rather less-discriminatingly which made him a popular attraction to town folk and tourists alike. A few did take exception to his language, especially in front of young children, although most people found it funny.

Pauline found it shocking. The worst Pauline could bring herself to say was 'sugar', or when things were really serious, 'fluffin' heck'. Determined to break Jolly Roger of his bad habit, Pauline repeated the phrase 'God bless you' to the parrot numerous times a day. It worked in so much as Jolly Roger picked it up, but backfired in that he often added 'wanker' as a kind of suffix, so that customers were often greeted or sent off with the phrase 'God bless you wanker' much to Pauline's mortification.

Trudi was kind to Pauline in that she gave her a job and never said anything nasty to her face but it was actually Trudi who came up with the name 'Pious Pauline'. She rarely put Pauline on the till as the girl couldn't sell a bag of hamster feed without saying something like: 'God loves this hamster as much as He loves you so He'll know if you don't take good care of it' or handing over a squeaky toy with the information that: 'The spots on your Dalmatian are reminders that sin can stain the purest of souls'.

Once, when Terry Gideon came in to enquire if they could stock frozen mice to feed his pet python, Pauline had seized the cross she wore round her neck and thrust it toward him like he was a vampire. 'Satan loves the serpent,' she hissed.

Trudi had to drag Pauline into the stockroom to calm down while her husband Ryan apologised to Terry.

Ryan had been all for sacking Pauline, but Trudi refused. She had her reasons. Firstly, she didn't pay Pauline very much, even after five years Pauline was still on the wage Trudi began her on at sixteen, and she was very happy doing the muckier jobs in the pet emporium. Secondly, Ryan had rather too much of an eye for the two teenage girls who they'd employed before Pauline. Pauline he barely glanced at. Thirdly, Trudi had some heart. At twenty, Pauline had lost her mother to cancer and now lived alone in the little bungalow. Her life was work in the pet store and the Grace Home Mission group.

A couple of years later, Grace Home shut. The league abandoned their quest to restore morality in Mapton. It seemed to be a lost cause. Only Pauline and a few other members of her faith were left to carry on, and they gradually drifted away too.

Pauline was left isolated, a strange young woman in fuddy-duddy clothes with out-of-step religious views, in a small seaside town, looking for a cause.

She was also biologically at her reproductive peak, hormonally charged, and sexually frustrated, even if she was too repressed and inexperienced to recognise it.

And Pauline was lonely.

This made her the perfect target for bad boy Jim Sutcliffe when Mapton became the centre of scandal and media attention following the rumour that the Paradise Holiday Park was going to turn into a camp for swingers.

Here was the cause. Moral outrage created the protest group Mapton Knights, led by Gina, and its rebel splinter group, Mapton Crusaders, led by Andy Timmis. The Crusaders proved to be the fierier, flag-waving, rabble-rousing bunch and it was to this side, and particularly to Jim, one of the main provocateurs, that Pauline was drawn. Excited, envisioning herself as a modern Joan of Arc fighting the righteous cause, Pauline was swept into Jim's irresistible orbit.

But Jim wasn't who he appeared to be. It was Frank Manning who discovered the truth about him, and by that time Jim had fled Mapton, leaving destruction in his wake.

Part of the damage he left behind was Pauline's heart and her sense of moral shame. She had done sinful things with Jim – things which she believed should only be done within the sanctified walls of a marriage. She had fallen.

Pauline felt such shame she could hardly face people for a while. Then Frank came to see her asking questions about Jim, who had disappeared by then, and she had to admit she didn't even know Jim's last name even though she had 'known' him carnally. Frank hadn't flinched or turned away from her. He had told her that she wasn't the person who should feel ashamed; the shame belonged to Jim. He had exploited her innocent nature and used her.

Pauline had denied it. No, the sin was hers, she insisted, even if Jim was the tempter.

'He got you drunk, I remember,' Frank said. 'On cider I think.'

'Cider's only apple juice though,' Pauline said. 'I was drunk on lust.'

Frank shook his head. 'Cider's made from apples, but it's alcoholic. It's stronger than beer. Did Jim tell you it's just apple juice?'

Jim had done just that.

Frank was such a nice man. He had come back to see her when he found out who Jim really was, and explained it all to her.

For a few months afterwards, Pauline felt lost. She avoided going into Mapton, other than work. She certainly wouldn't have come to the diner on her own, like she had today. She knew people laughed at her, smirked behind their hands, rolled their eyes when she walked in. But before Jim she'd always felt she had the higher ground – God knew her worth – and they wouldn't be laughing so hard in the next life. But lately she had proven she was just as sinful as them and had tasted the apple of knowledge (and really enjoyed it).

Pauline prayed daily for the chance to redeem herself. With Grace Home boarded up she had no church to go to so one day she walked to St Bart's. Even though it was C of E, it was still God's house so she tried the door, found it open and went inside.

Inside, the cool, hushed interior, with its hints of century-old must and dust motes swirling in hazy sunlight strained through stained glass, made her draw in breath.

Pauline shuffled into a pew to kneel on a red hassock and closed her eyes to pray. She didn't know how long she knelt there before she felt a presence at her side.

Opening her eyes she peered up to see the most beautiful male face smiling down at her.

'Are you an angel?' Pauline asked.

The angel laughed gently. 'What a lovely question?' he said. 'But I'm afraid not. My name's Reverend Michael Rivers. I'm the new vicar at St Bart's.'

He had listened when Pauline blurted out a spontaneous confession listing her sins, which didn't just include carnality, but also (under Jim's influence) involvement in a pub fight, participation in a near riot, name-calling, vanity and pride.

'Jesus has forgiven you.' The vicar told her gently. 'Because you have already repented. Punishing yourself with regret is to deny His love. He wants you to move on. Do you know the best way to do that and to forgive yourself?'

'What?' Pauline sniffled.

'To help others,' the vicar said. 'To be useful.'

'I tried,' Pauline said. 'I wanted to volunteer at the animal sanctuary – I love animals – but Eleanor Branwin didn't want me.'

The vicar smiled. 'It just so happens that I require help. I'm currently without an assistant – a secretary of sorts – to take phone calls and make appointments, and such. Do you have any experience with that sort of thing? I'm afraid it wouldn't be paid at first.'

'I work part time at the pet shop,' Pauline said. 'I take phone calls and do stock takes and things like that. I don't serve the customers very often because I say the wrong things. I talk about God which people don't like.'

The vicar had a beautiful laugh. 'I don't think that would be a problem here,' he said, gesturing around the church. 'Do you?'

Pauline giggled.

Half a year later, here Pauline was, confident enough to sit in The Last Resort Diner on her own, secure that she had a place in her community. Not only had the vicar asked her to call him Michael, two days prior to that he'd said she was indispensable, which meant he needed her.

Feeling needed by the most handsome man in Mapton – probably the entire country – was heady stuff indeed.

Allowing herself to day dream, perhaps just a little too much, as she spooned a half-melted marshmallow into her mouth, Pauline was startled out of her reverie when someone slid into the booth.

She looked up to see Frank on the seat opposite.

'Hello Pauline,' he said. 'Do you mind if I join you for a few minutes while I wait for my order. I'm taking lunch over to Grazja at the sanctuary.'

Pauline beamed at him. She had a soft spot for Frank. He was one of the few people who had always been kind to her, even after she'd behaved badly towards him during the Jim period. Frank had been on the other side of that pub fight.

'Of course,' she said. 'How are you?'

'Good,' Frank said. 'Can't believe it's almost Christmas again! What's this I hear about St Bart's Christmas Eve blessing for pets?'

'It was Mayor Gina's idea. She thought it would be good for getting people into St Bart's. We're going to hold a service where people can bring their pets. It'll be early – six o' clock – and there will be another proper service at midnight like usual.' Pauline leaned forward to whisper. 'It's a surprise, so don't tell anyone, but we've got a donkey and I'm going to be Mary and ride it down the aisle.'

Frank raised his eyebrows. 'Wow,' he said. And again. 'Wow.'

'Yes!' Pauline nodded. 'It's going to be amazing. We've got a Joseph too, and Gina's going to lead the procession.'

'That's going to be quite a service,' Frank said. 'All those pets and a donkey and the mayor, not to mention excited kids.'

'It's going to be beautiful,' Pauline said.

Frank patted her hand. 'I'm sure it will be. That's a lot for the vicar to handle though.'

'Oh, the vicar can handle anything,' Pauline felt herself swell with happiness. 'And he's got me. He says I'm indispensable to him.'

'Does he?' Frank looked interested.

'Yes. If I could afford to, I'd work as his assistant full-time,' Pauline told him.

Frank looked puzzled. 'But wouldn't you get more money if you went full-time?'

'Oh no,' Pauline said. 'If I went full-time as the vicar's PA I'd have to give up my job at the pet shop. I get paid for that.'

'Don't you get paid as the vicar's PA?' Frank asked, frowning.

'Oh no,' Pauline said. 'That's voluntary work for the church. Michael says he would pay me but with the repairs St Bart's needs, there's not enough in the budget at the moment.' She felt a thrill at using the vicar's name so casually.

'You seem quite close to Michael,' Frank said. 'Does he talk about his previous church?'

'Not really,' Pauline said. 'Mostly about St Bart's. Why?'

'No reason,' Frank shrugged. 'He's still quite new – a bit of a mystery. The local ladies certainly seem to like him.'

Pauline giggled. 'I know!' she said. 'It's because he's so handsome.'

Ang brought over Frank's order, bagged and ready to go.

Frank slid out of the booth. 'Thanks Ang.'

Pauline watched him zip up his coat.

'It was lovely seeing you, Pauline,' he said. 'Do me a favour will you – just be careful around the vicar. If he asks you to do more than feels right, come to me.'

Pauline wasn't quite sure what he meant. She really didn't mind working for free. 'Okay,' she said vaguely. Then, perking up: 'You should come to the Christmas Eve service. See me play Mary.'

Frank cocked his head to one side as though thinking. 'You know what?' he grinned. 'I'll be there.'

He waved goodbye and was gone, as were Pauline's cookies and hot chocolate.

It was time to get back to St Bart's.

January Blues

Stella woke on the last Wednesday of January to find Gerta asleep next to her and something suspiciously carrot-like on the bedside table next to a propped-up postcard.

Groggily, she focused. The object was a carrot of sorts, but a chocolate one wrapped in orange foil with a green flourish on top. She reached for the postcard. It was an old one, blank on the back, which always made her laugh. Split into four rectangles it showed the boating lake, the seafront, and the funfair, but the fourth picture featured a kitten. It was one of those fluffy, blue-eyes kittens that were popular on cards and tins in the seventies and it had absolutely no relation to either Mapton specifically or the seaside in general. It was as though whoever made the postcard couldn't think of anything else Mapton had to offer, or just couldn't be bothered.

Stella flipped it over to see Rick's scrawl.

Sorry you're having a tough time, honey. We can talk later. Didn't want to wake you as you seemed to need a lie in. I'll drop Gerta off at nursery. She can come with me to the diner till then, give you a bit of peace.
Peel this carrot however you want!
Love you! Rick xxxxxx

Stella welled up. She didn't deserve such a good man; she'd been awful to him yesterday. She'd actually thrown a carrot at him. It was infuriating when he got all chef-like and made a fuss about doing things a certain way. Who cared how a carrot got peeled? But throwing the carrot at him with the force of real fury behind it? Not okay. It was the fury that scared her. At that moment, with the peeler in one hand and the root veg in the other she'd felt such an enormous sweep of rage that hurling the carrot was the least damaging form of release she could find.

Of course it hadn't released anything. Instead she'd immediately felt a rush of self-disgust and dismay at the hurt and astonishment on Rick's face, and still underneath it that anger.

When she'd burst into tears, it wasn't so much out of regret, or to garner sympathy, but out of an inability to articulate this terrible illogical feeling of anger she'd felt for days. Beneath the anger was an even worse feeling of deep sadness and loss.

It was ridiculous. *She* was ridiculous.

She had absolutely nothing to feel angry or sad about. She had the perfect life!

Stella unpeeled the chocolate carrot from its wrapper and munched on it morosely. Rick must have got it from Jill's deli.

Rick was so sweet. She was so lucky. Why couldn't she feel it? Why did the sight of him sometimes make her grind her teeth?

Thinking back, Stella could pin-point the date she'd first felt this over-bearing sensation of things being 'off'. It was the drag club outing. She'd woken up that morning with a strange feeling of underlying panic, and been irritable all day. The sore boobs had been the tip-off that it was hormonal. After Rick had sleepily reminded her that last time they'd been this sore she'd been pregnant, Stella had stayed awake most of the night, veering between excitement at the possibility of being pregnant, and 'Uh oh! What have we done?'

She'd had an IUD fitted a few weeks after Gerta's birth, but had it taken out a year ago. She and Rick weren't desperate for another baby; they'd discussed it a lot and decided that if another one came along they'd rather it be while Gerta was still small so there wasn't too much of a gap between them. Despite a healthy sex life, nothing had happened since and they'd been starting to discuss Stella using an IUD again. They were both inclined to feel that Gerta was enough.

Stella had hurried to the chemist the next morning to get a pregnancy test. It had come out negative, and then later that day she had started her period.

She'd been surprised by how crushed she was to not be pregnant. She'd put a brave face on it with Christmas and all that entailed. Christmas Eve had been distracting in any number of ways, and Gerta's excitement carried her through the rest of it.

The weeks since she'd felt awful. Not every day. There were days when she felt much better – really good in fact – and days when she just felt a little blue and on edge. And then there were mornings when she woke feeling like this.

Oh God, she didn't think she could face tonight. It was Girls Night again, and this time Elliot had been invited too. She'd felt as though her nerves were made of glass, ready to shatter.

Stella sank her head on her knees and began to cry.

A Night to Remember

Elliot hated January with its grey skies and post-Christmas emphasis on cutting down and cutting back. He was glad it was nearly February, although that was nearly as bad. At least his husband Tim's twenty-eight day detox would be over then.

Tim had put them both on a low carb, no alcohol diet for a 're-set' after their Christmas indulgences. Elliot went through the motions of this at home for Tim, who did tend to gain the pounds easily. Outside the house was another matter.

Tonight, he'd raided the secret stash of peanut M&M's kept in the glove compartment of his Audi as he drove to Mapton for an evening fitting with Gina.

This was his second meeting with her this month. Her trip to the Christmas drag night seemed to have worked wonders on her attitude towards him although he wasn't naïve enough to believe it had erased an underlying homophobia. For many of her generation it was societally ingrained.

It was a start, and he'd genuinely enjoyed his last fitting with her.

Grazja had driven her over to his shop where Gina had 'oohed' and 'ahed' over his bespoke creations in the back, and gone crackers for the hen night paraphernalia in the front. She'd spent a satisfying amount of money on a variety of funny items. She'd wrinkled her nose at the chocolate willies on display. 'None of them,' Gina had said, mouth turned down. 'Being chocolate don't make 'em any prettier. Shouldn't be on show where kiddies can see 'em.'

'I don't sell stuff for kids,' Elliot said. 'We never get them in.'

'Don't matter,' Gina said. 'Only knobs on public display should be on doors and drawers.'

'I'll bear that in mind,' Elliot said, catching Grazja's eye.

'You should be used to it,' Grazja said to Gina. 'Rock cocks sold in Mapton.'

'I know!' Gina said. 'Who'd want to suck on one of them! Disgustin'. And sugar boobs. I tried to get the council to vote ban 'em' but no one cares. Stan says it's part of seaside tradition – a bit saucy like. When I was a girl saucy meant a nudge and a wink not an erect penis next to the pick n mix.'

Elliot was laughing.

'Oh no,' Gina continued, turning puce. 'Now you made me say the 'p' word and I hate that too.'

'I would pay to see your act,' Elliot said, wiping tears away.

'It's not an act,' Gina said, although she was grinning.

'No, it true, Gina hate penises,' Grazja said.

'Now you said it too,' Gina cackled. 'Stop it!'

'Does your fiancée know about this?' Elliot asked. 'Or are you waiting to tell him on the honeymoon.'

'Ooh, yer cheeky bogger,' Gina cried. 'George knows I don't hate 'em in the right place and time. I just don't want any staring me in the face.'

That was it for Elliot. He was gone. He collapsed into howls of laughter.

The fitting had been a lot of fun after that. He even persuaded Gina to order a corset to go under the dress, one that would support everything it should without cutting her in half.

After Gina and Grazja left, Elliot realised he'd forgotten about the one thing he was dying to hear about. He'd read about it on the local news, 'Pandemonium at Pet's Christmas Service', but he wanted to hear it from Mayor Pontin herself. Gina seemed to create drama and headlines whatever she did. His Glinda side was almost envious.

He'd been delighted, then, when Gina rang and asked if he'd like to combine the next fitting with a 'girls' night in' they held at Stella's on the last Wednesday of each month. 'You being an honorary girl.' Gina said. She'd said this as though she was bestowing some great honour on him.

Intriguingly, Gina said he'd know it when he found Stella's house because it looked like a small castle.

It actually did. Even in the winter's dark evening he could make out four turrets. It was a red brick castle on a small scale. Not an old one of course; a Victorian representation of one. But still pretty impressive, especially for Mapton on Sea, the poor little raggedy sister of Skeg.

He was looking forward to meeting Stella. Stella Distry was a successful artist. Tim had bought two of her paintings – limited editions not the originals – and loved her work. Elliot could take it or leave it. Tim hung them in his study where he worked from home as an accountant. Their tiny dog Princess Alys kept him company, or rather Tim kept her company as she refused to be alone. The din she made when they tried to leave her on her own was unbearable, which meant that they either had to take her with them, or book her favourite dog-sitter, Sandi, who charged more than the average childminder, and ate everything in the fridge.

Tonight Elliot had gone to his book club group in Lawton, one of whom had a morbid fear of small dogs. They didn't come much smaller than Alys.

Elliot had asked Gina if he was okay to bring Alys along.

'Fine by me,' Gina said. 'I love dogs. Stella's got a nasty cat but he hates me so he won't hang around.'

'Why does he hate you?' Elliot asked.

''Cuz I hate him,' Gina said. 'I don't like cats. They're sneaky and snooty.'

'Wake up sleepy head,' Elliot said, lifting Alys off her pink velvet car cushion. 'We're here.'

Gina opened the door to him.

'What kind of chuffin' breed is that?' she asked, staring at Alys in his arms.

Alys stared back with her black, slightly bulbous eyes. She was weighing Gina up, Elliot knew. Two divas meeting.

'This is Alys,' Elliot said, waving her paw for her. 'She's half Dachshund, half Chihuahua. They're often called a Chiweenie, but Alys prefers Dachshuahua. (He pronounced it 'dahks-wah-wah').

'Does she now? Not heard of them; daft name' Gina said, peering at her. 'Ain't she pretty though?'

Elliot relaxed, as did Alys, who had heard the word 'pretty' enough to know it meant something nice about her. She wagged her tail.

'Aw,' Gina said, stroking her head. 'Look at you. Look at that diamante collar. Ain't you a princess?'

'Tell me about it,' Elliot rolled his eyes.

'Gerta's going to love her,' Gina said, leading him through the hall. 'Gerta, come see what Elliot has brought,' she called. She gave him a sharp look over her shoulder. 'You remembered to bring the dress, didn't yer?'

'It's in the car,' Elliot said. 'I'll pop out and get it in a minute. I bought some snacks to share too.'

105

'You can add them to ours,' Gina said. 'We got 'em laid out on the coffee table.'

A little girl appeared out of the room they'd just reached, squealing with delight when she saw Alys. 'A doggie' she cried. 'Is it for me?'

'No duckie,' Gina said. 'She's not for you but I'm sure Elliot will let you play with her. She's alright with kids ain't she?'

Elliot bent down to Gerta 'As long as you're very gentle with her,' he said kindly.

Gerta nodded seriously. 'I'll be sooooooo gentle,' she said. 'I'm good with doggies. You can ask Tiny.'

Elliot put Alys down and let her dance over to Gerta, who very carefully crouched to stroke Alys.

Gina waved him into the room, which turned out to be a large comfortable lounge.

Stella had her legs folded under her on one of the two sofas, sipping a large glass of red wine. Elliot had met her very briefly at the drag night but that had been as Glinda. She wore her hair long and curly, her make-up was the expensive sort that gave an 'au naturel' glow but Elliot thought she looked quite tired despite it.

She smiled at him. 'Hi Elliot, nice to meet you again. So this is what you look like when you're not Glinda?'

'Not so tall, not so glamorous,' Elliot said.

'Would you like a drink? We've got red, white, beer, Babycham, soft drinks – tea, coffee- you name it.'

'Would you be able to do me a white wine spritzer?' Elliot asked. 'I'm driving.'

'Ooh, posh,' Gina said. 'They say gay men are sophisticated.'

'Gina!' Stella said.

'What?' Gina threw up her hands. 'It's a compliment.'

'I think I can rustle up a spritzer,' Stella smiled apologetically, pushing up from the sofa.

'Mummy, mummy,' Gerta ran in with Alys in her arms. 'Have you seen the puppy? She's even prettier than Tiny.'

'She's not a puppy,' Elliot explained. 'Alys is a full grown dog.'

'But she's so small,' Gerta shook her head in wonder. 'And long.'

Alys preened under the attention as they all looked at her.

Elliot swore she could bat her eyelashes.

'Tiny is very small because he's just a puppy,' Gerta explained. 'He was going to be my dog but I let someone else have him.'

Elliot was hearing a lot about Tiny whoever he was.

Stella frowned. 'Oh dear,' she said. 'I didn't know you were bringing your dog.' She shot Elliot such an accusatory look he almost stepped back.

'Gina said it was okay.'

'It is okay,' Gina said. 'Stop being a mardy-arse, Stella.'

Stella glared at her, then sighed. 'Sorry,' she said to Elliot. 'It's just that Gerta really wanted a puppy for Christmas . She was obsessed with a puppy at the sanctuary – Tiny – but it wasn't going to happen. She's been okay since. I just can't take it if she starts up again.'

Elliot glanced at Gerta, who was intent on smoothing Alys's coat rather than listening.

'Gi' over, Stella,' Gina said. 'Kids are always asking for things. Don't mean they get 'em. You just say no.'

'Well, you be the one to do it, then,' Stella snapped. 'All I hear is that Grandma Gina says 'she could have it but Mummy wouldn't like it.' 'I'm always the bad one.' Stella stamped out. Elliot was taken aback. This wasn't quite the fun atmosphere he'd been expecting.

'Don't mind her,' Gina shrugged. 'She's been in a right mood since Christmas. Needs a holiday I think.'

Gerta piped up. 'Mummy threw a carrot at Daddy yesterday.'

'Did she?' Gina sounded delighted. 'Why?'

'Don't know,' Gerta said. 'Throwing the carrot made her cry and that made me cry and then we all had a nap.'

'Well I never,' Gina said. The doorbell rang. 'That'll be Grazja.'

Elliot watched Gerta play with Alys, who had flipped onto her back for a tummy rub. They were both very cute, but Elliot was disconcerted by Gerta's presence. He'd looked forward to a raucous evening of smutty girls' talk but having a four year old in the room would surely curtail that.

In fact, not a lot about the way the evening progressed turned out as he hoped, although some of it really was fun. Grazja's hair, Gina's corset, and Alys's singing. But it hadn't ended well, particularly for poor Alys.

Tears and Tantrums

Grazja was running late by the time she arrived. She rang the doorbell even though she had a key to the house. When she wasn't staying over at Frank's Grazja lived in the annexe connected to Stella and Rick's property but she chose not to enter the house freely out of respect for their and her own privacy. They, in turn, didn't enter her annexe unless invited.

Gina answered the door, wearing her cerise, fluffy dressing gown, in readiness, Grazja assumed, for the dress fitting. She shrieked when she saw her. 'Bloody 'ell! You look like a new woman.'

'Stella,' she yelled. 'Come and see Grazja's new do.'

Stella emerged from the kitchen holding a wine glass. She stopped, gaping. 'Wow! Is it...?'

'Real?' Grazja blushed under their scrutiny. 'Yes. Not another wig. I had it done today.' She touched her hair self-consciously. It felt so strange and light after years of long hair.

'You sneaky bogger,' Gina said. 'Didn't mention that, did you?'

'Elliot knew,' Grazja said. 'I wanted surprise you and Stella.'

'You did that all right,' Gina replied. 'Dint she Stell?'

Stella was still staring at her in a way that made Grazja nervous.

'You not like it?' she asked Stella.

'What? Yes, no ... I mean yes, I love it. You look amazing.' Stella's smile seemed a bit forced. 'Better go show your new best friend. He's in the lounge with Gerta.'

Grazja found Elliot sitting neatly on the floor supervising Gerta as she fussed over a tiny, silk-eared dog in a diamante collar. This must be the famous Princess Alys.

As Elliot glanced up, Grazja saw his face light with delight. 'OMG!' he said, springing lightly to his feet. 'You are a STAR! Eva has outdone herself.'

Grazja stood on display as he assessed her.

'Turn around,' he said. 'I want to see the back.'

'I'm not shop mannequin,' Grazja grumbled, embarrassed but pleased.

'Wonderful,' Elliot gushed. 'You have a beautiful neck. It deserves to be seen.'

'Thought you're gay,' Gina said. 'You sound like you fancy her.'

'I can appreciate beauty without wanting to shag it,' Elliot said. 'Sexual attraction and aesthetic appreciation are not the same thing. Although they're not mutually exclusive either.'

'Ooh, la di da!' Gina chanted. 'Why don't you just say she looks good but yer don't fancy her?'

'You know, darling,' Elliot smiled at Grazja. 'You look so good maybe I do fancy you tonight!'

Grazja laughed, blushing at all the attention. 'Stop it. You all being stupid. It just a haircut.'

'And a colour change,' Gina said. 'It really does make a difference, don't it Stella? You better keep Rick away from the new Grazja.'

Stella didn't look amused. 'He likes long hair,' she said. 'He doesn't go for the androgynous look.'

Elliot pulled a face at Grazja. 'Miaow! I think someone's got a touch of friend-envy. Don't worry, darling, it happens to the best of us. Glinda's positively green with envy at your new 'do.''

Grazja smiled but she was quite hurt by Stella. She hadn't expected this undertone of competitive hostility from her best friend. But maybe she hadn't given Stella any reason to show this side before?

Before she could ponder this more, the funny little dog entrancing Gerta started to sing.

Singing was a kind word for it. A tremulous high pitched howling was a more suitable description but Elliot seemed to think his dog had the voice of a soprano.

'It's the song,' he cried, clapping his hands. 'She always sings to Mariah Carey. Turn it up.'

In the background Stella's TV was tuned to Christmas pop classics video channel, and Mariah Carey was prancing about on the screen in a red, white fur trimmed mini dress, warbling 'All I want for Christmas is You.'

Gina grabbed the remote and turned up the volume.

Princess Alys threw back her head and really went for Mariah's famous five octave range.

It was hilarious. Gerta began clapping along, and Gina laughed so hard tears leaked out of her eyes and she cried. 'I'm going to pee meself if she don't stop.'

'Who Mariah or Princess Alys?'

'Both o' them.'

Mariah hit her final impossibly high 'youuuuuu'. Princess Alys matched her. Poor little Gerta clapped her hands over her sensitive young ears while Gina cried 'Uh oh!'

Grazja automatically turned to exchange a grin with Stella, as they so often did. Only Stella wasn't there – she had left the room. Grazja considered going to find her when Gerta let out a little cry.

'Grazy where your hair gone?'

Gerta hadn't paid attention when Grazja had entered the room. Even with all the commotion over

Grazja's hair, the little girl only had eyes for Princess Alys. Now, she'd finally noticed and her face reflected her shock.

Gerta was very close to Grazja, who'd accepted a child-minder job with Stella when she'd first returned to Mapton a year before. It was only recently that she took the decision to retrain as a veterinary nurse and had begun to work with Eleanor Branwin at the sanctuary. Gerta was enrolled in pre-school now so the transition hadn't been too painful but she still regarded Grazja as her own 'Grazy'. It was obvious from Gerta's furrowed brow that she wasn't happy with this sudden change.

'I had my hair cut,' Grazja said, crouching down to Gerta.

Gerta's mouth turned down. 'I don't like it,' she said. 'You don't look like you. I like your long brown hair.'

'I'm still me,' Grazja said. 'Still your Grazy. You'll get used to it.'

'Won't,' Gerta said, eyes filling with tears.

Grazja pulled her into a hug, but Grazja drew back sharply. 'You don't even smell like you,' she declared, bottom lip trembling.

'It is only shampoo and hair stuff,' Grazja said. 'I smell just like me after I wash hair.'

'Will your real hair come back then?' Gerta blurted, chest hitching.

Grazja sighed. 'It will take longer than that to grow back,' she explained.

Gerta started to cry and Princess Alys began to whine, whether in sympathy or opposition, Grazja didn't know.

Stella returned bearing a large pizza and some plates.

'What's going on?' she frowned. 'Gerta what's wrong?'

'She alright. She just shook up by my hair change,' Grazja said.

Stella shot her an annoyed look. 'I'm not surprised,' she snapped. 'You didn't give her any chance to prepare for it.'

Grazja was stung. She adored Gerta but she didn't need to ask permission of a four year old to get her hair cut, or anyone else for that matter.

Gerta had begun to properly bawl. Stella tutted, dropped the plates and pizza rather heavily onto the coffee table, and marched in to sweep Gerta into her arms.

'She's overtired,' Gina said. 'Best put her to bed, Stella.'

'Noooooo!' Gerta wailed, hearing the dreaded words. Her wail continued into the hall as Stella carried her out of the room.

Grazja felt her earlier buoyant mood rapidly decreasing.

'Maybe we should do the fitting another time,' Elliot said.

'No,' Gina shook her head. 'I'm not having a little tantrum ruin our evening. I want you to get on wi' me dress. Go get it out of the car Elliot.'

'Okay,' Elliot said. 'If you're sure.' He patted Princess Alys. 'I'll be back in a second sweetheart. Don't panic.' He turned to Gina. 'She hates it when we leave. She might make a fuss.'

Alys watched him leave the room with interest. It wasn't until she heard the front door open though and his footsteps outside that she started to bark and ran for the door.

Elliot had closed the door behind him so she started to scrabble at the paintwork.

'Don't worry duckie,' Gina said, swiping a fragrant pizza slice as she went to the Dachshuahua. 'He's coming right back. Here, have some of this.'

Princess Alys seemed to forget her distress the moment the pizza was waved in front of her nose. She sniffed it once and then gobbled it enthusiastically.

'I don't think you should feed her that,' Grazja said. 'Elliot might not like it.'

'What he don't know won't hurt him.' Gina retorted, as Alys snuffled for leftover crumbs. 'Shall we have another one before he gets back?' she mock-whispered to Alys.

'No, Gina!'

Gina ignored the advice, enticing Alys over to the coffee table to feed her a second slice of melted cheese heaven.

'You'll make her sick,' Grazja said.

'Gi'over. Only thing makes dogs ill is chocolate. They can eat anything otherwise.'

Princess Alys made very quick work of the pizza and would have probably begged for another slice if she hadn't heard Elliot's return.

By the time he got into the room Alys was waiting eagerly for him by the door and Gina had picked up a paper napkin to wipe her mouth and fingers as though she was the one who had devoured the pizza.

Typical Gina, Grazja thought, genuinely irritated by her friend. She wished she'd stayed in bed with Frank.

Stella brought Gerta back into the room with the proviso that any more tears and it was straight to bed for her. Gerta beelined towards Princess Alys. She gave Grazja an exaggerated wide berth, holding her hands to the side of her face like blinkers, and settled next to the dog.

Wonderful, Grazja thought. I too hideous to look at.

Stella noticed the gap in the pizza. 'Oh, good you've started. Would you like some pizza, Gerta?'

'Yes please Mummy,' Gerta said. 'I give some to Princess Alys.'

'Oh no,' Elliot interjected. 'It's too rich for her tum. 'Here,' he said, reaching into the leather satchel he'd brought in. 'I've got some biscuits for her. Give her these.'

Grazja raised an eyebrow at Gina who ignored her.

Elliot unzipped the dress from its cover. It was really taking shape now, skirts spilling out in a froth of white from the fitted bodice.

Gina slid off her dressing gown to reveal a mid-thigh length corset in nude.

It set them all laughing, even Stella creasing up, restoring their usual comfortable camaraderie.

'What's so funny?' Gina cried, striking a pin-up pose, one hand behind her head, pointing her toes to push her calf into a curve mimicking Betty Grable. With her blue-veined pasty skin, wobbly thighs and skinny ankles it wasn't quite so becoming.

'Oh dear Lord,' Elliot said. 'I'll never be able to unsee that image.'

The next half hour passed pleasantly, a mix of banter and giggling. Elliot plied his craft with skill, making adjustments and taking notes, while Gina chaffed and chivvied, as Stella and Grazja drank wine, ate pizza and snacks, commenting from the sidelines.

Stella allowed Gerta one slice of pizza, handing it to her on a plate. Once things got going with Gina's fitting, none of the adults paid much attention to the little girl and her doggie friend, so missed Gerta sharing the fat-loaded dough bake with Princess Alys, then sneaking yet another slice.

It became appallingly apparent how much pizza the Dachshuahua had snaffled when Princess Alys began to vomit on Stella's carpet.

'Have you given her pizza?' Elliot demanded of Gerta.

Gerta started to wail again.

Stella lost it then. To everyone's shock she ordered them to leave.

'Yer can't just chuck us out,' Gina objected. 'That's rude.'

'It was rude to bring an uninvited dog,' Stella retorted. 'Henry's been cowering under my bed since it got here.'

'Well you don't have to worry,' Elliot said, cradling a drooping, ill-looking Princess Alys. 'We shan't be coming again.' He strode out, leaving Gina in her half-finished dress.

'Now look what you've done,' Gina yelled. 'If he don't finish my dress I'll never forgive yer.' Picking up her skirts and avoiding the pool of vomit, Gina went after Elliot.

'I'll help you clear that up,' Grazja said to Stella. At the sound of her voice, Gerta, clinging to Stella's leg, peered up at Grazja. Seeing her hair again she let out another sob, pressing her face into Stella's thigh.

'No, thank you,' Stella said. 'I think you'd best go. You're only upsetting her more.'

She said this with such bitter resentment that Grazja simply nodded and walked out.

#

'I can't believe you let her eat that stuff,' Tim chided when he'd arrived home to find Elliot cleaning up Alys's mess. 'Poor baby. She's too delicate for crap.' He cradled the dog, who looked pitiful.

'I didn't let her,' Elliot protested. 'Stella's little girl sneaked it to her.'

'Should we take her to the vet?'

'No, she's fine. Hopefully it's all out of her system now.'

'Poor poor baby,' Tim said, dropping a kiss on Alys's head. 'I'll never let Daddy Elliot take you with him again.'

'Fine by me,' Elliot said. 'God, what a night.'

'What's Stella like?' Tim asked. 'Was her house filled with marvellous art?'

'To be honest, she's a bit of a bitch,' Elliot said.

Tim's eyes widened. 'Really? Do tell.'

Elliot told him about his evening. 'She basically threw us out,' he ended.

'I suppose it's because she's an artist,' Tim said. 'They're temperamental. Did you ask Gina about the Christmas Eve fiasco at St Bart's?'

'Aw,' Elliot groaned, slapping his forehead. 'I forgot to ask again!'

Getting Serious

Frank kept looking over and grinning at her.

Grazja laughed. 'Eyes on road,' she said. We not want an accident.'

'Sorry,' he said, fixing his attention on the road ahead. 'I just have to keep looking at you. I love your hair like that.'

'Does that mean you not like it before?' Grazja asked slyly.

'No, I liked it before. I'll like it again if you go back to it. It's not just that you look great with it blonde, it's that you look happier.'

'They say blondes have more fun,' Grazja said, touching her new haircut. 'Maybe it's true.'

'I like it because you've done something for yourself,' Frank said.

'What you mean?'

'You do so much for everyone else,' Frank went on. 'You help Gina and Stella, look after Gerta, work with rescued animals, not to mention buying the land for the new sanctuary…'

'I sound like a saint,' Grazja protested, embarrassed.

'You put up with me,' Frank said.

'This is true. I am a saint.'

'I'm just saying, that this is the first time I've seen you do something for yourself; something just to make you feel good.'

'Pah!' Grazja dismissed him. 'I do lots to make me feel good.'

Inside she was quite taken aback by the observation, although she knew that a deep-rooted part of the reason she had taken so long to show Frank her blonde wig was that he would view her as self-indulgent and vain. When she had finally revealed her purchase and shyly tried it on for him, the effect on Frank had been electrifying. That had been on Christmas Eve, and it was fair to say that if Santa had crashed through the ceiling they wouldn't have noticed. They were lucky, in fact, to not have crashed themselves, through the bedroom floor into the Kleen and Gone launderette below Frank's flat, so vigorously were the bedsprings singing.

'I not know you had a thing for blondes,' Grazja had gasped afterwards.

'I don't,' Frank replied. 'Just for you in that wig.'

When Grazja decided to take the plunge and have her hair chopped and bleached, it wasn't to please Frank, or for her sex life (although that was a bonus) but because the way she looked in the wig made her feel good about herself. It suited her so much why not make it permanent? She didn't need a persona to slip on and off.

She'd mentioned her decision to Elliot who was ecstatic.

'Who does your hair?' he asked.

'Beryl Finch Hair in Siltby,' Grazja said.

'Oh dear Lord, no! Elliot shrieked. 'Just the name conjures up old dears and blue rinses.'

'They do okay job,' Grazja said.

'I'm sure Beryl does do 'okay',' Elliot said. 'But you deserve more than okay. You deserve a fabulous cut and colour. I know just the person for the job. She'll cost more than Beryl but it will be worth it. Trust me.'

So Grazja had trusted him and booked in with head stylist and salon owner, Eva, in Lawton.

It was worth it. Eva had even marched her out of the salon so she could examine Grazja under the cold light of a grey day to assess the exact type of blonde that would suit Grazja's skin tone best.

'It has to work for you in daylight, electric light and moonlight,' Eva told her, looking herself like a sable haired Bettie Page.

Grazja had been a little intimidated by Eva and the salon. Beryl Finch Hair was more in her comfort zone.

To Grazja's alarm, Eva cut her hair shorter than the wig. 'Relax,' she'd advised, pushing Grazja back in the chair. 'With those cheekbones you can take it.'

The whole process took hours, cost a fortune, and made Grazja, who was happiest when busily useful, feel trapped. A dozen times Grazja decided she wasn't going to go through this again just for the sake of vanity. Then she looked into the mirror and saw the attractive, vibrant woman looking back at her and reconsidered.

Frank, who'd come to Lawton with her, pottered around town, ate lunch, and quite happily amused himself while she was in the chopping chair, dropped his jaw when he met her outside the salon.

'You're gorgeous,' he said. 'It suits you even more than the wig.'

Frank had driven back to Mapton faster than he normally did, with Grazja begging him to take the bends more slowly before they spun off the road or veered into another vehicle. At home they made use of the couple of hours available before Grazja was due at her monthly girl's night in, so that when Grazja did get to Stella's, not only did she have a dramatic new haircut and colour, but also a certain glow about her that she felt rather too conscious of. Fortunately, the haircut and styling was so strong that even after Frank's eager caresses it fell back into shape.

Not everyone had appreciated her new haircut. Gerta's reaction had been a shock - but Gerta was a little girl who didn't want her Grazy to change. Stella's reaction had been far more hurtful.

She discussed it now with Frank as he drove them to the animal sanctuary. Grazja usually drove herself to work but today Frank had volunteered to help Dan build a new shed so he'd be there for the day and could drive them both home.

'Some people don't like it when a friend changes,' Frank said.

'I not change. Only my hair.'

'But you look quite different,' Frank said, wiggling his eyebrows. 'Sexier. More confident.'

'I not sexy before?' Grazja teased again. From the reactions she kept getting she was beginning to wonder if she'd previously been invisible.

'I'd find you sexy in a potato sack with a colander on your head,' Frank laughed. 'You know what I mean. But sometimes people find it hard to accept when a friend changes. They come to rely on them being one thing, and handle it badly when they do something unexpected.'

'How you get so wise?' Grazja poked his arm.

'Years of listening to confessions.' Frank said. 'I don't how many times I heard 'Father I have sinned. I envied my friend's win on the bingo/ encouraged my friend to buy a dress that didn't suit her/ran a key along my work colleague's new BMW, etc., etc.'

'Nice,' Grazja said.

'Human nature.'

'So you think Stella envious?'

'It's possible. Definitely. I'd have thought Stella was above showing it though.'

'Me too,' Grazja sighed. 'I didn't expect it from Stella. Just goes to show, you never really know people.'

'You know me,' Frank said. I've told you all my darkest secrets.'

Grazja cocked her head at him, her smile impish. 'You never know someone completely,' she said. 'How I know you don't leave toenail clipping in bathtub?'

'Well, there's one way to find out,' Frank said lightly. 'Move in with me.

Rumours

'I've discovered something about our slippery vicar,' Frank said.

Rick quirked his mouth. 'Oh yeah?' He'd just bought them pints from the bar in The Diving Helmet, and seated himself across from Frank at the round wooden table.

Rick was tired. Things weren't going well at home and he needed this pint. And a few more.

Frank looked around to check no one was in earshot. It was a quiet Tuesday evening in late February; two youths were potting balls on the pool table in the family room, and a couple of other tables were taken, but otherwise there was no one near. The publican, Sugsy, was watching the news on the TV and commenting about it with Andy Timmis who was perched at the bar, drinking Fosters and munching on a bag of cheese and onion crisps. Over that, the usual selection of yesteryear pop hits played through speakers.

Things didn't change quickly in Mapton, including the charts.

'He's married – or was,' Frank said, leaning towards Rick. 'His wife left him for another man. It was quite the scandal in his last parish.'

'Poor bloke,' Rick said.

'Maybe.' Frank looked unconvinced. 'But from what I discovered sounds like she had good reason to go.'

'Oh!'

'Yes,' Frank said.

'How'd you get this info?' Rick asked.

'You know our weekend away in Chester? It was partly because the reverend came from that area,'

Frank confessed. 'I attended the service at his previous church on Sunday morning.'

'Sneaky,' Rick said. 'What does Grazja think of your new obsession?'

Frank looked a little sheepish. 'Says I'm being too judgemental and too nosy. I said, what did she expect? I am an ex-priest. But she puts up with me.'

Rick laughed.

'Anyway, I avoided the churchwarden – Mrs Beaton. She was quite ferocious when I spoke to her on the phone in December. Wouldn't hear a word against the Rev. Rivers.'

'So who'd you get to spill the beans?'

'There's always someone willing to gossip,' Frank said. 'You know – the one who always starts with 'I'm not one to gossip but…'

'Oh yeah,' Rick nodded. 'I hear that a lot.'

'I found a couple happy to talk after the service. I said I'd been expecting to see Michael take the service. That I was an old friend looking him up. Did he still live around here? That got the ball rolling. Irene – they were a married couple, Irene and John – was pretty eager to talk. I could see it straight away –you know the look? Eye lights up at the prospect of sharing something juicy.

Rick nodded. 'Yep, and they don't want to spread rumours but…'

'Yeah, so I could tell she wanted to talk so I gave her a bit of a push. I said 'I'd been surprised when Michael chose to go into the church because he'd a real eye for the opposite sex when we were younger. Bit of a ladies' man.'

'Machiavellian,' Rick said. Taking a sip of his beer.

Frank shrugged. 'Anyway, turns out there were rumours that the rev had a bit of a thing going on with a young woman employed as his administrative assistant.'

'Like Pauline,' Rick said.

Frank's face was serious. 'Exactly. Although to be fair Irene's husband wasn't happy – kept repeating it was just a rumour. No evidence, and Irene shouldn't be spreading it about. She got annoyed and said 'Why did his wife leave him then? She'd been doing his administration before he took Judy on. Laura didn't just take-off for no reason, did she?''

'I suppose John had a point though,' Rick said. 'Just because his wife left him didn't mean he was having it off with his assistant.'

'No,' Frank said. 'But we've seen the effect he's had on the women around here haven't we? That's the reason I'm asking questions. I saw him talking to Stella yesterday in the Co-op. She looked as enthralled as every other woman. Grazja admitted she'd felt it too. It's like he casts a spell.'

Rick had himself felt the vague draw of that spell. It bothered him more to know Stella might fall under it. A prickle of unease ran down his spine. She'd been so up and down lately; just not herself. She'd had a period of depression a couple of years ago but it didn't last long and it wasn't the same as this. She'd been tired and down, irritable yes, but not like recently when some days she seemed to barely suppress a nameless rage. Everything he said and did seemed to be wrong.

She certainly hadn't mentioned running into the gorgeous vicar. But then they hadn't engaged about much lately, other than matters regarding Gerta.

'You find out anything else?' he asked Frank, pushing his thoughts aside.

'Only that it wasn't long after his wife left him that the reverend applied to move to another parish. And that the girl – Judy– quit her job after he left, although she could have stayed in position as administrator to the next vicar.'

'Doesn't sound good,' Rick said. 'What are you going to do? Tell people. Warn Pauline?'

'I don't know,' Frank sighed. 'I could do with tracking this Judy down, and Laura perhaps, his wife. Find out what went on.'

'Agreed,' Rick said. 'You can't cast aspersions without evidence to back it up.'

'So,' Frank said. 'How are plans for the big wedding going?'

Rick groaned. 'I think Stella may kill Gina.'

'Erm,' Frank cleared his throat. 'How is Stella?'

He sounded tentative. Rick cocked his head to the side to consider his friend.

'Okay,' he replied cautiously. 'A bit tired, I think. Why? Has Grazja said anything?'

Frank looked uncomfortable. 'Erm, she mentioned Stella kicked them all out of your house last Girls Night.'

'What?' Rick frowned. 'Kicked them out. What does that mean?'

'Well, Elliot brought his dog along and she was sick in the lounge, and according to Grazia, Stella lost her temper and told them all to get out.'

Rick digested this. 'I knew the dog was sick - Gerta told me. I don't believe Stella kicked them out. That's not like her.'

'Well,' Frank squirmed. 'I don't suppose it was quite like that. But I know Grazja was upset when she got home. I don't think she and Stella have really spoken since.'

'That's too bad,' Rick said. He knew Frank was inviting him to talk. Perhaps he did need to - the situation with Stella was getting to him - but he hadn't been raised to share his feelings, especially with his male friends. As open to listening and friendly banter as he was, Rick was at heart a private man. All he said was: 'They're friends; they'll sort it out.'

Wedding Lists

Today Stella was having an up day. She felt suffused with energy which was very welcome because Gina had her working through a wedding job list long enough to use as a hallway runner.

At the moment they were busy writing out wedding invitations. For a woman who had spent most of her life with very few friends, Gina was sending out a lot of invitations.

'This is practically all of Mapton and half of Siltby,' Stella said.

'I don't want to offend anyone,' Gina said.

'Since when?'

'Shut up,' Gina dismissed her. 'I'll have a big wedding if I want one. Half of 'em won't come anyway.'

'This is a royal size wedding,' Stella said. 'I don't think the function room at the Helmet is going to be big enough.'

'I were thinking that,' Gina agreed. 'Better to have the reception in the community hall. After all, makes sense, me being mayor.'

'About that - you might not be mayor by the time of your wedding,' Stella said. 'So 'You're invited to the wedding of Mayor Gina Pontin to George Wentworth' might not be accurate. Not that it matters really.'

'What d'you mean?' Gina scowled. 'Of course I'll be mayor.'

'The mayor can change every year,' Stella reminded her. 'The councillors vote in a new mayor in May like they did with you last year.'

'Oh, that,' Gina said. 'They'll choose me again won't they? Martha Seaton was voted in three years running.'

'That was unusual,' Stella said. 'Before her I think it was a different mayor every year.'

'They'll pick me,' Gina said. 'Who else is there?'

'All the other councillors. Any of them could be chosen.'

'I meant who else is there like me?' Gina said.

'Nobody like you,' Stella said.

'Exactly,' Gina concluded. 'I'm the best mayor Mapton's ever had.'

'Of course you are.' Stella chuckled.

'Glad to see you're in a better mood,' Gina said, stamping the side of her fist down on a self-seal envelope. 'Stick yer bogger.

'Yer've been a right mardi cow lately.'

'Thanks.'

'I thought I'd die of embarrassment when yer kicked us out of yer house.'

'I know. We've been through this.'

'You're lucky we all forgave you. I tode Elliot yer had bad PMS.'

'I did' Stella said. 'Can you let it go now?'

'I would,' Gina said. 'But's it's not like you've been a barrel o' laughs since is it? You and Ricky alright?'

'Fine,' Stella lied. She couldn't understand it but she seemed to have gone off her husband. It frightened her to admit it but it felt true. And confusing. How could she have gone off Rick? And in a short space of time? He hadn't changed.

Then there was Michael Rivers.

She'd run into him last week in the Co-op. Awkwardly, she'd been clutching a packet of pantyliners and when she saw him walk smiling towards her she'd grabbed a magazine off an adjacent shelf to slip the packet under. The liners were Tena

Lights because recently, much to her dismay she'd started to leak a bit of pee – not much, just a drop or two – which hadn't ever happened to her before, even after the birth of Gerta. She prided herself on the strength of her pelvic floor muscles.

The vicar, who she hadn't seen since the unfortunate events of his Christmas Eve service for pets, was as handsome as ever. More so, perhaps.

His smile pulled her into his orbit. Stella knew by now that this was the effect the vicar had on women, but when he looked into her eyes, wasn't it just a little more intense? Didn't it feel as though he was really seeing her?

Rick's blue eyes, which she'd always loved because they reminded her, sexily, of a faded pair of lived-in Levi's, seemed lacklustre compared to the startling, black-ringed cerulean of the vicar's eyes.

'Hello again,' the vicar said. 'Fantastic to see you Stella. In fact, I've been thinking about you; I have a bit of a cheeky request.'

'Oh?' Stella asked, trying to look cool but sure her cheeks were flaming under that gaze. 'That sounds intriguing?'

'I know you're not a believer,' the vicar said. 'But would you consider donating one of your works – a small painting or sketch – to the little auction we're planning to raise money for a 'meals on wheels' service?'

'I thought we had that service?' Stella said, trying to gather her thoughts.

'Ah, it seems we did until fairly recently,' the vicar said. 'I believe the scandal with a local abattoir and meat factory put a stop to it.'

The vicar leaned in. 'I hear the less said about that the better,' he winked.

Stella could smell his aftershave, a pleasant scent of lemon and sandalwood. She had a sudden mad urge to stretch up and kiss him.

He stepped back again. Stella shook herself, trying to focus on what he'd meant.

The abattoir that the vicar alluded to had been slaughtering donkeys and horses and who knew what else to supply to the meat and food packaging plant Bestjoint who donated meat to the local meals and wheels scheme (not to mention cut price to cafes and holiday parks) on the recommendation of ex-deputy mayor Tom Turner. Tom (who Stella and most Maptonites knew as Pirate Tom) just happened to be on the board of, as well as heavily invested in, Bestjoint. Mysteriously, Tom and his wife Phyllis had taken the opportunity to take an extended trip to Spain from which they had not yet returned.

'I'll see what I've got,' Stella said. 'I'm sure there's something I can donate.'

'Wonderful. Thank you,' the vicar said. 'When you've made a choice, come and see me. My door's always open.'

By the way he looked at her Stella was sure it was.

'You listening?'

Stella came back with a start. 'What?'

'You listening,' Gina said. 'You're miles away. I said, have you ordered them flowers like I asked.'

'Yes,' Stella said, hoping Gina wouldn't notice her cheeks burning.. 'That's done.'

'Only I were thinking,' Gina said. 'I don't think I want Flo's Florists to arrange them.'

'Why not?'

'Pam's better,' Gina said. 'You should see her arrangements at church.'

'You hate Pam,' Stella said.

'That's a wicked unchristian thing to say,' Gina cried.

Stella blinked. 'Okay. You dislike Pam.'

'I don't dislike her,' Gina countered. 'I just don't like the way she hangs her smalls out for all to see. I like *her* though.'

'Ask her to do your flowers then,' Stella said, knowing perfectly well that Gina's U-turn on Pam was all about what she wanted from her.

'Actually, I was hoping you could ask her for me,' Gina admitted.

'Why?'

'Because although I like her I don't think she likes me,' Gina said.

'I wonder why?'

Stella stood up, stretching. As she turned Gina yelped.

'What you got on your jeans? Blood?'

'What?' Stella tried to twist to see. 'Oh no! My period finished four days ago. I must have started again.' She felt dismayed. She was wearing a light pantyliner; for the blood to have soaked through her jeans, it really was a heavy flow, not a few spots. This wasn't normal for her at all.

'I tell you, that's one thing about being older, yer don't miss the monthly curse,' Gina observed. 'You better not have got any on me chair. I only bought that new cushion pad last week.'

Pam's Passion

Pam Stimson discovered bliss in arranging the church floral displays. She'd always loved cut flowers in her home, and felt she had a real knack for creating pretty bouquets, but volunteering to do the church ones had allowed her to develop a hobby into a true artistic ability.

The vicar said it was her God-given gift, and she believed he was right. She knew in her bones where exactly the right bloom should go, how a feathery fern spray could elevate an arrangement to perfection, and when to subtract from an over-stuffed vase to find an elegant balance.

Pam popped into the church most days, ostensibly to fuss with her flowers - plucking out a wilting rose here, replacing a sprig of baby's breath there - but also in the hope she'd see the vicar.

Michael. He'd asked her to call him Michael.

She felt guilty about it. She loved Ray without doubt, yet being in the presence of Michael was like bathing in light.

Oh, she knew all the other women fancied him, and along with a couple of men. Her friend Tony, for example, who ran a B&B in Siltby with his partner Simon, cooed over the vicar's movie-star looks.

But their interest in Michael was shallow – precisely because of his looks – whereas Pam felt her connection to him was deeper.

It was the way he looked at her, as though his soul saw her soul. Ray adored her Amazonian flesh and bones but Michael saw through to her dainty and delicate feminine core.

They had a connection. Pam felt sure of it. She just wasn't sure of what to do about it or whether she actually wanted to do anything at all.

She really did love Ray.

Pam suspected Pauline Watkins had a crush on the vicar too. She didn't feel jealous, although Pauline got to work closely with him; instead she pitied Pauline, with her terrible clothes and badly cut hair. It was all too easy for a naïve, lonely girl like Pauline to fall for a man as handsome and compassionate as the vicar. Sad too, Pam thought because surely Michael had only offered Pauline her job out of kindness.

Mind you, Pauline was proving to be surprisingly good at running things administratively. Which only went to prove that the vicar really could see what was inside of people.

Pam just hoped that Pauline wouldn't be crushed if or when she realised Michael wasn't attracted to her the way he was to Pam.

Pauline appeared now, out of the gloomy recess of St Bart's where she worked in the office next to the vestry.

She clapped her hands together when she saw Pam's new display.

'It's beautiful, Pam. We're so lucky to have you.'

Pam noted the 'we'. It was Pauline's habit to use the plural pronoun, as though she and the vicar and the church were as one.

Pam stepped back to assess her work. Pleasure suffused her as ever when she saw her finished creation.

'Thank you,' she said. 'I love doing it.'

Pauline beamed. 'I wish I was creative like you,' she said with such sincerity that Pam experienced a warm rush of affection towards the frumpy young woman.

'Would you like to get some lunch with me?' she impulsively asked. 'I was thinking of going to the diner.'

Pauline looked startled but pleased. 'Okay, I'd like that. But I just need to text the vicar. Let him know I've gone out.'

Pauline didn't have to text, because just then the old, oak doors to the church creaked open and the vicar appeared, holding the door open for Stella Distry to slither past him clutching a rectangular package under her arm.

Michael and Stella were laughing about something; a joke just shared was clear on their faces, and Stella had her pretty face turned up to his in a manner that gave Pam a nasty jolt. They looked inappropriately intimate.

Michael spotted Pam and Pauline, giving them a little wave as he and Stella started down the nave towards them.

Pauline waved happily back.

Did they both look a little flushed? Pam narrowed her eyes at Stella, who with her lustrous dark curls and luminous eyes, managed to look both angelic and alluring in the soft shafted sunlight streaming through the stained-glass windows.

And she was wearing red lipstick. When had Pam ever seen Stella wearing lipstick? Unlike her grandmother Gina, who smeared her lips in tangerine orange or glaring pink, Stella favoured a natural look, a subtle gloss at the most.

Pam, who loved classic powder and paint, often thought Stella could use a little colour. She would have been pleased to see her making an effort, if the effect of it was not so flagrantly aimed at the vicar.

'Pauline, Pam,' Michael said. 'Stella has donated a painting to auction off. Can you imagine? An original work by Stella Distry.'

Pauline did her usual clap. 'God bless you!' she cried at Stella. 'How wonderful.'

Stella blushed prettily, one hand going protectively to the brown-paper wrapped rectangle under her arm.

'It's only a little piece,' she said. 'You might change your minds when you see it.'

The vicar – Michael – laughed as though she'd just made the wittiest comment he'd ever heard.

'A Stella Distry is a Stella Distry,' he said, cupping her elbow and ushering her past them. 'We'll look at it in the vestry.'

'I'm going to lunch with Pam,' Pauline called after him. 'Is that alright?'

'Of course,' the vicar said, hardly glancing back. 'Have a good time.'

'You scarlet woman,' Pam thought hotly, glaring at Stella's retreating back. 'You Jezebel.'

Michael never even looked at Pam's beautifully arranged flowers, only at Stella.

Reluctantly, regretting her suggestion of lunch, Pam followed Pauline out of the church, leaving the vicar alone in the clutches of the red devil.

Bridesmaids

'Here, try this on,' Elliot commanded her as Grazja took the white knee-length dress he'd handed to her. 'It should be your size but I have one smaller and one larger if not.'

He steered her towards the changing room in the front room of his shop. The shop itself was closed and shuttered as it was seven-thirty on a Wednesday evening.

Grazja had come straight from work. George had dropped Gina off at the sanctuary as he didn't fancy the longer drive in the dark to Skegness, so that Grazja could give Gina a lift from there.

Grazja hadn't seen Stella since January. Both of them had claimed to be too busy to make plans. Grazja genuinely was busy. Between her veterinary nurse course, her hours at the sanctuary, and the time she spent with Frank, the weeks were flying by. But the truth was that, initially, she'd avoided Stella at first out of hurt, convinced Stella should be the first to reach out and apologise. Then, as the days stretched out, Grazja flip-flopped between stubborn resentment versus wanting to reach out and reconnect. At least, she'd told herself, they'd see each other at the bridesmaid's fitting. The date had already been in the diary.

Tonight, Stella's choice to stand them up seemed to confirm that she no longer cared about their friendship. Grazja felt tremendously hurt.

'What she doing that more important?' Grazja demanded.

'The vicar's roped her into helping with his charity auction,' Gina said.' Can't believe she's agreed to it. Never wanted anything to do wi' the church before.

She's donated a picture, and tonight she's doing some sort of radio interview to promote the auction.' She laughed. 'Our vicar could persuade the devil to come to church.'

Gina gleefully flounced about in her Judy dress. It only lacked the final details, and Elliot was also in the process of customising a bonnet into the huge white hat that matched the dress in the film. He was still 'sourcing' a parasol.

Between his fancy dress suppliers and his drag contacts there wasn't much Elliot couldn't find.

But as tonight was really about fitting Gina's bridesmaid – Grazja – and matron of honour – Stella – into their dresses, Grazja thought it was particularly rude of Stella to cancel.

Elliot hadn't made the bridesmaid dresses. Instead he'd ordered them off the rack and was again intending to customise them with flourishes that mimicked the details of Gina's gown.

'How does it look?' Elliot called.

Grazja stepped out of the changing cubicle wearing the white dress. It fitted perfectly.

'Excellent,' Elliot said. He stepped forward to fluff the full skirt. 'I'll add a couple of ruffles, and you'll wear a crinoline style lace petticoat to make it chime with Gina's dress.'

Gina tottered about looking like a wedding cake.

'Bloody hell, this dress is heavy,' she said. 'Pity Stella couldn't come.'

'I think it very rude of Stella,' Grazja sniffed. 'It kind of Elliot to invite her after she'd thrown him out of her house.'

Elliot pulled an exaggerated sour face. 'Gina can give her the dress to try on at home. If she can be bothered she can drop it back herself and if not you or Gina will have to. I'm not coming to Mapton to chase her up.'

Gina shook her head, pursing her mouth. 'Dunno what's up with her lately. She's been like a teenager again, a moody little madam, one minute up, the next down. She's started wearing red lipstick; I ain't seen her in that since her teens neither.'

'Stella, red lipstick?' Grazja frowned. Even when they had a night out Stella always kept to subtle shades.

'I told her 'yer look like a scarlet woman.' You might as well write available for intercourse on yer forehead.'

'I didn't know red was considered so slutty' Elliot said. 'I must start wearing it. Glinda always goes for cerise.'

'Loads of women wear red lipstick,' Grazja protested. 'Not 'slutty. I don't like that word.'

'T'is,' Gina said. 'Men think it's a come on. Like blonde hair.'

Grazja glared at her. 'Blonde hair not a 'come on.'

Gina shrugged. 'Bet you've had more attention with blonde hair than you ever did with brown, especially from men.'

'It suit me more,' Grazja said. 'That's not a 'come on.'

'Not to you,' Gina said. 'But it is to men. They're dirty boggers. Don't take much for them to make assumptions.'

Elliot grinned at Grazja.

Grazja shook her head. 'Well, whatever men might think, not make it slutty. But it is change for Stella to wear red lipstick. Why you think she start?'

'Probably just a phase,' Gina shrugged. 'She wore a nose stud for a year when she went off to art school. Rick should gi' her another baby. That'd sort her out – broody I reckon, that's what wrong wi' her. Trying to get his attention.'

She dismissed the subject with an airy wave, and, cocking her head to contemplate Grazja's white dress, observed: 'Bit plain, ain't it?'

'It won't be when I've worked my magic ,' Elliot said. 'Trust me on the frou-frou, darling.'

'White's tricky,' Gina said. 'I hope Stella don't start her period on my wedding day. Took her by surprise last week – soaked right through her jeans and nearly ruined my chair cushion. I had to soak the cover in cold water.'

'Too much information.' Elliot wrinkled his nose, retreating to the boudoir beyond the curtain.

'That not like Stella,' Grazja said. 'She always know when to expect period.'

'I know,' Gina said, swishing her tiered skirts. 'She were a bit surprised. Said it weren't long since her last bleed.'

Gina glanced at the clock. 'Ooh, Elliot,' she called ''ave you got a radio? Stella should be on now.'

Will They Won't They

Stella felt giddy and guilty. Mostly giddy, although guilt insisted on hanging around like the twinge of toothache that was a harbinger of worse to come if left to fester but you ignored anyway because you feared a trip to the dentist.

Stella focused on the giddy high of a potential affair to avoid the feelings of intense anxiety and low mood running beneath, not to mention irritability and an inexplicable sense of loss.

She felt so restless, as though her life, which until fairly recently had seemed fine, was dull and joyless. Pointless even. Rick bored her. The jokes that once made her laugh seemed predictable and stale, his habits more annoying, his idea of moving to Lawton because of his pop-up kitchen entirely selfish.

Gerta was playing up at the moment, throwing tantrums like she had back in the 'terrible twos' stage. It was a relief to pack her off to pre-school in the mornings so Stella could head up to her studio where she feverishly (and secretly) worked on a portrait of Michael Rivers when she wasn't sitting with her head in her hands despairing.

Rick wanted to talk but she refused, and now she could feel him pulling away from her. She wanted to care, but she couldn't. She spent all her time thinking about when she could next see Michael.

Not that Stella was actually having an affair with him. Neither of them had openly acknowledged their mutual attraction or done anything more than flirt. Yet standing next to him in the vestry had been erotically charged. It was as though, by unwrapping her painting, he'd undressed Stella; it was her body his gaze caressed, rather than a small portrait of Mildred on her mobility scooter licking an ice-cream.

'Marvellous,' he'd said, turning to her. 'You truly capture the essence of a person. God has given you such a gift.'

Those were the words his mouth said, but Stella saw in his eyes something else entirely; something that made her flush with heat.

How could a vicar exude that much sex appeal? She felt like Hester Prynne inexorably drawn to Arthur Dimmesdale. Would Maptonites force her to wear a scarlet letter if she followed her desires?

She wanted him. She was sure he wanted her, but he was holding back, surely because she was married and he was a moral man. Nothing he said to her was explicit, but it was there. She felt it in the little touch beneath her elbow when he guided her into his study for their radio interview about the auction, and in the electricity that crackled when he'd held the door so she could squeeze past him. It was most definitely there when he smiled at her, in the way he held her eyes just a fraction longer than necessary.

Stella found him thrilling, tantalising. His interest in her made her feel alive and vital.

Invited to his home to do the phone interview with Radio Lincolnshire, Stella had felt sick with excitement and fear. She'd dithered over what to wear – not just what dress, but what underwear to choose. Not that she was intending to expose her underwear but what if… How much perfume was too much?

It hadn't been Michael who'd called her with the radio request, it had been Pauline, who cheerfully asked if she'd be available, and then casually added:

'Would you mind doing it with the vicar at the rectory?'

To which Stella had seriously replied that she wouldn't mind that at all.

'I'd love to be there,' Pauline said, 'but I promised Pam I'd help her paint Easter eggs. We'll be listening though.'

Rick was conveniently out of the way. He'd taken himself off to Lawton even earlier than usual to start prepping for the evening restaurant menu.

Sue had already agreed to babysit Gerta whom she had a special reason to be fond of, so Stella's way was clear.

After the phone-in interview with an over-jolly local radio DJ called Paul Scottie was over, Stella found herself sweating nervously. They'd shared the phone speaker, and now Stella hoped her perfume and deodorant masked her perspiration. Sitting so close she found the tension almost unbearable, anticipating what might happen next.

Nothing happened, as it turned out. Michael – he'd asked her to use his name – got up almost abruptly, and said he needed to catch the bell ringers before their practise session ended.

'Oh,' Stella said, springing to her feet. 'Um, yes. Of course.'

'That went well, I think,' Michael said.' Very well. You're a natural at interviews. We'll get a lot of interest in the auction with a Stella Distry to sell.'

'Good,' Stella said.

He smiled at her and took her hand. 'I can't tell you how much I appreciate your generosity.'

Stella's breath almost stopped. Instead of a thrill she felt anxiety; was her palm wet with sweat?'

Maybe it was because Michael quickly dropped her hand and ushered her smoothly out of the study, and out of the house.

The early spring evening smelled fresh with the tang of sea salt and the lingering scent of daffodils. The blood pumped so hard in Stella's ears she couldn't hear the peeling bells.

The vicar leaned in. 'Drive safe,' he said, before striding purposefully away towards the church.

Actually, Stella hadn't driven. Walking home in the dark, she didn't know whether the sick feeling in her stomach was crushing disappointment, or crashing relief.

Once she'd thanked Sue for babysitting and managed to get rid of her without too much chatting, and then got Gerta into bed and off to sleep, she could turn her mind, like a crush-afflicted schoolgirl, back to the object of her attention. She had to see him again as soon as possible. It was like a sickness.

Lying in bed she suddenly remembered she had a perfect excuse to visit St Bart's in the morning. Hadn't she promised Gina she'd ask Pam about the flowers for Gina's wedding? She knew for sure that Pam was going to be setting up the Easter display at St Bart's.

Heart racing with anticipation, Stella heard Rick's car in the drive, and snapped off the lamp. Feeling feverish and guilty, she closed her eyes when he came to bed and pretended to be asleep.

In the Early Hours

Grazja was awake in the early hours of the morning mulling over what Gina had said.

Stella was unusual in that her menstrual pattern was highly regular, and thus predictable, and her periods tended to be light, something Stella said she was grateful for as she remembered her mother having an awful time with heavy, painful periods.

Grazja knew all this because she and Stella were best friends and it was the sort of thing they'd shared with each other until recently.

Now Grazja was worrying that her own insecurities, her hurt at Stella's reaction to her hair cut, and a lingering resentment at Stella's lack of any apology had stopped her from seeing that her friend needed help.

Looking back at Stella's behaviour she could see times before Christmas, back to the autumn in fact, when Stella had seemed out of sorts. She'd stayed home on bonfire night due to a migraine that lasted three days; something that Stella put down to eye-strain from painting. Hadn't she looked tired and pale on the drag night outing, then mentioned another migraine between Christmas and New Year? Then she'd been in such a foul mood on that night in late January. No, it wasn't pleasant to have someone's dog be sick on your carpet, yet Stella was used to cleaning up after her aging cat, Henry, plus she did some voluntary work at the animal sanctuary, so it wasn't like she was squeamish. Her reactions, Grazja realised, had been so out of character.

Why hadn't she seen this sooner?

Frank had mentioned that Rick seemed a bit down lately, so he'd taken him for a pint but hadn't wanted to push him. Grazja supposed men didn't share so easily. Also Frank, when he wasn't with her, was quite fixated on doing a background check on the vicar. Maybe she and Frank should be paying more attention to their own friends?

Grazja ran through a few options, as Frank slept on beside her. As always happened in the small hours her mind latched onto the worst scenarios first. Changes in behaviour, migraines, mood-swings and personality disorder might mean a brain tumour.

Tsk, Grazja told herself. Use your nurse's brain. Stella could be clinically depressed and her brain chemistry imbalanced. She'd had depression before.

More likely a change in Stella's menstrual cycle and a change in her behaviour indicated some kind of hormonal fluctuation, and hormones were powerful things. You only had to look at how they affected teenagers.

And hadn't Stella sounded like a giggly teenage girl on the radio last night, not the sophisticated woman Grazja knew? It had been squirm-inducing, (although Gina seemed not to notice) the way Stella talked about the vicar. Grazja found it troubling; she well remembered the knee-trembling effect he'd had on herself. Even Frank admitted he'd felt the man's charismatic pull.

With Stella not herself, she'd be vulnerable to that sort of man. Grazja suddenly feared her friend could be about to make a terrible mistake – if she hadn't already made it. One that could destroy her marriage.

Red lipstick was a danger sign she couldn't ignore.

Rick on the Rocks

Grazja wasn't the only person awake in the early hours of the morning. Rick was too. It was becoming too familiar a pattern - awake in the small hours worrying about his marriage, wanting to reach for his wife's hand, and too miserable and confused to do it. Poor Gerta was getting grumpy, sensing the tension between Stella and himself. She'd started to throw the sort of tantrums they hadn't seen since she was two.

He wanted to make it all right, and yet how easy it was to see how couples fell apart, and how quickly it could happen. Snapped at by Stella, cold-shouldered, bombarded with angry tears (and carrots) or ground down by sulky silence, Rick had begun to withdraw, bit by bit. He came to bed late when Stella was either asleep, or as he suspected, pretending to be. The few times he'd nuzzled up to her, for sex, or a cuddle, or just a little warmth in the middle of the night, the way they always had, the rigid line of her backbone told him all he needed to know. He wasn't wanted. Not by his wife.

He got up early for the same reason as he came to bed late. So he didn't have to deal with Stella's rejection of him.

And Stella stayed in bed until he'd gone.

Then came the red lipstick. He never saw it himself. Stella wasn't wearing it for him; that much was clear. She was careful to take it off at home, and to be honest, Rick had stopped looking at her. They slid past each other with defences bristling, like two animals forced to share the same territory, eyes averted to avoid outright conflict.

It was much easier to let the distance between them expand, to let his own feelings of rejection and resentment quietly simmer, a noxious brew whose vapours were slowly poisoning him.

He heard about the red lipstick from locals. It was amazing how many Maptonites felt it necessary to comment on his wife's change of make-up. Some folk, like Sue, had shared opinions from a purely aesthetic viewpoint. 'Tell her she don't need it Ricky. Don't suit her.' Marjorie Suspring thought the opposite. 'Glad to see Stella making a bit more effort, Rick,' she said. 'She can look a bit washed out with that pale skin. That red lippy really brightens her up.'

'I'll be sure to pass that on,' Rick had said, his sarcasm bouncing unheeded off Marjorie's orange spray tan.

It was the other comments that bothered him more. The insinuation-laden banter, the implications dressed as jokes.

'Stella trying out a new look? You know what they say, 'new look, new man.'

'You paying your missus enough attention, Rick?

'Not a colour I'd wear to church, but not many vicars look like ours. Ha ha, that right, Rick?' Mildred threw this grenade just as she left.

Martha Seaton, Mapton's ex-mayor said: 'Give a woman the right lipstick, she can conquer the world.'

'I don't know why everyone is obsessed with Stella's lipstick?' Rick grumbled.

Martha patted his hand. 'Out of season we notice the smallest of changes,' she said. 'Small town life I'm afraid. She looks very striking, is all I'm saying. Eye-catching.' A pause, then: 'I heard Stella's donating a painting to the Meals on Wheels auction. The vicar knows how to net the big fish, eh?'

And that was the first Rick had heard about it. Stella was free to do what she liked with her paintings of course, but since when did they act so independently of each other? They used to discuss everything. All he said was: 'Yeah, a Stella Distry will raise a lot if the art world hears about it.' Inside his gut had churned.

Exhausted following his Wednesday night pop-up in Lawton, Rick finally slid out of bed to go open the diner early. He didn't bother to creep around in the darkened bedroom like he normally did so as not to wake Stella. To hell with her. Switching on the overhead light he banged open drawers as he yanked out underwear and a tee shirt, rattled the hangers in the wardrobe while he found his jeans, and slammed the lid down on the laundry bin.

Stella didn't respond beyond pulling the covers over her head and ignoring him.

He gave the bedroom door an extra hard slam as he exited. He wasn't worried about waking Gerta as she either woke early or could sleep through an earthquake. If she was up, he could usually hear her playing in her room, singing or chattering to her various dolls and cuddly animals, or scrambling around in her crayon box to produce her morning drawing. Most days they pinned at least one new drawing to the fridge door, while Stella kept the ever-growing archive of Gerta's art in a portfolio case in her studio.

Stopping outside her door, Rick listened, but Gerta was quiet. Opening the door to peer in, he was surprised to find her sitting cross-legged on her daisy-shape rug. Instead of playing with dolls or drawing, she'd tipped the contents of Stella's make-up bag on the floor and smeared thick scarlet lipstick over and around her mouth. She had it on her teeth too. A half snapped-off cylinder of crushed waxy red gunge lay on the rug.

Rick looked at the clownish lipstick. Normally he would have laughed, despite himself. Today his humour fled. No doubt this offensive slash across his darling daughter's face was the infamous lipstick he kept hearing about.

Spying his stony look, Gerta's expression went from 'caught in the act' to a mulish rebellious one that Rick recognised all too well. It foretold of an oncoming tantrum.

Jesus, he thought. I can't take this right now. This is Stella's fault; let her deal with it.

He forced a smile and said: 'Don't you look pretty. Go show Mummy. I gotta go open the diner now.'

Gerta seemed surprised out of mutiny. 'Aren't you going to make me breakfast, Daddy?'

'Not today honey. Mummy will do that. I got things to do. She's awake.'

'But I like your breakfast better,' Gerta whined, bottom lip trembling.

'Not today, honey.' He nipped in to give her a kiss. 'I'll tell Mummy you're up. See you later.'

He fairly leapt back out of her room, strode along the landing, hammered on their bedroom door, calling: 'Stella, Gerta needs you,' and was down the stairs and out of the house as though a lion was chasing him.

Desperately Seeking Stella

Grazja messaged Stella first thing: 'Got morning off. Coffee?'

She got no reply, but if Stella was working she probably hadn't looked at her phone.

Frank had left on some mysterious mission he'd said he'd tell her about later so at ten Grazja walked round to Stella's. She needed to clean her little annexe flatlet anyway; she'd neglected it, spending so much time at Frank's. They hadn't got any further with plans to move in together officially, but they'd started to casually look for a bigger place. Frank's place was fine for now but not big enough for a permanent home for the two of them.

She'd rung the doorbell but Stella didn't appear. Rick would be at the diner and Gerta at pre-school. Stella had probably popped to the shops after dropping her off and got caught up somewhere. Not with the vicar, Grazja hoped.

She sent another message: 'Need 2 talk.'

Checking her phone for the next half hour, Grazja occupied her time by cleaning her little kitchenette and bathroom, nipping to the window now and again in case she saw Stella come back.

She was being silly, she told herself; it wasn't urgent she talked to Stella. Yet Grazja did feel a sense of urgency now that she suspected what might be wrong. If Stella's hormones were going haywire she needed to get tested. If she was depressed she needed treatment. If she was about to jump into a destructive affair she needed a friend to talk her out of it.

After checking her phone about ten more times, Grazja decided to go to the diner. Perhaps Rick knew where Stella was.

The clouds that had greeted her this morning had begun to blow inland, scudded along by the fresh breeze coming off the sea. Mapton wasn't fully opened for the summer season but being the Easter school holidays there were more families on the promenade and beach than she'd seen for a while.

The diner was doing brisk business and Rick was busy taking orders and serving coffee.

'Hey,' he said, flashing her a warm smile. 'Not seen you for a while. What can I get you?'

Grazja noted the dark circles under his eyes. He looked strained beneath the usual smile.

She didn't want to ask him straight out if he knew where Stella was. 'I thought Stella might be here, fancy a coffee with me,' Grazja said.

Rick said: 'Nah, not her usual time to come to the diner. Is she not home working? You called her?'

'Messaged. Rung doorbell. She probably painting and listening to music,' Grazja shrugged.

'Probably,' Rick said, but he frowned. 'Want a coffee?'

Grazja realised a couple of people were waiting behind her. 'No, that's okay,' she said, turning to go just as Pete Moss, ignoring the waiting customers, squeezed in beside her. As a Mapton resident he considered himself entitled to queue jump the day trippers and out-of-towners.

'Usual,' he barked at Rick, who waved him away.

'I'll bring it over when I've served these nice people,' Rick said.

'Saw Stella heading towards St Bart's,' Pete said loudly. 'Better watch out, Rick. You know what the ladies are like for the vicar. He keeps reeling them in.' He gave Rick and Grazja a wink, retreating to hover by his favourite booth in the hope of scaring away the family currently sitting in it.

Grazja caught Rick's scowl as she said goodbye and hurried out, almost colliding with Pauline, who was coming in.

'Sorry,' they cried in unison.

'Oh, Pauline,' Grazja said. 'Have you come from St Bart's?'

'No, I've been cleaning at the rectory,' Pauline said. 'I'm on my way to the church after I've picked up some cake for me and Pam. We're working on the Easter flowers this morning.'

She announced this with pride. Then: 'Why?'

'I'm looking for Stella,' Grazja answered. 'Pete said he saw her heading to St Bart's.'

Pauline clutched at the little silver cross that hung at her neck. 'The red devil,' she gasped.

'Sorry?' Grazja said.

Pauline shot a look towards Rick in the diner. Grabbing Grazja by the hand, she pulled her a few feet along the prom.

'I don't want poor Rick to hear,' Pauline whispered loudly. 'I think Stella might be possessed.'

'What?'

At Grazja's astounded expression, Pauline seemed to get a grip on herself.

'Maybe not actually possessed, not yet, but she's certainly under Satan's influence.'

'Is she?' Grazja asked. It wasn't the first time she had seen Pauline go over the top. Pauline had once screamed 'sinner' at Frank in a pub.

Pauline nodded. 'She's become a jezebel, a painted lady. I didn't understand until Pam made me see it.' She dropped her voice, holding Grazja's eye with her fervent gaze. 'Stella is trying to tempt the vicar into adultery - sins of the flesh. The devil desires her to lead him into Hell where he will burn, writhing for eternity!'

Grazja couldn't help feeling that Pauline gained far too much pleasure from the emphasis she placed on the words 'flesh' and 'writhing'.

'Calm down,' she said in her best, brisk no-nonsense nurse voice.

Pauline blinked. She dropped her sweaty grasp on Grazja's hand. Her gaze seemed to clear. 'I do get het up,' she said. 'The vicar tells me to count to ten and then say the Lord's Prayer when I get into a tizz.'

'Why you think this about Stella?' Grazja asked. 'You mentioned Pam? Pam Stimson?'

Pauline nodded. 'She's my friend.' She swelled up. 'I didn't think anything of Stella being alone in the rectory with the vicar, until Pam pointed it out. Pam's clever - calls Stella the 'red devil'. I don't think it's only because of the lipstick.'

'When was Stella alone with the vicar at the rectory?' Grazja asked, trying not to sound alarmed.

'Last night,' Pauline said. 'For the radio interview. Did you hear it?'

'Yes,' Grazja said grimly. 'I assumed they'd gone to the radio station.'

'Pam said that Stella was trying to get her claws into our vicar, that's she trying to seduce him. It made

Pam's blood boil and Pam's ever so nice. I knew it must be serious to get her so het up. As soon as she explained I could see it! I could see the Devil working through Stella.'

Sensing a renewal of religious fervour, Grazja said sharply. 'It sounds to me like Pam is suffering attack from Green Eye Monster.'

'D'you think so?' Pauline asked. 'Is that another name for the Devil?'

'I mean Pam sounds jealous,' Grazja said. 'You say she in church this morning? Where Stella was going?'

'Yes,' Pauline said. Her hand flew to her mouth. 'Oh! You think there will be trouble?'

'Maybe,' Grazja said. 'I think we better go make sure there isn't.'

She set off with an impatient stride that left Pauline struggling to keep up.

'What do you mean, Pam being jealous?' she huffed.

'I mean maybe Pam want vicar for herself,' Grazja said. 'She jealous because she think Stella take him.'

For a minute all she could hear was Pauline panting behind her. Glancing back, she saw the frown on the girl's face, more puzzled than upset.

'I don't think Pam wants him like that,' Pauline decided. 'She just wants to protect him from being tempted.'

'And what about you, Pauline? You seem very attached to the vicar. Do you want him?'

Pauline blushed. 'I do love him,' she admitted. 'Sometimes I wish he'd marry me, but not to fornicate. Only if he wanted children of course. That would be my duty. But,' she added breathlessly. 'Michael is so pure it would feel wrong – like 'doing it' with Jesus.'

She looked so mortified that Grazja nearly laughed. Instead, she slowed and patted the girl's arm kindly.

'The vicar isn't Jesus. He's just a man, and it seems to me he holds far too much influence over the women in this town.

'Come on, let's make sure our friends don't do anything stupid.'

Green Eyed Monster

Pam had started the day in a foul mood, and she took it with her to church, jabbing daffodil stems into the spiky frog at the bottom of a vase with unusual vehemence.

The job should have given her pleasure; she'd been looking forward to creating the Easter display for weeks and had planned it to perfection, with an abundance of narcissi and hyacinths for colour and scent, passion flowers to signify the Passion of Christ, and Easter lilies to celebrate His resurrection. To these stars she would add forsythia and spring foliage. Then she would dangle painted egg baubles from delicate sprays of pussy willow dotted around the church, as well as more eggs in little yellow and green raffia baskets.

Instead of joy, Pam felt angry and unsettled. It was all Stella Distry's fault, the floozy. If she hadn't started throwing herself at the vicar, Pam wouldn't be feeling so damned upset.

That red devil had a lot to answer for. What did she think she was playing at? A married woman (that poor Rick) with a child, trying to mislead a man of God with her flirty mannerisms and scarlet lipstick.

Pauline didn't see it of course. She only had eyes for the vicar anyway, and she thought it was nice that Stella was helping the church even though she was a self-confirmed heathen.

'That's the vicar's gift,' she said. 'Even non-believers want to help him. That's how he draws them to God.'

Pam didn't think Stella had the remotest interest in God; she wanted to get her hands on the flesh of the vicar.

Pam felt that the soul to soul attraction between herself and Michael was purer than mere lust; it was a spiritual connection (although she couldn't deny the allure of a physical one) and likely to stay that way out of mutual respect (and her love for Ray).

She didn't want that delicate, gossamer-fine, unspoken connection between herself and the vicar to be broken by Stella's influence on him. Michael might be a man of God, but he was still only a man, and they were weak when it came to women.

Just look at Adam and Eve and how that had turned out.

Discovering that Michael had invited Stella to his home had made Pam tremble with panic. The thought of them alone together of an evening, it wasn't right.

'Why can't they do the interview in your office?' she demanded when Pauline mentioned it.

''Because of the bells,' Pauline explained. 'It's practice night. Too loud for a radio interview.'

They were painting the moulded eggs for the displays at Pam's kitchen table. The eggs were actually toys, very realistic and made of rubber. If you dropped one it bounced. It was easier than blowing out the eggs the way they had in school.

Earlier in the week, Pam had let Ray take an egg box filled with rubber ones to the diner where he'd pretended to drop them each time someone new came in, until Ang had threatened to ban him if he did it one more time. There was only so much fun to be had from a repeated joke.

'I don't trust that woman,' Pam blurted. 'She's got an eye for the vicar.'

Pauline laughed. 'Everyone loves the vicar,' she said.

'Yes, but she's out to seduce him,' Pam insisted. 'Have you seen the way she is with him, always touching him and simpering. And that lipstick she wears.'

'Stella?' Pauline asked, wide-eyed. 'But she's married to Rick? Who would want to cheat on Rick? He's lovely.'

'That red devil, that's who,' Pam hissed. 'She wants to get her claws in Michael, mark my words.'

Pauline blinked. 'Oh, you call him Michael too?'

'That's his name isn't it?' Pam said, immediately feeling that she'd given something secret away.

'Yes,' Pauline said, frowning slightly. 'Most people call him vicar.'

'He asked me to call him Michael,' Pam said defensively.

'Oh,' Pauline nodded. She looked a little crestfallen. 'Me too.'

This gave Pam pause. 'Maybe because we're part of the inner-congregation,' she said. 'Those who work closely with him.'

'Yes,' Pauline agreed, brightening. 'We are closest to him.' She glanced at the clock on the wall, a big bright sunburst shape, and said: 'The interview should be on soon. Let's listen to it.'

To Pam's ear, Stella's soft, well-spoken voice, which she had always admired (especially compared to Gina's grating tones) seemed suddenly sultry and artful, a honeyed trap to catch a man.

Pam was seized by an uncharitable spite towards the woman. Nobody else in Mapton had a posh voice like that - well, the vicar did but you'd expect that – and it just showed what an affected stuck-up cow Stella was.

Listen to her talking about 'her work', giggling when the vicar spoke, answering the DJs questions like she thought she was so special. And Michael, falling for all of it, saying what an honour it was to have *the* Stella Distry devote her work and time to such a good cause; what a coup it was to have an original Stella Distry to auction off; how it showed she not only was a part of, but really cared about her community.

Pam was offering a bespoke flower arrangement to some lucky bidder but it, or other lots, didn't seem to warrant a mention.

It made her blood boil, it really did.

And then came the final straw as Paul Scottie asked. 'Stella, you admitted you're not religious yourself. What made you donate to the church?'

Stella gave a little low giggle. 'Michael can be very persuasive,' she said.

Pam and Pauline looked at each other. 'Michael,' they echoed.

Pam and Pauline had spent the evening winding themselves up with all the devious wiles Stella would use to seduce their vicar, if it wasn't already too late.

Pauline even went so far as to wonder if Stella was demonically possessed.

'No, course not,' Pam said. 'She's just rich and pretty and thinks she can have whatever she wants, like how she first waltzed into Mapton and stole Rick straight off.'

'But you call her the red devil,' Pauline said.

'Because of her lipstick,' Pam explained. 'Not because I think she's possessed.'

Pauline looked unconvinced.

Pam had a restless night, twice almost knocking Ray out of bed with her tossing and turning. He'd left early to go fishing much to her relief. She didn't think she could hide her mood today, and if he'd asked, she couldn't tell him the truth because mention of the vicar had the same sort of enraging effect on him that the smell of bleach used to have on her old cat, Mirabelle, who would bite Pam's fingers if she smelled bleach on them. Pam continued bleaching her dishcloths, but she opted to wear rubber gloves when she did so to keep Mirabelle content. She did much the same with Ray over the vicar. She hadn't stopped going to church or arranging the flowers but she didn't talk about the vicar in their house because it upset him. Since they'd swapped Sunday morning sexy time to Saturday mornings, Ray had somewhat settled down.

For a few months Pam enjoyed the frisson of loving two men. One physically and emotionally, the other spiritually (and alright, she could confess to herself, physically in her imagination too).

Now Stella Distry was causing Pam to feel horrible, burning jealousy and threatening to ruin the purity of her connection with Michael by corrupting him.

At this moment, decapitating a lily with uncharacteristic force, Pam hated Stella.

That was when the door to the church creaked open and in walked the red devil herself.

Unholy Kerfuffle

Stella had been rudely awoken that morning by Rick switching on the overhead light and slamming drawers and doors. She'd almost jumped out her skin when he'd hammered on the bedroom door, yelling: 'Stella, Gerta needs you,' leaving her to stumble out of bed in a panic, thinking something terrible had happened, only to find a lip-stick smeared Gerta on the edge of tantrum, and Rick nowhere to be seen.

She'd cursed him roundly. No wonder she was thinking about another man, she'd told herself. Again swept by a jittery craving to see Michael, she remembered her plan to visit Pam at the church.

After dropping Gerta off at pre-school, and forcing herself to chat with some of the other mums, Stella ran a few errands as though this was just a normal day and she wasn't in the grip of a strange fever.

She returned and paid a fine on an overdue library book that she'd found under Gerta's bed, and picked up some of Henry's favourite cat treats at Petz. (As well as wild bird seed to fill the feeders so that Henry could chitter through the window at the birds as they fed. Even in his younger days Henry had been more voyeur than active hunter.)

Gerta - the little minx - had completely ruined her only tube of red lippy, so Stella purchased a new one at Kiss & Makeup. Her urge to wear red wasn't just about attracting Michael. It countered this terrible nagging sense she had that she was disappearing, fading in the way old polaroids did over time.

She chose a shade called Crimson Passion, paid for it and slicked it on using the mirror in the shop, completely ignored by the bored-looking teenage girl manning the till. Next she visited the bakery and bought two Belgian buns. Pam, she knew, loved a Belgian bun. This, Stella figured, would act as sweetener to her request that Pam take on the flower arrangements for Gina's wedding. Plus, if Michael was there - fingers crossed - he'd admire her generosity.

As Stella approached St Bart's, she found herself flushed with sudden heat. It was hard to believe just how the possibility of seeing Michael affected her. Even in the beginning with Rick she hadn't broken into a hot sweat. She couldn't say it was pleasant but it must mean something profound about the chemistry between herself and Michael.

Checking no one was about, Stella nipped around the side of the church into a cool shadow to fish a packet of baby wipes out of her bag. She kept these for Gerta's sticky fingers (and Gerta's inclination to pick up all sorts of filthy things off the ground) and was grateful now that they were to hand to swipe under her sweaty armpits. She flipped open a compact mirror, primped her hair, made sure her lipstick wasn't smudged, and finally felt ready to go in.

Inside the church, enveloped by the smell of beeswax, must, and heady narcissi, it took Stella's eyes a moment to adjust to the gloom after the bright daylight.

She saw Pam surrounded by buckets of flowers and floristry paraphernalia, arranging a display in front of the altar.

Stella set off down the knave towards Pam, expecting to see Pam's pretty, dimpled smile of welcome, her own smile already curving up. Instead Pam watched her approach with a stony expression, one Stella had seen turned on Gina but never toward her. Disconcerted, Stella kept her own smile in place, realising with bewilderment that Pam's stare was less stony, than actually hostile.

Stella had always got on well with Pam, often acting as a soothing barrier between Gina and Pam when neighbourly relations got fraught. Pam's line of frilly babydolls had appeared in a number of Stella's Mapton paintings. They evoked a joie de vivre that Stella enjoyed about Pam, encapsulating the way in which Mapton folk tended to live their lives according to their own quirky preferences.

Had Gina gone and done something horrible?

Before Stella could greet her, Pam said coldly: 'He's not here.'

'Sorry?'

'He's not here,' Pam said. 'So you've wasted a trip.'

Stella stopped, thrown. 'I don't understand,' she said. 'I'm here to see you, Pam.'

Pam, yanking a large lily out of a bucket, gave a snort of derision. 'I'm sure you are,' she said. 'Wearing your red lipstick.'

Stella touched her lips, stung. She instantly understood the insinuation. It was too close to home. 'I don't understand what you mean,' she lied. 'I came to see you Pam. I was going to ask a favour and I bought you these,' she said, thrusting the paper bag of Belgian buns at Pam.

Pam looked at the bakery bag, lips curling. 'Oh, I can guess the favour you want,' she said. 'You can't drag me down to your moral level with a couple of buns.'

'What is that supposed to mean?' Stella shot back, temper shooting up like mercury in a thermometer.

'Don't pretend with me,' Pam spat. 'I can see what's going on, you hussy. A married woman, acting like a slut around our vicar. You want me to keep quiet about it, don't you? But I know where you were last night even if poor Rick doesn't.'

Stella was swept with a wave of guilt and embarrassment that quickly transformed into rebellious outrage. Adrenaline surged through her. Incensed, she hissed: 'How dare you? You have no idea what you're talking about. I was going to ask you if you'd do the flowers for Gina's wedding! And if anything it's you who's been throwing herself at the vicar. Ray's been moaning about it at the diner. Look at yourself, do you really think Michael's going to look at you? It's embarrassing.'

Pam began to shake like a volcano about to blow. Lunging forward she smacked Stella hard across the face with the lily.

Losing it completely, Stella lowered her head and charged Pam, butting her in the sternum. Pam oofed as her breath was knocked out, but grabbed Stella and wrestled her into a headlock.

They shuffled back and forth, Pam grunting as she held on, Stella screaming as she tried to writhe free.

That was the point when Gina entered the fray.

#

Gina had also noted that Pam was going to be arranging the Easter flowers in St Bart's that morning. Gina didn't trust Stella would remember to ask Pam about doing the flowers for her wedding - she'd been acting so funny lately - so Gina decided she would have to ask Pam herself. She'd be extra nice about it; make sure to compliment Pam on her Easter display first. She'd pick up four Belgian buns at the bakery. Gina liked to go large with gestures.

When she entered the church she couldn't quite take in what she was seeing. Two figures wrestled in front of the altar, one large, holding a struggling smaller person into a headlock. The scene crystallised and Gina recognised the pair as Pam and Stella. Horrified, she dropped the Belgian buns, and started down the knave, screaming 'Ger off her you cow!'

Gina launched herself onto Pam's back, grabbing her hair, yelling 'Let go of my granddaughter.'

Pam staggered under the unexpected attack but didn't relinquish her grip on Stella who flailed, face red and gasping for breath, knocking over buckets of water, smashing flowers underfoot.

Angels and saints on the stained glass windows looked down impassively on the fracas below.

Gina yanked out a bunch of Pam's hair. Pam squealed and let go of Stella as she grabbed for Gina. Stella stumbled away, face-red, gasping for air as Gina slid off Pam's back.

Pam turned on Gina and began slapping at her. 'Ger off, ger off,' Gina shouted, protecting her head with her hands.

Stella, regaining her breath, saw her grandmother under attack and plunged back in, clawing at Pam.

A loud male voice cut through the frenzy.

All three of them froze, like kids caught in an act of supreme naughtiness.

They turned to face the vicar.

Except it wasn't the vicar; it was Frank Manning, half way down the nave, gaping at them in horror. A few paces behind him, Grazja and Pauline looked equally appalled.

Next to Frank, an attractive blonde woman appraised the situation with cool calmness.

'Let me guess,' she asked in a pleasant, low tone, which never-the-less carried clearly. 'You're fighting over the vicar?'

'Who are you?' Gina bristled.

'I'm Laura Rivers,' the woman said. 'The vicar's wife.'

Rick Roars

It had been blessedly quiet first thing in the diner, a time Rick usually treasured; just him, the sound of the surf, and the coffee machine burbling and hissing as it warmed up. Mark wouldn't be in until eight at the earliest, when the grill really fired up. Before that Rick could handle the few early birds who came in.

Frank used to be a regular early customer in the days before Grazja, but now he had a reason to stay in bed a bit longer, he'd transferred his visits to late afternoon out of season, when the diner was quiet again and he and Rick could catch up.

This morning the quiet was less soothing for Rick. It gave him time to churn over his domestic problems but provided no answers.

By late morning, the diner was busy, and he'd managed to blot his thoughts out with work and chatter, but then two things occurred that got him thinking. Grazja had come in looking for Stella, seeming strangely anxious about finding her, not that she said that. Rick could see it in her manner though, and the fleeting alarm on her face when Peter Moss (that idiot) made his snide remark. 'Saw Stella heading towards St Bart's. Better watch out, Rick. You know what the ladies are like for the vicar. He keeps reeling them in.'

Rick did know what the ladies were like around the vicar.

Outside, Grazja and Pauline were involved in animated conversation, about what Rick couldn't hear, but he caught the pitying look Pauline shot him through the glass, and it added to his growing disquiet. They were talking about him, that much was clear, and if he was being pitied by Pious Pauline, then God knows he'd become a sad case.

Lunchtime trade was brisk, and Rick had no more time to think. Peter was hogging a booth to himself, nursing an endless coffee, while families waited to be seated. Rick asked him to finish up as they needed the table. Peter, looking affronted, huffed out, mumbling about being mistreated as a loyal customer. Rick didn't care, and he knew Peter would be back all too soon. Recently he seemed to live at the diner.

By four o' clock the day-trippers had set off for home as the unusual Easter warmth bled out of the day with the sinking sun, and the diner was quiet, except for Peter who'd slunk back in and was sipping another coffee in his favourite booth, tucking into a muffin, and reading the Lawton Post. Rick didn't have the heart to comment. Peter was a lonely man he reckoned.

Mark had finished for the day, and Rick was wiping down the counter, thinking about the friggin' vicar. Since the vicar's arrival hadn't Stella started changing? She'd donated a picture to the church fund-raiser, started wearing that fuck-me lipstick, pushed Rick away. Jealousy rose like reflux, sour and acid, tightening his chest, burning his heart.

Then Ray came in, plonking himself down at the counter.

'Hey Ray,' Rick said, trying to raise his normal smile. 'What can I get ya?'

'Tea please, Rick, and one of those millionaire shortbreads.'

'Coming up,' Rick said, flipping a teabag out of a canister, and turning on the hot water tap on the coffee machine. 'How's things?'

'Pam got home from church looking like death warmed up. Says she's got a migraine - never seen her look so pale. Gave me a scare. Anyway, I left her to a bit o' peace in bed with the curtains closed.

'Sorry to hear that,' Rick said, setting a mug down in front of Ray with the bag still steeping. He retrieved a slice of millionaire shortbread from under a glass dome. 'Hope she feels better real soon.'

Ray nodded. He shifted uncomfortably and leaned forward, lowering his voice.

'Heard Stella on the radio last night,' Ray said. 'Being interviewed with the vicar. You want to be wary of that man, Rick. You know the trouble I've had with Pam. Women aren't safe around him. I overheard Pam and Pauline catty-talking. They were spitting nails that Stella did the interview at the vicar's house alone. Bitching about her red lipstick.'

Blood thundered in Rick's ears. He thought Stella had gone for a bridesmaid's fitting while he was at work in Lawton. Boy, was he stupid!

Peter Moss, still stinging at his earlier lunchtime exit, chose his moment to pipe up: 'They say women wear red lipstick to make their lips look like their private parts. You think Stella's doing that for the vicar, Rick?'

Rick leapt across the counter and was on Peter before he even knew what he was doing. He grabbed Peter up by his collar and shook him.

'That's it,' he yelled in his face. 'You come in every day, often twice, buy one lousy coffee and an occasional cake, then treat this place like your own personal office and piss my customers off – the ones who actually spend money. Now you insult me and my wife. You're out of here.'

Peter flailed back, protesting, but Rick had a grip on him and began dragging him towards the door as Ray watched, flabbergasted.

Frank entered just as Rick hauled Peter to the exit. He gaped, astonished.

'Out of the way, Frank,' Rick growled. 'I'm throwing out the trash.'

Frank stepped swiftly aside. He could see Rick would brook no argument.

Peter wind-milled his arms but to no avail. Rick had him out of the door and onto the promenade where he abruptly let him ago.

'And don't come back,' Rick said. 'You're barred.'

He slammed the door behind him as he returned inside to find Ray and Frank goggling at him.

'What'd he do?' Frank asked faintly.

'Said my wife was wearing her vagina on her face,' Rick spat.

'Oh!'

'Rick,' Ray breathed. 'What I said, I didn't mean to upset you. I think it's my fault…'

'No, it's Pete's fault.' Rick said grimly. 'He offends at least one customer every day but he went too far. You're right, Ray. You're not telling me anything I didn't suspect. I've just been ignoring it. It's time for me to go see the fucking vicar.'

'I wouldn't do that right now,' Frank said, stepping in front of Rick.

'Why? My wife with him?'

'No,' Frank said. '*His* wife's with him.'

Hormones and Handkerchiefs

A week after the mortifying fight in the church, Stella sat in her GP's office and listened as her friend, Dr Sarah Graves, confirmed what Grazja had come to suspect. Based on various symptoms and backed up by blood tests, Stella was going into premature menopause.

'I'm only thirty-five,' Stella said, feeling numb.

'I know, it's unfortunate but it happens I'm afraid,' Sarah said. 'The good news is with HRT we can treat it,'

'Stop it?' Stella asked, hopefully.

'No, not stop it,' Sarah said. 'HRT doesn't stop the menopause, but it will replace the hormones you lose and level things out for you if we get the balance right. We should be able to get you back to feeling like yourself.'

'Have I done something to cause this?'

'Not at all,' Sarah said. 'We don't know why it happens to some women. It might be genetic. Did your mother or Gina go into early menopause?'

'My mum died in her early thirties,' Stella said. 'Gina's never mentioned it but I remember her getting hot flushes when I was a teenager so she would have been in her fifties then, so no, not early.'

Stella put her face in her hands. 'I can't believe it,' she said. 'Are you sure?'

'Well, your estrogen levels are very low and all your other symptoms point that way. Mood swings, bladder issues, heavy and erratic periods, hot flushes, irritability…'

'Sore breasts,' Stella picked up. She hesitated. 'Wanting an affair?'

Sarah shrugged. 'It's not on the official list of NHS symptoms but from what I've heard, and what I've read many women when they hit peri-menopause and full menopause leave their partners, or have affairs and so forth. Evidence is mostly anecdotal at the moment. Menopause hasn't been taken seriously or been extensively studied until recently. We're beginning to understand that hormones affect every cell in your body. Right now yours are in massive fluctuation. Menopause isn't a straight line of gently falling estrogen levels; it's far more up and down with levels sometimes surging up or plunging, and like hormonal changes in your teens that can leave you feeling very emotionally out of sorts.'

'I do feel like a teenager again in some ways,' Stella admitted. 'I'd forgotten those feelings of awful longing for something – you don't know what – just that you're restless and desperate to escape.'

She felt tears welling. 'What does this mean about having children? We think Gerta is all we want but recently... Does it mean I'll be infertile?'

Sarah gave her a sympathetic look. 'It makes things more difficult, certainly. You are still having periods so technically it's still possible for you to get pregnant – that will be true on HRT too – but unlikely. Another term for pre-forty menopause is premature ovarian insufficiency. The decline in egg production is what's driving the early menopause. If you do want to conceive you might need to consider IVF treatment.'

Stella pressed her palms against her face again. 'I can't believe it,' she repeated.

'Look,' Sarah said, with a swift look at the clock. 'I suggest we get you started on HRT right away - a combination of estrogen and progesterone because you're still having periods. The progesterone will protect you from a thickening womb-lining which can lead to cancer. It does this by giving you a monthly period until we think you've probably stopped naturally and can go on just estrogen. It might take a while to find the right HRT for you. My advice is to not make any life-changing decisions until you've settled into the HRT and then see how you feel. We can discuss any further options once you're feeling more balanced. I'm also going to prescribe you a vitamin D and calcium supplement.'

Grazja had offered to come with Stella to the surgery, and so had Rick, but Stella had reassured her she was fine to go on her own. She was grateful to Grazja for persuading her to have her hormones tested, but still acutely embarrassed by what had happened in the church last week.

Rick didn't know about the fight – at least she hoped he didn't. She couldn't bear for him to know. Grazja promised her that Frank hadn't talked to anyone about it and had no intention of doing so. But Pauline might gossip or Frank might change his mind and decide that Rick deserved to know. Or Pam would confess to Ray, and he would tell Rick.

All she'd told Rick was that Grazja thought her hormones were out of synch and had persuaded her to see her doctor. They'd both carefully sort of danced round the unspoken rest.

And, as far as Stella knew, all the talk in the town had been about the revelation that the vicar had a wife, not about herself and Pam and Gina.

The shock had broken more than a few hearts in the parish and had filled even more pews over the Easter weekend as Maptonites flocked to have a good look at the mystery wife. Rumour had it that she had previously run off with a younger man.

It had yet to be verified by any respectable source.

Stella would never forget the moment Laura Rivers announced who she was, jolting them into the grubby reality of their ridiculous scuffle.

She'd been so cool about it, as though she'd seen it all before, sweaty, hysterical women scrapping over her husband's attention. At the same time she hadn't laughed or put them down, instead she'd insisted they calm themselves by taking some time to breathe in deeply. Stella had the feeling the woman was going to sit them all down and sort everything out in an efficient, yet kindly, manner before sending them home for tea and reflection.

It never happened because the vicar had entered the church at that moment.

As his wife turned towards him Stella saw his utter shock and then his face infused with incomparable joy.

That was her signal to flee. The vicar barely registered Stella as she barged past and charged out of the church. Gina and Grazja came barrelling out after her, followed by Pam and Pauline who split off in an opposite direction.

They made their way to Gina's in dazed silence, until, sitting in Gina's lounge (with George thankfully out and Ginger Rogers scurrying for the kitchen) Gina exploded.

'What the bleedin' hell's going on, Stella? I can't believe you were scrappin' wi' Pam.'

'You were fighting with her too!'

'Only cuz she was about to kill yer,' Gina yelled. 'And what's this about fighting over the vicar? You been acting like a floozy?'

Stella burst into tears. Grazja stood between her and Gina.

'Stop now, Gina. She's upset, can't you see? Almost hysterical. Go make tea.' She pointed in the direction of the kitchen.'

Gina glared pugnaciously but Grazja calmly stood her ground, still pointing kitchenwards.

Gina finally backed down, stamping towards the door. 'I'm not making you two a cuppa,' she grumbled. 'Just meself.'

'Fine,' Grazja said. 'Give us few minutes please.'

Grazja held Stella while she sobbed. 'I'm so stupid, so stupid,' she moaned.

'Not stupid,' Grazja said. 'But not right. Something wrong Stella. I think it might be your hormones. Let me take you to Sarah, get a test.'

Gina returned with three mugs of tea as Grazja knew she would, and half a pack of ginger nuts.

'I take Stella to doctor,' Grazja told her.

Gina looked alarmed. 'Doctor? Did Pam do her damage? I'll have her.'

'No, no,' Grazja said quickly, although she could actually see bruises forming on Stella's neck. 'I think Stella might have hormone imbalance.'

Gina snorted. 'She's got something imbalanced,' she said. 'Way she acted today.' But she sat down on the other side of Stella, who was still sobbing, and pulled her granddaughter's head onto her shoulder. 'C'mon on yer silly bogger. Stop yer blortin'. Let Gina and Grazja sort you out.'

Their friend, Dr Sarah Graves worked a half day on Thursday but she'd agreed to squeeze Stella in after her appointments, and took a blood sample to test.

Now Stella had the results and she reeled from the shock of them as she exited Sarah's office.

She wanted to call Grazja. She wanted to call Rick. But she hadn't the strength right at that moment for either option, so she left the surgery without calling either.

She was so immersed in her own spinning thoughts that it took her a moment to register the woman trying to greet her in the carpark. At first the 'hello' seemed like a distant sound, then Stella's ear picked up on the close proximity of the second 'hello?' and her focus sharpened onto the woman in her path.

It was Laura Rivers, the vicar' wife.

Blood flooded Stella's face. She could feel the humiliating flush as she stared at Mrs Rivers, scarlet-faced.

Laura Rivers' smile was warm but concerned.

'It's Stella, isn't it? Are you alright?'

'I'm fine,' Stella blustered. 'Um, thank you.' All she wanted to do was get away from this woman, witness to her disgrace, and the wife of the man she'd made a fool of herself over.

She didn't even feel jealous towards her, only humiliated and terribly embarrassed.

As she began to move past, Laura put her hand lightly on Stella's arm.

'I'm glad I bumped into you,' she said. 'I've been wanting to talk to you.'

'I'm sorry,' Stella said 'I...' She didn't know what to say. Her panic must have shown because Laura jumped in with: 'No, no. Don't be sorry. I haven't got anything bad to say. I just wanted to explain some things to you. Please, let's go somewhere and have a chat. I hear there's a great American-style diner.'

'No!' Stella said, more sharply than she meant to. 'That's my husband's diner.'

'Ah,' Laura smiled. 'I see. Yes, not the best place. Is there somewhere else – somewhere we can have a cuppa but talk quite privately?'

Stella thought about her own kitchen, but she wasn't comfortable with that. Mapton wasn't a private sort of place.

'Are you in a car?' she said. 'We could drive to Siltby. It's only a mile along the coast. There's a nice pub that does morning coffee. It has a lot of nooks and cubby holes to sit in.'

'Perfect,' Laura smiled. 'Are you in a car? I can follow you or give you a lift.'

'I walked,' Stella said. 'If you give me a lift there I don't mind walking back along the seafront.'

Stella couldn't quite believe she was doing this, but giving Laura directions allowed her to avoid feeling too awkward on the drive and gave her something to focus on other than her recent shock diagnosis and this peculiar situation.

The Barrel in Siltby was a hotel as well as a pub, thickly carpeted and plush compared to Mapton's hostelries. Aside from a larger, open restaurant area, it was divided into smaller wood-panelled drinking rooms, with book-lined cubby holes, and sound-muffling flocked wallpaper.

'This is nice,' Laura said, looking round as they entered the dim interior.

Laura insisted on buying Stella a coffee and tea for herself. They carried them to a corner table, well away from earshot of the bar or any of the few other customers.

Stella was glad she didn't see anyone she knew. Not that she was doing anything wrong but any sighting of the vicar's wife was ripe for speculation, and Stella wasn't able to deal with being pumped for any juicy information.

'Look, Mrs Rivers...' Stella began, not knowing quite what she wanted to say.

'Laura, please.'

'Laura, I'm very sorry you had to witness our fight in the church. I'm very ashamed. I don't know quite how it happened. It's not how I usually behave...' Stella felt the usual tears starting. Oh, how frustrated she was at feeling like a human fountain. 'I'm sorry,' she repeated. 'It's not just about the fight - I've been given some upsetting news.'

Laura nodded. 'I thought you looked upset. Can I help? A trouble shared?'

Stella was about to shake her head no, when the words tumbled out unbidden. 'My doctor says I am going through premature menopause – ovarian inefficiency or something. I'm only thirty- five!' She half sobbed, half laughed. 'I suppose I should be grateful I've got an excuse for acting so stupid lately.'

Laura's expression was kind and sympathetic. ' That's terrible for you. I'm so sorry. But I doubt you've done anything too stupid,' she said.

Stella gave a sharp laugh. 'You know I did. You saw it.'

Laura smiled, genuine amusement dancing in her eyes. 'It was quite a sight,' she admitted. 'But I've seen a few foolish squabbles over my husband.'

Stella gulped. 'What do you mean?'

Laura sighed. 'It's why I wanted to talk to you really. You needn't feel so bad if your feelings for

Michael got a bit out of hand, especially given what you've just told me.'

Stella flashed hot then cold. 'He told you about us? I mean, not that anything happened between us...'

'It wasn't going to happen,' Laura said gently. 'That's what I wanted to explain. I've seen it all before – the effect Michael has on women – some men too – can be very powerful but he doesn't intend it in the way you might think.'

Stella didn't understand. She shifted uncomfortably.

'Michael's gift,' Laura seemed to choose her words carefully, 'is more than just his physical beauty. It's that he makes people feel desired – wanted – needed even.'

Stella felt nauseous. That was exactly how Michael made her feel when he looked into her eyes. Of course, she knew other women found him attractive. Half the town had a crush on him, but she'd been so certain he looked at her differently.

'He's had affairs before?' she asked. 'Oh, sorry... you must...'

Laura stopped her. 'No, not affairs,' she said. 'Michael loves three things: God through Christ, the church, and his flock. His mission, always, is to create believers and bring them into the fold. He's not interested in people sexually. He doesn't want an affair with them. He's interested in recruiting them to the church. He's interested in their souls.'

'By making them fall in love with him?' Stella asked, suddenly furious.

'Are you really in love with him?' Laura asked gently. 'That's the thing. Lots of people have thought they're in love with him but in reality they're not. They have a crush on him because they feel seen and special.

Mostly it's people who are a bit lost or feel they need something.'

'Weak-minded, you mean,' Stella said. 'Like me?'

Laura looked surprised. 'That's not what I meant at all. Look, the crushes are powerful – as I said it's not the first time I've seen a scuffle for Michael's affections, but they actually do fade. Well, mostly – I only know of one woman who genuinely fell in love with him – but usually it does fade and that's because the person realises they've found the thing they really needed, and it isn't Michael himself.'

'I don't understand,' Stella said. 'What do you mean?'

Laura took a sip of tea. 'Take Pauline and Pam for example,' she said. 'I've talked to them both. Pauline – sweet girl, a bit odd, but sweet – she was terribly upset about the fight in the church. And clearly quite distraught to discover Michael is already married. But we had a lovely chat once she'd calmed down. She'd been allowing herself to dream that one day she might marry Michael. I asked her why and she said so that she would feel truly part of the church (and of course because Michael is so handsome). She misses her parents and being needed. I pointed out that she's already found her new place as part of the St Bart's family, and seems to have found her true calling helping organise the vicar's duties. He thinks she's wonderful at her job. She went away quite happy I think.'

Stella scoffed 'And I suppose Pam has discovered her true calling to floristry. Calling me a slut and getting me in a headlock was just her way of showing it. Nothing to do with her feelings about Michael.'

Laura blinked. 'Actually, yes. We had a heart to heart. Like you, she's tremendously upset and embarrassed about what happened. Hadn't left her house in days. Seeing me, she said, had been like having a bucket of ice water thrown in her face. She realised how foolish she'd been. She doesn't want Michael – she loves her partner Ray – she wanted the way he made her feel - that her special skills in floristry are vital to St Bart's and that she's an artist. She was heartbroken imagining she could never express her talents in the beauty of St Bart's again.'

Laura sighed, twisting her wedding ring. 'I blame myself,' she said quietly. 'If I hadn't left him it would never have got this far. I've always acted as a balance before. And of course he didn't mention he was married. Why would he? What man would, given the circumstances?'

Stella was startled. Tentatively she asked: 'Are the rumours true then? Did you leave him for someone else?'

Laura looked up. 'Ah, news travels fast. I suspected people knew by some of the looks I've been getting. Yes, I left him for a much younger man. Pretty scandalous for a vicar's wife wouldn't you say?'

Although she smiled ruefully, Stella recognised the sadness and pain in her eyes. For the moment she forgot her own troubles. She reached out to touch Laura's hand.

'Who am I to judge?' she said. 'We all have our own reasons.'

Laura took Stella's hand and squeezed it gratefully. 'Thank you,' she said. 'I know a lot of people won't feel that way.'

'Well, I do know that it can't be easy having a husband who uses his sexual charisma to lure women into Christianity.' Stella said this as lightly as she could.

Laura shook her head. 'No,' she said. 'That's not easy. Although it's not quite fair; Michael doesn't really use his sexuality – not on purpose. When he gives you that look, the intense one where he seems to be looking into your soul and your heart flips inside out – you know the one?'

Stella knew that look all too well. It was very strange talking about it to the perpetrator's wife but she nodded, yes.

'Well, Michael is sort of looking into your soul. At least he's searching for a connection with you that will bring you into the church. His intensity and interest in you at that moment is entirely genuine but it isn't sexual. The irony is...' Laura stopped and bit her lip. 'Oh dear, I shouldn't be saying this. I've never told anybody but...'

'Go on,' Stella said. 'Whatever you tell me it's between us. I mean it.' She did, and Laura must have seen it because she went on after a swift look round to check no one was listening.

Stella half expected Laura to tell her that Michael was gay. She didn't, she said: 'Michael isn't really sexual at all. Despite his looks, despite his charisma, he doesn't really experience sexual feelings. He doesn't really have a libido.'

'Oh!' she said, taken aback 'Really?'

'Really,' Laura said. 'Or hardly any. Some people don't, you know? It's perfectly normal. It's only a problem if you're in a relationship and one wants to and one of you doesn't.' It was Laura's turn to flush red and look embarrassed.

Stella felt slightly stunned. It was hard to accept that someone who made you almost swoon with his gaze didn't feel that sort of frisson back. Plus she'd assumed that all men wanted sex. Even Rick, adorable and civilised as he was compared to a lot of men, seemed to have an unspoken quota of sex that needed to be fulfilled each week. Not that it always was, especially recently.

'That can't be easy in a marriage,' she said, cautiously.

Laura grimaced. 'Hence after fifteen years I ran off with someone else.'

Stella suddenly felt the grip of a new panic. In all her focus on herself and the vicar, it hadn't occurred to her that Rick, too, might seek solace elsewhere.

She forced the panic aside.

'Anyway,' Laura said overly-brightly. 'That's in the past. I'm back now. I'm sorry, I shouldn't have burdened you. I'm supposed to be helping you…' She looked anxious.

'It's fine,' Stella reassured her. 'If you want to talk about it…'

Laura nodded. 'Maybe I will sometime. If we become friends. I hope we do.'

'I think we will,' Stella said, touched. 'But I have to warn you, I'm an atheist.'

'Ah,' Laura nodded. 'Did you tell Michael that?'

'The first time we met.'

'No wonder he was interested in you,' Laura said. 'He likes nothing more than to convert a non-believer.'

'But that's awful,' Stella said. 'It's wicked, even.'

'Not from Michael's point of view. When he gave you the 'look' he was looking at a soul in need of saving, not trying to seduce you. Did he actually ever say anything suggestive or flirtatious? Do anything untoward?'

Stella felt confused. She tried to remember. Despite the recent delirious atmosphere of sexual tension and ripe possibility she couldn't actually name a single obvious word or action to support her case.

'He seemed to touch my elbow a lot,' she said weakly.

'He does that to most people,' Laura said. 'Shepherds them.'

'He asked me to auction a painting of mine.'

'He knows a good opportunity when he sees it. Any chance to raise money for the church or a charity he'll capitalise on it. This is his way – anything to do God's work and do good as he sees it. That's what makes him so attractive. His passion is entirely spent in doing that work; the intensity you feel in his gaze is down to that passion; the fact that he smoulders like a Lothario is, I said, an irony. But his intentions are pure. He just wants to help people find their way into faith.'

Stella had all sorts of angry retorts she could give to the last statement, but she found they died on her tongue. Laura had been kind to her. Instead she asked: 'I can't believe I fell for it. I'm not usually that sort of person. I wasn't looking for anything.'

'To be honest,' Laura said. 'I don't think you're the usual type. I think you've been unlucky – susceptible because of your hormones.'

She put it delicately but Stella agreed. 'My head's been such a mess, and my body. I just didn't know why. I've been looking for answers in the wrong places.'

Stella leaned across the table to squeeze Laura's hand again. 'Thank you. Thank you so much. Don't worry about what you told me. I won't tell.'

'Thank you,' Laura said. 'I'd really appreciate it. I hope it's helped.'

'It has,' Stella said. 'A lot.'

'Do you want a lift back or do you want to walk?' Laura asked as they finished up and left the pub.

Stella had intended to walk but she was struck with a sudden longing to see Rick.

'A lift would be great,' she said. 'I have a prescription to pick up and a husband I need to hug.'

Peace Offering

On the Saturday two weeks after Easter, Pam nervously twitched her curtains, waiting to see if Stella would bring Gerta round to Gina's as she did most Saturday lunchtimes.

Pam wanted Stella to arrive and also dreaded it. She had prepared two pretty spring bouquets using flowers cut from her own garden – one for Stella and one for Gina. They were a peace offering and an apology, especially towards Stella.

Pam had experienced one of those very rare moments – usually an unpleasant incident – which, like a sudden blow to the head, completely alters your perception.

It hadn't actually been the announcement by Laura Rivers that she was the vicar's wife that had delivered this blow to Pam, but seeing the expression of horror on Frank Manning's face. In her mind's eye Pam envisioned Ray, not Frank, witness to this disgraceful scene, and in a searing flash of clarity she beheld herself. Her feelings for the vicar shrivelled as quickly as a balloon popped by a pin.

Pam never wanted Ray to know about her fight in the church. Of course he already knew about her crush on the vicar. They'd had plenty of rows about it, even though she'd denied it. Her shame made her so ill, that she couldn't get out of bed for three days. She'd told Ray she had a nauseating migraine which was actually true, but she didn't reveal the cause of it.

Then Laura Rivers came to see her. What a wonderful and generous thing that woman had done. Pam didn't care what the rumourmongers said about her; she had made Pam feel so much better about the whole thing and pointed out what she had gained was the discovery of her true talent and a place where her skill was appreciated.

Laura also swore that she hadn't said a word to the vicar about the scene in the church nor to anyone else. If it ever did get around, it certainly wouldn't be from her lips.

Pam was fairly certain that no one other than the six people present at St Bart's that day knew about the fight. Not one person – Sue Mulligan or her marauders, Peter Moss, the gossips at the Co-op, any of the usual suspects in fact – had given any hint they knew. No sidelong looks, or smirks, nudges to friends, or whispers behind hands. Pam was so relieved.

She had managed to avoid Gina since then. With Gina living across the street in George's house, they at least no longer had adjoining gardens - although Gina still owned her house, having yet shown no sign of selling or renting it. Gina living opposite made it easier for Pam to keep a surreptitious eye on her neighbour's movements, so that she could try to time her own comings and goings not to clash with Gina's.

But the day had come when Pam felt she must be brave and reach out in reconciliation. It wasn't the first time they had needed to patch up neighbourly relations. Since Gina's first arrival they'd had to do it a few times, with varying degrees of success. Last time, it had been Gina's turn to apologise, an event so rare that Pam had actually hugged her, hopeful this would be the beginning of a new era. Gina had predictably returned to type.

Still, Pam very much felt that she needed to be the one offering an apology this time, to both Stella and

Gina. It felt like the right thing to do, no matter how unappetising.

Pam heard a car approaching and twitched the curtain again. It was Stella, drawing up in the close. She could see Gerta perched high upon her child seat in the back, waving her hands around.

Pam dropped the curtain and closed her eyes, taking a moment to gather her courage before embarking on her perilous task. As ready as she could be, she picked up the bouquets and set off.

Stella seemed oblivious to Pam's presence as she helped Gerta out of her seat, and gathered a few bags together. Pam cleared her throat, about to announce her presence, when Gina ran out of her house and shrieked. 'You stop right there, Pam Stimson. You leave my girls alone.'

Stella whirled round, then froze. Gerta looked at Pam with interest. 'Pretty!' she said, seeing the bouquets.

Gina barrelled out of her gate, springing between her girls and Pam like a protective family dog, hackles up, teeth bared.

George appeared at the door, frowning. 'Everything alright?' he called.

'Fine,' Stella called back. She motioned Gerta towards him. 'Go and say hello to Grandad George' she said. 'Mummy and Grandma are just going to have a chat with Mrs Pam.'

'Okay,' Gerta said. 'Grandad,' she shouted waggling her glitter backpack. 'I've got something to show you.'

She ran down the path to George's embrace. After a nod from Stella he hurried the little girl inside.

Pam withstood Gina's glare. She held out the spring bouquets winningly. 'I came to apologise,' she said. 'I, I don't know what came over me. I'm so sorry, Stella.'

'You should be,' Gina started. 'We could have you up for assault.'

Stella moved forward, shushing Gina. 'I'm sorry too,' she said softly. 'I've been so ashamed of myself. I've been intending to come and see you.'

'Have yer?' Gina demanded. 'First I've heard of it.'

Pam and Stella ignored Gina. Pam smiled shyly at Stella, offering her a bouquet. Stella took it, smiling back. 'Thank you,' she said. 'It's beautiful and I don't deserve it.'

'I called you some awful things…' Pam started.

Stella shook her head. 'We both said awful things. I haven't been … I wasn't myself. I don't think you were either.'

Pam felt a loosening in her chest. 'I wasn't,' she agreed.

'It's like we've been under a spell,' Stella said.

Gina snorted.

Pam looked more closely at Stella. 'Have you talked to Laura Rivers?' she asked tentatively.

'Yes,' Stella nodded. 'She was very helpful.'

Pam beamed. 'She's a wonderful woman.'

'I agree.'

Gina hooted disbelief. 'I don't know what you two are taking but it's addling your minds. One moment you're fighting over the vicar, next minute you think his wife's the bees knees.'

Pam turned her attention to Gina. 'These are for you,' she said. She didn't offer them yet. She knew Gina well enough to know it would take more than that to make peace with her. 'I wondered if you'd let me arrange the flowers for your wedding?'

Gina blinked. In a trice she changed from a growling dog to a favoured pooch being offered a sausage. She laughed and clapped her hands. 'I'm glad we're all friends again. Come in and have a cuppa with us, Pam. I can tell yer what I want. Gi' me them bunches; I'll stick 'em in some water while I put the kettle on.'

As they followed Gina up the path to the house, Pam exchanged an amused look with Stella. It was one they'd shared many times before, and it felt good.

A Certain Smile

By the end of May, with two weeks left until the big day, wedding preparations were going smoothly. Elliot had finished Gina's dress, trimmed her bonnet, and sourced a suitable parasol.

'Why ever does she need a parasol?' Sue Mulligan had said to Stella one day, when they'd bumped into each other outside the diner.

'Who needs a veil or a train or a thousand seed pearls on a wedding dress?' Stella replied. 'None of it's necessary but if it makes the bride feel special what's the harm?'

'Suppose so,' Sue said. 'Best not to put it up inside the church though. Reckon that would be asking for bad luck, like putting an umbrella up inside. Same thing really. Still, a hat and a parasol; that's Gina all over.'

'Livin' it large,' Stella laughed. 'What are you going to wear to the wedding?'

Sue pulled a face. 'Not been invited,' she said.

Stella looked horrified. 'Oh Sue, oh no! I can't believe we missed you out. That can't be right?'

'Not surprising,' Sue said. 'What with my indiscretion with George that time.'

'That was ages ago,' Stella protested. 'And you made up afterwards. You should come – at least to the reception afterwards.'

'Nah,' Sue said. 'I'm alright, honestly. Me and Tiny got plans that day. Haven't we?'

Tiny was Sue's puppy, but not 'tiny' at all. At seven months he'd grown into a gangly, long-legged cutie, with the brown and white patches of his Jack Russell sire and the large head of his Great Dane mother.

He no longer fitted into the basket attached to Sue's mobility scooter but loped alongside her on a lead as they zoomed along the promenade. So far, Sue seemed to be handling him just fine, even though he had the energy of any toddler. Folk speculated that he'd get too big for Sue to cope with, what with her arthritis and mobility issues, but Rick disagreed with them. He'd told Stella that Tiny was the best thing to happen to Sue since the death of her beloved dog Scampi. Nurturing Tiny had re-energised her and given her a new purpose. He'd brought her joy. He was particularly proud of the part four-year old Gerta had played in bringing Tiny and Sue together.

'Are you sure?' Stella asked, looking pained. 'Everyone will be there.'

'Not everyone,' Sue said. 'Eleanor Branwin flat out refuses to go. She's giving me and Tiny an extra dog training session that afternoon at the sanctuary. She loves seeing him.'

'Ah, I see,' Stella said. It was true; Eleanor would much rather spend her time worming a pet, mucking out a pen, or stitching up a barb wire wound in a wild animal's side, than attend a social event, especially one as antithetical to her nature as a wedding. Spending an hour or two training a dog and its owner would be Eleanor's idea of a good time socially, and one where she could simply wave them off after the designated time was done without any social niceties and awkward leave-taking. Not that Eleanor would even bother doing that. When she wanted to leave she just got up and left.

'She's so rude,' Gina had complained, when Eleanor had returned a flat 'no' to the wedding invitation. 'I wouldn't have asked her and Dan, if it weren't for Bing

Crosby livin' with 'em. I'd like him to come to the reception.'

'You don't want dogs at the reception,' Stella had said.

'I do,' Gina said. 'Ginger's coming, and I've told Elliot he can bring Princess Alys if he keeps her away from the food. We don't want more pizza incidents.'

'Grazja told me it was you who fed Alys pizza, not just Gerta. Kept that to yourself, didn't you?'

Gina had rolled her eyes. 'She were fine wi' the bit I gave her. It were Gerta giving her the rest what made her sick.'

'Gerta's only four,' Stella had pointed out. 'You're not.'

'It were your fault for providing the pizza,' Gina had countered. 'Plus your mood that night woulda made anyone sick. Yer seem a lot better, duck. Them pills working you think?'

'They're beginning to,' Stella had said. 'I'm feeling more like myself.'

'What's going on between Pam and Gina?' Sue asked her. 'I saw them coming out of Flo's yesterday, chatting and giggling like a pair of schoolgirls. Since when have they been such pals?'

'Since Gina asked Pam to do her wedding flowers,' Stella explained. 'Gina can be charming when she wants something doing for her.'

Sue pulled her mouth into a sour bow. 'Never seen that side of her myself,' she said. ''spect they'll be back to fighting like cat and dog after the wedding's over.'

'Perhaps,' Stella laughed.

'Anyway, nice to see you, love. Got to go, Tiny needs his run,' Sue said. 'Give that husband of yours a big kiss from me. I just saw him but I can't climb the counter to wrestle him into a snog.'

'Will do,' Stella smiled. 'See you Sue.'

As Sue manoeuvred her scooter onto the promenade she called: 'Glad you've stopped wearing that lipstick. Didn't suit you; everyone said so. You're pretty enough wi'out it.'

Day trippers at two of the outside tables turned to examine Stella, who quickly ducked towards the door. Maybe she should start wearing blue lipstick? See what people thought of that, as it seemed that everyone in Mapton had an opinion on her brief sojourn into red lippy and felt the need to share that opinion now that she'd stopped wearing it.

It really was a very small town.

#

Rick glanced up as Stella came in. He was struck by the brightness in her eyes, which for a time had lost their hazel gleam. For months those eyes had been dull and introspective, or hard and angry, or red-rimmed from tears. So often she'd looked at him with weary resentment or flashes of irritable disdain. It had been too long since he'd seen them shine with the smile he cherished. The one she gave only to him and to Gerta; the spark of pure pleasure in seeing someone you loved.

He saw it now and answered with his own smile.

It had been a rough year so far. The discovery that Stella was going through premature menopause came as a shock. It had brought them pain for sure, forcing them to consider the improbability of having another child, and how much they might want one, but God, it had also been a relief to Rick, to be told there was a medical reason for Stella's behaviour. It wasn't simply that she'd stopped loving him. Because it had begun to feel very much like she had. Rick had been through one divorce; he didn't want another. His first had come after his own mental breakdown and had felt less like a loss than a necessity. He and Justine's marriage had been more of a business partnership (with sex) and when he walked away from the business, Justine had walked away from him. He'd viewed the end of his marriage as a failure, but not as a blow to the heart. Splitting from Stella would be more than just a blow. It would be catastrophic. She and Gerta were his heart.

The day he ejected Peter Moss from the diner, he'd been all fired up to punch the vicar's lights out and drag Stella home.

It was only Frank's intervention that had stopped him going caveman.

'I wouldn't do that right now,' Frank had said, stepping in front of Rick.

'Why? My wife with him?'

'No,' Frank said. '*His* wife's with him. I collected her from Skegness station and dropped her off today.'

'What?' Rick was stunned.

'Eh?' This was Ray. 'Wife?'

'I tracked her down,' Frank said. 'Persuaded her to come to Mapton. Took her along to the church earlier.'

Ray looked dumbstruck for a moment. Then a slow, slightly malicious smile curled his lips. 'That explains why Pam came home feeling so ill. I bet there'll be quite a few ladies with migraines when this news gets out.'

'Ray,' Frank said. 'I need a private word with Rick. Would you mind…?'

'Oh no, no' Ray said,' not at all.' He left his tea, hesitated and picked up the shortbread. 'Too good to leave,' he muttered.

'I owe you a tea next time,' Rick murmured.

'Don't be daft,' Ray said, hurrying out. 'You don't owe me a thing, Rick.'

The bell rang behind him.

'Actually,' Rick frowned. 'He's right. I didn't charge him. He got the shortcake for free.'

After his burst of aggression towards Peter, the after effects of adrenaline left him shaky. Frank steered him to a booth and sat him down. Then he went to the door and flipped the sign to closed, poured himself and Rick a coffee, added a cookie for Rick, who needed the sugar, and sat down opposite his friend.

'It's about Stella,' Frank began.

'Oh God,' Rick sunk his head in his hands. 'It's true then. She's having an affair with that bastard.' He thought he might vomit.

'No, no,' Frank shook his head. 'Stella's with Grazja. Grazja's worried about her. She's persuaded her to go to see Sarah Graves.'

Rick's head jerked up. 'Stella's ill? What... serious? Jesus.'

'No, just shut up and listen,' Frank said. 'Eat some of that cookie and drink your coffee. You'll feel better.'

And that had been the first Rick heard about a potential hormonal imbalance. At first he was sceptical. That would have to be some major hormonal imbalance to make Stella change so much. On the other hand, it was preferable to grasp onto that than believe that Stella had fallen out of love with him. So Rick had gone along with Grazja's advice (via Frank) that he didn't get confrontational with Stella, at least until the test results were back. Hold back, and play nice and be understanding for a while longer (as though he ever did anything else?) was what Grazja suggested. It wasn't easy because his own hormones, particularly testosterone, were in turmoil, boosted by stress and jealousy and frustrated sex drive. Yeah, he'd sometimes thought bitterly over the past few weeks, where was the treatment he needed to smooth his feathers?

Yet it gave him something to focus on. He started to read up on the female hormone system, something he pretty much thought he'd already known about in an enlightened male way. His knowledge extended to this: women were grumpy before periods, had babies and produced milk. Then they went through menopause, got a bit hot for a while, before it was over and done with, all helped along with a bit of HRT if they wanted it.

Oh my God, it was much more complex. Estrogen and progesterone, it seemed, affected every cell of a woman's body. Menopause brought a tsunami of unpleasant side-effects, mental and physical, and the rather terrifying statistic that sixty percent of divorces were instigated by women in their forties, fifties and sixties whose hormones told them 'no more'. Early menopause happened to a woman in her forties, but premature menopause could be much earlier. Rick read the symptoms. He wasn't as surprised, perhaps, as Stella seemed to be when she shared her results from Sarah's tests. He'd been preparing himself.

Sarah put Stella on a combined HRT and after two weeks the hormone replacement started to kick in. Stella gradually began to feel more like herself as the weeks went on and they started to talk. And talk. And talk. About so many things. Stella, obviously. About the vicar, who Rick still wanted to knock the teeth out of, despite Stella's reassurances. About what Rick had been going through. About the possibility of moving to Lawton and starting afresh.

It was too soon to make any big decisions, he knew that. Stella needed far more time to regain her equilibrium and come to terms with premature menopause and its implications for their family. They'd agreed on previous occasions to leave it another year, but then when Rick had been in Lawton on Wednesday he drove past a house he and Stella had always loved and saw a For Sale sign posted in front of it. He couldn't help himself – he collected the details from the estate agent handling the sale and had perused the information at least five times since.

Seeing Stella's happy smile now, as she approached the counter, he made the decision.

'Hi,' he leaned over to kiss her. 'I know the timing isn't great but take a look at this.' He pressed the print-out into her hand. 'It's that house we always admired. It's come on the market.'

Mapton Hens

Elliot's second trip to Stella's was much more welcoming than his first. She'd paid him an unexpected visit a couple of weeks ago with an apology, an explanation, and a request. They ended up having quite a heart to heart over a bottle of prosecco (a peace offering from Stella) and came up with a delicious little surprise to spring at Gina's wedding reception.

On this first evening of June, so different to the biting cold of his previous visit, Elliot rolled up to Stella's with a car full of specialised kit, a box of vintage Babycham glasses he'd bought on eBay and a crate of Babycham. Perry wasn't a drink Elliot would normally stomach but tonight was Gina's hen night, and they would all sink at least one glass of her favourite tipple in a toast to the Bride to Be.

He'd left Princess Alys at home with Tim. A Mapton hen night was no place for a diva such as Alys and she needed to keep her singing voice in tip-top condition a la Mariah.

Stella came down the path to greet him. He noted her eyes were brighter, her smile genuine, but she still looked a little frail and slightly sad. He hoped tonight's entertainments might cheer her up. She could do with letting go a bit.

'Hello darling,' Elliot said, catching her in an impulsive hug. 'Doing better?'

'Better,' Stella squeezed back. 'Not perfect but getting there.'

'Perfection is a bore,' Elliot declared. 'Fabulousness is our aim tonight. And fun, fun, fun. Help me unload my box of magic will you?'

Elliot's 'box of magic' covered a plurality of boxes and bags, vanity cases and two large wheelie cases.

'Did you bring the entire shop?' Stella asked, puffing as she trolleyed one towards the house.'

'Nothing like, darling,' Elliot said. 'Just a few necessities and a bit of glitter for our bijou affair.'

It was a limited-number hen party. Stella persuaded Gina to keep it small, as her wedding was going to be huge. Although people would come to the wedding for the spectacle and the free food and drink, she wasn't sure Gina would attract many hens to her pre-wedding celebrations as she wasn't a woman who had many genuine friends. The handful she could call 'friends' now was more than she'd ever had at any other time in her life.

'Who's coming?' Elliot asked.

'Me, you. Grazja, Pam, Pauline...'

Elliot stopped dead. 'Not Pious Pauline?' he said, delighted. 'The Virgin Mary who got thrown off the donkey at Christmas?'

Elliot had finally heard the details of the infamous Christmas Eve fiasco at St Bart's. He'd laughed so hard his mascara had run.

'Shh,' Stella looked behind her nervously. 'Don't call her that tonight, and don't bring Christmas up.'

'I won't,' Elliot said,' but I can't make any promises for Glinda Sparkle.'

'Don't!' Stella looked panicked. 'We don't call her Pious Pauline to her face. It's not nice.'

'Just behind her back,' Elliot said, enjoying himself. 'How splendidly bitchy.'

'Seriously,' Stella said. 'I don't want to hurt her feelings. I'm surprised Gina invited her, but I think Pam persuaded her to. She and Gina have been really chummy since Pam agreed to do her wedding flowers. Never thought I'd see that.'

'Didn't Gina once throw Pam's cat in the lake?' Elliot could hardly contain his excitement. These women were living legends to him.

'Has Grazja told you everything?' Stella asked.

'We had her and Frank around for dinner last week. The tales they could tell. We're thinking of moving to Mapton for all year round entertainment.'

Stella laughed. 'You'd get that all right. Sometimes I wish we didn't.'

'Anyone else coming tonight?'

'Oh, yes, I forgot. I invited Laura Rivers too.'

'Who's she?'

'The vicar's wife.'

Elliot's guffaw bounced around the street.

'You've invited the vicar's wife to a hen night drag party?'

'She's new in town,' Stella said. 'I thought it would be nice for her. And she's not what you'd expect. She's very open-minded.'

'Is she frumpy?' Elliot asked, envisioning a middle-aged dumpy matron in frumpy shoes.

'Not at all. She's elegant. Very attractive.'

Elliot was disappointed. 'What about Pauline?'

'Oh, she's frumpy,' Stella said. 'Hasn't got a stylish bone in her body.'

'Bad hair?' Elliot asked hopefully.

'Terrible.'

'Excellent,' Elliot said, feeling a swell of excitement. 'I can't wait to dress her up. I hope she wants a makeover. C'mon, let's get inside and get set up. This is going to be so much fun.'

It was fun.

Gerta, who in Elliot's mind had become a sort of devil-child (after feeding Princess Alys all that pizza), was thankfully out of the house for the evening. Rick had taken her somewhere or other. Elliot hadn't met Rick but imagined him as a stud-muffin cowboy in chaps. He was sure he'd be disappointed when he met Rick at the wedding, but until then he took pleasure in the picture he'd conjured up.

Earlier that day Frank had delivered a deep pink velvet dressing screen that Glinda sometimes used in her act. They'd placed it in front of the bay window, with the curtains drawn behind it to provide a make-do changing room. On the screen, Elliot artfully hung a variety of fancy dresses, from the high glam to the high camp. Frank had also delivered a wallpaper pasting table, which Elliot covered with a shimmering gold lamé cloth. Here he set up a dizzying array of make-up paraphernalia, a vanity case that opened to reveal a multiplex of unfolding cosmetics shelves, and (unpacked from a wheelie case) a range of wigs on stands. In the centre he placed a Hollywood-style make-up mirror framed by LED lights. Along the bottom of the table he lined up high-heels in a range of sizes and colours.

Stella provided a free-standing full-length mirror from her bedroom.

In the kitchen they carefully balanced the Babycham champagne-style glasses in a pyramid on the island work-counter, and placed out trays of nibbles, including dainty halved finger rolls of eggs mashed with butter and pepper and a large glass dish of Birds Eye trifle.

Elliot twitched his nose at the egg rolls. 'Très 70s,' he said. 'Washed down with Babycham. What a treat.' He grimaced.

'That's Eggs Yolka Polka,' Stella told him. 'It means something special to me and Gina.'

'Then it's a must have,' Elliot said quickly. 'And anyway, what's a hen night without a few eggs?'

'As long as we not laying them by end of the evening,' Grazja said. 'It all fine.'

At eight the doorbell rang and all three of them went to answer it, each bearing a different party prop.

They could hear the excited giggling and Gina shouted through the letter box. 'We're here. You gonna let us in?'

Elliot grinned at Stella. 'Ready?'

Stella took a deep breath. 'Ready,' she said, and opened the door.

Gina was dressed in her favourite red peplum dress from the eighties, channelling a look that was a cross between Joan Collins in Dynasty and Lucille Ball in old age. Her orange lipstick was so thick, Elliot had a moment's doubt that his drag plans for the evening could begin to compete.

'Tah Dah,' he stepped forward to drop a white BRIDE TO BE sash over Gina's head, wrestling it over the wide shoulder pads so that it settled diagonally across her torso. Then Stella came forward and placed a crown on Gina's head, proclaiming her Queen Hen and dropping a curtsy.

Gina roared with delight. Grazja handed her a plastic sceptre, and passed hen party tiaras out to Pam, Pauline, and standing a little behind them, Laura Rivers.

Gina pointed to Elliot's tiara, perched jauntily on his silver hair. 'Surprised you ain't come as Glinda Sparkle.'

'Just you wait,' he said. 'You might be surprised with what we've got planned.'

Elliot observed the newcomers with sharp, observant eyes, making swift assessments.

Pam's smile was wide and open, her face round and sweet as a little girl's. Despite her six-foot stature and brick-house build, she was clad in a pretty blue polka-dot dress. He could already tell she'd love the chance to play with clothes and make-up.

The vicar's wife was an elegant ash blonde. She had style but looked like she had a sense of humour.

Pauline was both a concern and a challenge. Her hair looked home cut with a pair of blunt scissors, held back with a hairband that had been chosen with zero consideration to how it might coordinate with the rest of her outfit, if that was what you could call a mismatched skirt and blouse paired with the type of shoes he'd imagined the vicar's wife might wear. He almost clapped with anticipation.

#

Grazja watched her friends with pleasure. They'd all popped their tiaras on (Pauline over her headband) and bustled, chattering and laughing, into the kitchen, where they toasted Gina with Babycham, showered her with party poppers, filled plates with nibbles, and headed to the lounge for the entertainment to begin. Once the Babycham had been used for the toast, everyone was free to select a tipple of their choice.

When the gold-rimmed Babycham glasses (with the Bambi-like faun stamped on the glass) were raised,

Pauline shyly asked. 'Babycham's not alcoholic is it? I don't drink.'

Grazja, suddenly remembering the last time she'd seen Pauline drunk, said: 'Actually, it is. Only about 6 percent, but it's perry – sparkling pear cider.'

'Oh, get it down yer,' Gina said, irritated by the interruption of her starring moment. 'One won't harm yer.'

'Just take a tiny sip for the toast,' Stella advised. 'You don't have to drink the rest. I've soft drinks too.'

So they had all clinked glasses and taken a sip of Gina's all-time favourite tipple, sweet and fizzy and champagne bright to look at, and Pauline, once she'd taken a first sip, had widened her eyes with pleasure, drunk the rest, and accepted a top up. Gina had clapped her on the back and declared: 'Once you taste Babycham you never want anything else'.

Grazja was keeping a careful eye on Pauline. She wasn't used to drink.

Contrary to Gina's claim, only Gina and Pauline stuck to the perry. Grazja swapped to white wine, Stella to a white wine spritzer, while Elliot, Laura and Pam chose gin and tonics.

Gina gasped when she saw the lounge decorated in hen party splendour; the balloons, streamers and banners glittered, while the gold lame-covered table and velvet screen beckoned like an altar set up to worship the Bride to Be.

Grazja grinned at Stella, who winked back, raising a glass to acknowledge the success of their hours of hard work.

It was good to have that connection with Stella restored. Her friend was returning, her smile more ready, her sense of self restabilising as the replacement hormones worked into her system. Grazja felt sad for Stella. It was one of life's mean tricks, stealing more than a decade of reproductive years from a woman, but Grazja knew there were worse things. Her own husband had been taken by cancer very young. Stella and Rick would find their way through.

Grazja watched as Laura sat down on the other side of Stella. The woman was still the focus of much speculation in Mapton and Siltby. Had she really left the vicar for another man, and what had brought her back? Grazja knew some of the truth from Frank, who had tracked Laura down. She had left with another man but was no longer with him when Frank found her. About that she hadn't said anything more to Frank, but when she'd heard Frank's suspicions that the reverend was a sexual predator, ready to exploit women like Pauline, she had laughed apparently. Then sighed. It wasn't what he thought, she'd said, but neither was it a new story. She'd return to Mapton with Frank to help ease tensions. And she'd stayed. The wattage in the vicar's bulb had dimmed a little since; the town women no longer seemed to flap around him like helpless moths, yet members of his congregation reported that he seemed happier somehow, although they couldn't say that he had ever seemed unhappy.

It occurred to Grazja that of all the people in this room, only Elliot didn't know about the fight that took place in the church. Funny, she thought, how an incident that could have been so destructive, actually bound this disparate bunch of women together. It was their secret still. Even Frank, witness as he was, was outside the group, although equally bound to secrecy.

Elliot interrupted her thoughts by ringing a bell for their full attention. When he had it, he flicked a remote towards the sound system and the opening strains to Madonna's Vogue started to play.

'Ladies,' he projected over Madge. 'Tonight to celebrate the coming nuptials of Queen Gina to King George of Wentworth...' (cheers) We shall sing... we shall dance... we shall dazzle with...' Elliot drew it out before suddenly tearing off his shirt and trousers (specially velcroed to rip apart easily) to reveal a glittering rose dress which spilled down waxed shining legs to the floor. 'A HEN NIGHT DRAG PARTY!'

'Yer what?' Gina shouted, crown sliding precariously.

Elliot swept a flourish towards the wares displayed on the table and screen. 'We're all going to dress in drag,' he said.' And I'm going to show you how to do it.'

'But we're already women,' Gina said. 'What's the point of that?'

'Drag isn't about gender,' Elliot said. 'It's about attitude! It's about fun. It's about sass. It's about celebrating.'

'We think it'll be fun,' Stella said. 'Who doesn't want to play dress-up?'

'I'm not sure I do,' Pauline said in a small voice.

'No one have to do anything they don't want to,' Grazja reassured her. 'But it will be fun. I know, because my blonde wig change my whole look.'

'Your hair's a wig?' gasped Pauline.

'No, not now, but I tried going blonde with one of Elliot's wigs before I do it for real.'

'Oh, I can't wait,' Pam cried. 'I love it! Look at all the make-up.'

'I'm game,' Laura smiled.

Everyone looked at Gina. This was her party. She narrowed her eyes, and for a moment Grazja thought they'd got this all wrong and Gina was going to kick up a stink, but then she pointed to a costume hanging from the screen. 'I want that Alice in Wonderland dress,' she said, 'and them stripey stockings.'

This made them all laugh, except for Pauline who really did look scared.

'I would so not have thought you'd pick that,' Elliot choked. 'So, this is the plan… you girls get to choose your clothes – don't worry, there's a few more things in the wheelie case if you can't find what you fancy. Then I, Glinda Sparkle, am going to give you a masterclass – or should I say mistress-class - in drag make-up. Once we've all got our slap on, I'll teach you to lip-synch and sashay. It will be a riot!'

While he'd been speaking, Elliot had stepped smartly out of his loafers (incongruous with his dress) and slipped into a ludicrously high pair of heels.

There was a small stampede towards the clothes, wigs, accessories and shoes. Gina grabbed the Alice dress and stockings, disappearing behind the screen while the other women held up gowns, fingered hairpieces, swapped items, dangled rhinestones and flicked feather boas, laughing as they showed each other, exclaimed over choices, cajoled and negotiated.

Elliot nudged decisions, and opened the last wheelie case to pull out more wonders.

Grazja had selected a towering black beehive wig, an off the shoulder black Bardot top, scarlet shiny spandex jeggings and stacked red glitter sandals.

She noticed Pauline hovering on the edge of the melee looking awkward and unhappy. Settling her choices on an arm of a sofa, Grazja shouted fiercely. 'These are mine. Nobody touch them.'

'Ooh, fierce,' Elliot said. 'You tell them girl.'

He frowned at Pauline's lack of involvement and looked like he was about to say something, when Pam tugged on his elbow to show him her choice.

'I think this will actually fit me,' she said, glowing with pleasure. 'So many beautiful dresses are too small for me.'

'I don't design for itsy-bitsy pixie girls, honey,' Elliot said. 'I design for drag queens and magnificent women.'

Grazja took this opportunity to nudge Pauline towards the door. 'C'mon,' she said, 'Let's top up the drinks and nibbles.'

Pauline nodded. She was pale and sweating.

Grazja led Pauline back to the kitchen. 'Are you okay?' she asked the girl. 'I notice you look uncomfortable.'

Pauline squirmed. 'Elliot's a homosexual, isn't he?' she semi-whispered.

Aha, Grazja thought. Of course, I should have realised. It made sense with Pauline's upbringing and hellfire beliefs that she'd be homophobic.

'He's gay, yes,' she said, keeping her voice neutral. 'You feel this a problem for you?'

Pauline nodded. 'It says in the Bible that a man should not lie with a man as he would with a woman.' She dropped her voice into a hiss. 'It is an abomination. My dad always said 'It was Adam and Eve, not Adam and Steve!'

Grazja nodded thoughtfully. 'I've heard that joke too, and I raised Catholic so I know teachings against homosexuality. I be honest, I don't believe them, and Bible has been translated many times – difficult to know what original Hebrew said, yes? But I say this, Jesus preached to be kind and to love thy neighbour, whoever they may be. Agree?'

'Yes, but sinners will burn in hell,' Pauline said, looking genuinely upset. 'When I'm looking at Elliot I see that.'

Grazja suppressed a snort. 'Then you must see me burning in Hell too. And Pam, in fact probably all of us. I have sex with man who is not my husband, as does Pam. The Bible say that is sin. You not want to be friends with us?'

Pauline looked stricken.

'You believe in God as ultimate power?' Grazja asked.

'Of course!'

'It is God who decides who go to Hell. Not you, Pauline. Not even the vicar. So you don't have to worry about Elliot, or any of us. You do as Jesus say and be tolerant and kind to others. You let God decide what comes after, eh?'

Pauline digested this. A light came into her face. "But if you do not forgive others their sins, your Father will not forgive your sins,' it says in Mark.' She started to positively glow. 'I'll forgive Elliot his sins.'

Grazja raised an eyebrow. 'I'm sure he'll be very pleased to know it,' she said wryly and then hastily added: 'Actually, don't mention it to him.'

Pauline nodded. 'I can go back to the party now,' she said, 'but I don't want to dress up.'

'Why not?'

'I put on my prettiest outfit,' Pauline said. 'I was so excited. I don't want to change it.'

Grazja smiled. 'That very good reason,' she said. 'You stay just as you are.'

Pauline almost skipped to the door. 'Plus,' she called back to Grazja. 'You're all going to look like whores.'

Elliot walked into the kitchen just as Pauline ran out.

He eyed Grazja, who was choking on laughter.

'Did I hear Miss Frumpy say we all look like whores?' he asked.

Grazja grasped the kitchen counter. 'Yes,' she spluttered. 'And she not even joking.'

Elliot laughed. 'Cheeky moo! Just wait till I get her 'whored' up.'

'No,' Grazja said, pulling it together. 'Pauline not want to dress up. She put on her best outfit, she not want to change.'

'You're kidding?' Elliot gasped. 'She looks awful. I have to do a make-over.'

'She feel pretty as she is,' Grazja said. 'You leave her be.'

'She'll feel much prettier when I've waved my magic wand. Some heels, a bustier for uplift, a pencil skirt, a good brow plucking …'

'No, no,' Grazja stood up to him. 'Why women have to fit into that stereotype to be considered 'attractive'? Pauline wants to be who she is, like you do. You want to express who you are; she wants to express who she is. Why no one able to accept each other?'

'Ouch!' Elliot said. 'Someone's stroked your fur the wrong way.'

Grazja sighed. 'Sometimes I feel like I spend my life smoothing everyone else's fur the right way.'

Elliot's expression softened. 'I think you do,' he said. 'Come on, I'll be kind to our homophobic little friend.'

Grazja startled. 'You know?'

Elliot rolled his eyes. 'Call it reverse 'gaydar '. It's not hard to spot.'

'Not her fault,' Grazja said. 'She had very intense religious upbringing.'

'Which is why I'll be kind to her,' Elliot said, guiding her out of the room. 'But on one condition.'

'What that?' Grazja asked.

'You let me give you some padded hips and much bigger tits.'

'Want to make me more stereotypical woman, Elliot?' Grazja teased.

'I want to make you look hilarious as hell.' Elliot said. 'And until I get my slap on and my 'do' done, call me Glelliot. Glinda's on her way.'

Hungover but Happy

Gina sprawled supine on the sofa with a bag of frozen peas wrapped in a tea towel cooling her brow.

It was the morning after her hen party. Rick had deposited Pam and Gina off at their respective homes after taking Pauline to her little house first. He'd returned home the previous night to find a house full of singing drag queens in various states of dress and inebriation. Pauline was the only one make-up-less and wearing her usual sort of attire yet even she had succumbed to the lure of a feather boa, a tinsel wig, and a few glasses of Babycham.

George had hurried down the path before Gina had even clambered out of the car. It took the two of them to extract Gina and Pam out of the back seat, Rick getting more glimpses of his grandmother-in-law's knickers than he ever wanted to see. This, along with the tops of her stripey stockings and a petticoated dress that Rick failed to recognise as Alice in Wonderland but struck him as more Bette Davis in Whatever Happened to Baby Jane, was a sight he thought he'd have nightmares about for years to come.

'If you can manage Gina,' Rick told George, 'I'll take Pam.'

First they had to separate the women, who'd fallen into a drunken good-bye hug as though they'd been lifelong friends who would never see each other again.

'C'mon love,' George prised Gina away. 'Let's get you to bed.'

'Ooh, George,' Gina cackled. 'It's always intercourse wi' you.'

George cleared his throat apologetically, thanking Rick for escorting Gina home, and guided her up the garden path.

Rick knocked on Ray's door, supporting a gently swaying Pam. When Ray answered he said: 'This is yours I believe.'

Ray goggled at Pam, towering above them in her platform heels, swathed in a fishtail gown that left little to the imagination.

'Bloody hell, duck, you look beautiful.'

So Rick told Stella and Stella told Gina later, but for now Gina only knew that she'd had a wickedly good hen night, and that her head didn't hurt anything as much as she'd told George it did. She was enjoying his tender attentions too much, the cups of tea he brought her with chocolate Hobnobs, and now even a foot rub. It was all part of her starring role as the Bride to Be and to be milked as much as possible until the Big Day.

'Did you enjoy it, love?' George asked, pressing his thumb into the arch of her right foot, which was sore due to those ludicrous heels she'd come home in.

'Oh I did,' Gina sighed. 'It were brilliant, George. Absolutely brilliant. At first I was a bit disappointed we weren't going out on the town, but you know what? We had so much fun. Stella was right to hold it at her house. Elliot threw us a drag party. I thought, what do I want a drag party for? I'm already in me make-up and glad rags. But you know, it were like being a little kid again and playing dress-up with outrageous clothes. And wigs. Did you see me wig, George?'

'I did,' George said. 'Gave me a bit of a fright this morning. You left it on the bedroom carpet and I thought it was an animal got in. Then I realised what it was. Good thing Ginger didn't attack it, think it was an intruder.'

Gina chuckled. 'If it don't look and smell like food Ginger ain't bothered.' She wiggled her left foot for a massage. George dutifully moved on.

'You should have seen Grazja. Elliot stuffed some big fake boobs up her top and made her wear this hip padding. Can you believe it? Those drag queens think of everything. She looked like Dolly Parton if Dolly wore a black beehive. Them fake boobs were hilarious on Grazja, but I think she looked better having proper hips – English hips – gives her some shape. She's too straight, that's what I tell her.'

'I think Frank likes her the way she is,' George said.

'Well, he probably got a shock last night then,' Gina sniffed.

'I'm surprised Elliot let you keep all the stuff,' George said. 'Pam was still wearing hers too.'

'Oh, we're not keeping it,' Gina said. 'Elliot stayed the night at Stella's so he said we could get it back to him today. He won't be leaving 'til after lunch. Never thought I'd be good friends with a gay man, never mind one who did drag. Learnt some stuff last night, George. Make you lose the last of your hair, some of it.'

George touched the white tufts that clung to the sides of his head. 'Best not tell me,' he smiled. 'Want a bit o' hair for our wedding photos.'

Gina took the soggy pea-packed tea towel off her head and fidgeted into a sitting position.

'Do you know how drag queens wear them tighty-tight dresses without their whatnots showing?'

George did not.

Gina leaned forward and pointed at her crotch. Lowering her voice she said: 'They tuck 'em up. Like push up all behind somehow. Sometimes they use tape.' Her eyes were wide and round. So were George's and slightly watering.

'We asked Elliot and he told us. We fell about laughing.' She let out a guffaw. Then abruptly stopped and fixed George with a serious look. 'But that's not what shocked me most. You know what did?'

George swallowed. 'No love, I can't imagine.'

'Most of 'em lip sync.'

George looked really alarmed. 'I don't understand, love.'

'I know,' Gina nodded. 'Lip sync. They synchronise their lip movements to song lyrics, you know, like pop stars used to do on Top of the Pops.'

'Oh,' George said, looking relieved. 'Why's that shocking?'

'I thought Elliot sung all them songs at his Christmas drag show. I thought he was an amazing singer, remember? I thought he could do all them voices himself – Judy, Dean, Frank, Doris. But turns out he was lip syncing. They all were.'

'Ah,' George nodded. 'I remember now. Bit of a cheat.'

'That's what I think,' Gina said. 'According to Elliot it's an art form but I'm not convinced. He tried to teach us but we kept singing along to the songs out loud like you do, so he gave up.

'It got me worried though. We got Dusty booked to sing at our wedding…'

'You don't think Dusty lip syncs?' George asked, looking aghast.

Dusty Velour was a popular wedding and cabaret singer in those parts. She sang every year at the switch on of Mapton's Christmas lights.

'That's what I wanted to know,' Gina said. 'We're not paying what Dusty charges if she's not really singing the songs. But it's all right. Elliot knows Dusty. She sings for proper.'

'That's good,' George smiled at her. 'It's going to be a wonderful wedding, love.'

'I know! People are going to talk about it for years,' Gina crowed.

'I meant for us,' George said. 'I'm a very lucky man.'

'Aw, George,' Gina blushed. 'Ger off wi' yer!' Trying not to smile, she snuggled back onto her cushions, put a limp hand to her forehead and said: 'I still feel a bit peaky. Make me another cup o'tea would yer, duckie.'

George, as always, obliged.

Fresh Pastures

Rick and Stella went to view the house in Lawton only a week before the wedding. It was a crazy thing to do, they both agreed. The timing was terrible, with Stella still settling into her HRT and last minute wedding preparations taking up so much time and energy. Stella had hoped that once they stepped inside the house it would feel all wrong.

It didn't. It felt wonderful. As though the house knew they were the right people for it and welcomed them in.

The Lawton house was so different to their beloved Mapton home, the red brick Victorian 'castle' with its stubby turrets, high ceilings and Gothic arches. Built by a nineteenth century entrepreneur who brought the railway to Mapton when it was just a fishing village and developed it into a resort, the land around it had been sold off in the late fifties for housing, so that it stood out as a peculiarity in a street of modest, pebble-dashed homes.

Stella's studio was in the north turret which had two windows and let the light flood in, yet it was quite small and cramped for her needs.

The Lawton house was also unusual compared to the mix of Georgian and Victorian that filled the centre of town and the new builds on the periphery. It was a striking white art deco build from the early thirties, with large light filled rooms, set amidst a mature garden. The previous owners had added a purpose built granny flat behind the main house, as well as a large standalone garden room. Both these additions had wonderful light, and as soon as Stella saw them she could envision the spacious studio either one would provide.

'I love it,' Rick said, when they were out of earshot of the estate agent.

'I love it too,' Stella said. 'Shit!'

They'd long admired the house, always commenting when they drove past it. Suddenly there was a chance it could be theirs. They stayed up all night talking about it, weighing up the pros and cons – Gerta would have access to better schools and a wider social circle; they'd still be only forty minutes' drive from Mapton, so not too far from friends, family and the diner, nor too far from the sea. Lawton had better shops in terms of variety, more pubs and eateries, a clientele for Rick's pop-up kitchen, a small but thriving music and theatre scene.

In short Lawton was more upmarket, or as Gina said about it, 'posh and a bit up itself.'

Ah, Gina. For Stella, Gina was a major obstacle to moving. For herself, because after a decade of estrangement from her grandmother, Stella couldn't believe how close they had grown in recent years. For Gina, because she would take a move away as an entirely personal rejection.

Yet after the past few months Stella found she wanted a fresh start. Rick really wanted it, and Gerta was young enough to be flexible, as long as she was with them. And they'd all still be close to Mapton. Stella kept repeating this to herself. She would not be abandoning Gina.

The estate agent rang to tell them that an offer had been put in for the Lawton house. The offer was under the asking price, and did they want to counter? They needed to act quickly if they did.

The timing was terrible, so close to the wedding, but the time itself felt right.

Rick put in a counter offer and they spent a tense few hours waiting, texting each other back and forth throughout a day already packed to bursting with work and preparations.

Stella was with Gina when the acceptance came through. She could see her phone screen flash but her hands were busy, encased in thin plastic gloves massaging 'Pumpkin Spice' colour crème into Gina's hair.

'Make sure you get all of it even,' Gina said. 'And don't dye my ears again.'

Stella had only once dyed Gina's ears. She'd been fifteen and in a snit but Gina never forgot, nor it seemed, forgave.

Gina usually did her own colouring with various degrees of success, although she had it cut at Beryl Winch's regularly. Beryl didn't (and wouldn't) stock her favourite Pumpkin Spice (which was more pumpkin than spice in hue). For her wedding she asked Stella to do it to ensure full root coverage and to reach the tricky back bits.

Gina had been growing a fringe in time for her wedding. She was determined to have a rolled fringe like Judy Garland's in Meet me in St Louis. Although she was booked with Beryl for a trim on Friday morning, she had warned her not to cut the fringe too short.

It had been very strange, seeing Gina with a longish curtain of hair over her forehead, especially as the ends were orange but the roots were distinctly grey.

'Nice bangs,' Rick had commented.

'Yer what?' Gina said.

'Daddy calls my fringe 'bangs',' Gerta piped up. 'It's American.'

'Well, that's just daft,' Gina huffed. 'Don't make no sense.'

'It does,' Gerta said. She flipped her own fringe to and fro, lightly slapping her forehead each time. 'My fringe bangs on my head Grandma Gina. See.'

They'd laughed. 'Oh aye, you're right duckie, they do,' Gina said, copying with her own fringe. 'Clever so and so.'

Stella didn't get to check her phone until Gina's colour had set, been rinsed, conditioned and dried.

'They accepted our offer,' Rick's message said. 'OMG! Really doing this.'

Stella's stomach flipped over. Excitement, terror, disbelief, anticipation. All those feelings swept her at once.

'Who's that?' Gina asked, turning from the mirror where she was examining her blazing colour and scrutinising her roots.

''Just Rick,' Stella said lightly, slipping the phone in her pocket. 'Shall we have a go at curling your hair and fringe? We need to practice.'

She and Rick had agreed it was best not to tell Gina until after the wedding. Most moves didn't happen quickly and they hadn't even had time to really think about getting their current home on the market. Gina might react better when she was married and felt settled. Either way, her big day was the first priority. She had waited a long, long time for someone to love her like George did – not that she'd made it easy for anyone, including George.

Stella wanted to see Gina happy.

Fresh Pastures Too

Stella wasn't the only one ready for a new start. Grazja was too. Only she had no intention of moving away from Mapton, instead she was going to make living there a more permanent arrangement.

She had finally decided to move in with Frank.

So far, she and Frank were the only people who knew about Stella and Rick's offer on the Lawton house.

It made Grazja sad to think of Stella not living in Mapton. They'd still be around of course, visiting Gina, and she assumed that Rick would still be running the diner part of the time as he did now, but it wouldn't be the same as having them there. A friend within walking distance, who could just pop by for a cup of coffee, or go out with for an impromptu drink, or bump into on the street was something Grazja had come to value since living here. She had Gina and other friends, but Stella was her best friend, her confidante and special to her.

But circumstances changed constantly. Grazja knew that better than many people. Life was a fickle and inconstant thing, and not to be trusted to care for what you wanted, nor even for what you needed. Pragmatic by nature, Grazja accepted that, and simply got on with it as best she could.

Gina, now there was a woman who fought life. She would not be happy about Stella moving away.

'She has abandonment issues,' Grazja told Frank. 'Look at what she did to get Stella to Mapton. Caused her own accident so Stella had to come look after her.'

'They're only moving to Lawton,' Frank said. 'Not back to London.'

'Ah, but Gina sees things black and white,' Grazja said. 'You love me or hate me, you with me or leaving me, nothing in between.'

'It'll work out,' Frank said. 'Does this mean the castle will be up for sale?' He looked at her, half-smiling. Do you fancy living there? You have the money to buy it.'

They hadn't talked much more about moving in together for real, even though Grazja spent most nights in his flat, with many of her possessions migrating over to it. Frank had brought it up a couple more times since January, but hadn't pressed when Grazja had been unwilling to absolutely commit. He knew she was adjusting to living life unburdened of the needless guilt she'd carried so many years. He was willing to wait.

That didn't mean Grazja hadn't been thinking about it. She did want to live with Frank and had even identified a potential home but it had a factor that might well put him off. It put her off at times, but it was a house she was very fond of and had happy memories of.

It was Gina's bungalow. Gina had moved across the road to live with George but she hadn't yet sold or rented out her own house. Grazja suspected Gina was hedging her bets, hanging on to her place in case George popped his clogs or (knowing how Gina thought) left her. Once Gina was officially married she might be willing to let it go.

'Gina's place!' Frank said. 'Really?'

'It good size for us, near to sea front, I like it.'

'But we'd be living opposite Gina,' Frank pointed out. 'She'd be popping around all the time to see you, not to mention complaining about any changes we made.'

Grazja shrugged. 'I would make sure she didn't. I handle Gina. But I really like that house and she my friend. Also we get to have proper home together, yes?'

She had him on that one. Frank would agree to live in a musty, bat-ridden cave if it meant they'd be together.

'So, she's selling then?'

'Not yet,' Grazja. 'But I put possibility to her after wedding.'

'And if she doesn't want to?'

'Then we find somewhere else to make nest together.'

Frank looked so elated she thought he might take off like a rocket. He lifted her off her feet and danced her along the galley kitchen. After only a few steps they bumped into the washing machine set beneath the sink.

'That's why we need a bigger house,' Grazja laughed.

Too Good to be True

'We cannot wait.' Elliot told Gina down the phone. 'I can't wait, Princess Alys can't wait, and Tim can't wait. It's going to be the wedding of the century.'

'I'm getting the collywobbles,' Gina admitted.

'Cold feet?'

'No, don't be daft,' Gina said. 'I mean me tummy's doing flips cause I'm nervous it won't go off all right.'

'It'll be perfect, Elliot reassured her. 'Pam and Pauline picked up their dresses on Wednesday. OMG, they are so excited. I can't believe I managed to pull that out of the bag in time.'

'I can't believe I asked Pam and Pauline to be my bridesmaids' Gina said, sounding genuinely puzzled. 'I'm going soft in me old age.'

Elliot laughed. 'I think it's lovely. I'm hurt you didn't ask Glinda though.'

'Oh ger on wi' yer,' Gina huffed. 'I ain't having you sashaying down the aisle behind me in your ten inch heels distracting everyone. It's my day.'

'It is,' Elliot agreed. 'It's your day. What are you doing tonight? You need something calm and soothing so you're fresh in the morning.'

'Me 'n' Stella are going to watch a Fred and Ginger film over at my house, while Rick keeps George company at home,' Gina said. 'She'll be over in about an hour.'

'I don't understand,' Elliot said. 'You mean George is going to Rick's?'

'No,' Gina said. 'I forget you haven't known me long. The bungalow I live in with George, well, that's his house. I lived in the one across the road, next to Pam's. Me 'n' George were neighbours yer see. That's how I got to know him. Didn't much like 'im at first, him being a man; just like all the others I thought. Only want one thing and once they've had it leave you as soon as look at you again. But turned out George wasn't like that. George is a good' un. The best of 'em."

'And now you're going to marry him.' Eliot sighed dreamily.

'I am,' Gina said. 'But I still own my bungalow across the road so me and Stella are going to use that tonight. I'm here right now. It don't seem right for the bride and groom to be in the same house night before the wedding.'

'Makes sense,' Elliot said. 'Blimey, you and Stella have got some money between you with all your property. My friend told me about that big house she and Rick are buying in Lawton. Wonder if they'll sell the castle when they move?'

'Yer what?' Gina said. 'Who told you that?'

Elliot said. 'Janette. She's an estate agent in Lawton. Really excited she is to be handling the sale – big commission on this one if it all goes through. Couldn't wait to tell me she was representing Stella Distry. Actually seemed disappointed when I said I already know her. Janette's a bit of a gossip actually. I'm not sure she should be talking about her clients. Surely that's confidential?'

On the end of the phone Gina was silent.

Elliot suddenly said. 'Oh my God. You didn't know? I'm really sorry, oh...' He sounded panicky.

'Of course I bloody knew,' Gina spat out. 'Why wouldn't I bloody know?'

She terminated the call.

#

Gina, deep down knew it had been too good to be true. She was smelly little Gina Pontin after all, always unloved, pushed out, and neglected. Sooner or later it always came – betrayal, rejection, abandonment.

She had allowed herself to dream; thought she could have what others seemed to have so easily.

First it had been her parents. The drunken father whose casual revelation of her true parentage had devastated Gina and her absentee mother who lacked a scrap of maternal instinct. Later it had been Maggie, Gina's best and only friend, a friendship she fiercely cherished and needed that ended in a bitter feud over a love-triangle, the results of which would end in dire consequences.

Maggie had been the first person Gina had loved and felt truly loved by. Although platonic, their bond was deep, and their friendship passionate and intense. Maggie's rejection of Gina, and Gina's subsequent revenge had all the hallmarks of a Shakespearean tragedy playing out into untimely death and intergenerational strife.

Gina endured the loss of her daughter, Ivy, in a car crash only because she now had her beloved granddaughter, Stella, to raise. Yet when bereaved teenage Stella struck up a friendship with Maggie, unaware of the bitter enmity between the two women, Gina was consumed by terrible jealousy. Her subsequent actions led to a tragic event that Stella hated her for. Once Stella left home for university she never looked back, cutting her contact with her grandmother to the minimum.

Again Gina was alone, unloved, pushed out, rejected.

If, as an adult, Gina brought these things on herself, she could only admit that on the rarest of occasions. From childhood she had learnt in the hardest ways to be tough, to grow spines that repelled close contact, or spray insults, skunk-like, as a defensive reflex to deter intruders who might breach her barriers.

On the few occasions she had dared to love they had all abandoned her. Her parents, her best friend, her lover, her daughter, her granddaughter – all of them.

Stella had hurt the most. Her daughter, Ivy, hadn't meant to leave her. Death had stolen her; it wasn't a decision on Ivy's part to reject Gina. As much as Gina had tried, she perhaps wasn't the best mother in the world – far, far better than her own – but as a single mother it had been a struggle, and Gina and Ivy muddled through but weren't the closest of mother and daughters. It was easier when Stella came along. Gina had found it much easier to be a fun grandmother and weekend visits were treats for both of them. As a child, Stella adored Gina and Gina basked in her adoration. They played games, went shopping, watched old movies, made Eggs Yolka Polka, and danced around Gina's kitchen. At the end of the weekend Gina simply handed her back to Ivy where, as far as Stella saw it, boring school and regular grey life resumed. When Ivy died, the reality of bringing up a bereaved and sulky adolescent in Gina's little house in no way matched the nostalgic glory days but Gina still loved Stella fiercely. She couldn't bear to share her, especially with Maggie.

Those years when Stella had left home – so eager to go she'd practically run out of the house – were the loneliest for Gina.

She had her dogs - first Fred Astaire, and next Bing Crosby – but she missed Stella desperately. She railed at the unfairness of it; Stella should be grateful Gina took her in, gave her food and shelter, clothes, and love. She railed at Stella, resented her, badgered her when she got the opportunity, and loved her. And all the while the secrets Gina had kept from her granddaughter gnawed away at her; truths that might have healed the wound between them – a wound inflicted by Maggie's final triumph, her final nose-thumb at Gina Pontin; her death on Gina's doorstep.

Stella had blamed Gina, the last few nails banged into the coffin of their deteriorating relationship. She had continued to blame Gina for years, and Gina, who deep down blamed herself too, refused to talk about it. Instead, she did what she knew how to do best. She protected herself by taking the offensive. Gina grew even more prickly, even more abrasive, until even the neighbours she'd been on reasonable terms with for years on Bobbin Street, started to avoid her.

It was then, after she took retirement, that she decided to sell up her Nottingham house and move to the coast. Mapton, run down and more difficult to get to than Skegness, was also more affordable. She'd always liked trips to the seaside and felt the coastal air would be good for her. Bing Crosby would love it. Stella might be lured by the thought of the seaside to visit. It was the chance for a new start.

Stella didn't visit. She didn't visit for five years. Gina grew even lonelier. She made fresh enemies, fought off the polite advances of her neighbour George, encouraged Bing Crosby to behave badly and gained a reputation for being rude and curmudgeonly.

All the while Gina longed for a reconciliation with Stella and went about it in her usual wrong way, sometimes sending passive aggressive messages (I don't suppose you have the time to see your old gran?), a sprinkle of emotional blackmail (you'll regret not treating me better when I'm dead) but mostly plainly aggressive (stop being a sulky cow. You should be grateful for all I've given you) and so forth. Stella either didn't respond, or sent vague excuses.

George, who Maptonites quietly agreed had a streak of masochism, (his first wife had been a horror), remained friendly towards Gina, and in desperation she eventually asked him to help her execute a rash plan to bring Stella to Mapton.

The plan had worked, astoundingly, considering how foolhardy it was. All the good things that happened for Gina since had been as a result of that mad idea.

Gina and Stella reconciled. Stella fell in love with Rick and stayed in Mapton, then had Gerta. Gina made friends, had family, won a seat as town councillor and then as mayor. And George, after winning Gina's heart, proposed.

Gina Pontin was wanted. The big wedding day was supposed to be public proof of that. It was why she needed it to be in June, when tradition dictated and the most popular girls she knew in her youth had their weddings; it was why she wanted a white, spectacular wedding dress (even if it was an unusual one); why she wanted Pam's perfect eye for her flowers; why nearly the whole town was invited; why she had worked so hard and driven so many bargains to get the wedding she wanted.

It was to show the world that she, shabby little neglected Gina Pontin had made it.

Except she hadn't. Gina knew now that she would always be abandoned. It didn't matter that George wanted to marry her tomorrow. The day after he might leave her. He might die, or walk out of the door, or announce he had made a mistake. Nobody wanted Gina for long. Not even her own flesh and blood.

Elliot's news was proof of that. He had thrown that bucket of cold reality into Gina's face. Stella, her beloved and most treasured, was going to leave her again. And this time she had gone behind Gina's back.

If Stella could do that to her, anyone could. George could. He would one way or another.

The wedding was a sham as much as that long-ago harvest festival basket had been. Who would really believe it could be hers?

Grief and rage took Gina over; so familiar a response she welcomed it.

Going to the kitchen drawer she grabbed a pair of scissors and headed towards her spare room where her Judy dress hung, waiting.

Panic Stations

Stella was just packing some nibbles to take round to Gina's when she got a panicked call from George. Grazja and Frank had already arrived, ready to babysit Gerta for the evening and were drawing pictures with her at the kitchen table.

Gerta was very excited to be the flower girl during the wedding, having rehearsed her role to scatter flower petals before the bride about a thousand times in the last week. She'd demonstrated the action at least ten times in the preceding hour, and Stella was happy to hand her over to Grazja and Frank. Grazja had a calming effect on Stella's daughter, as she did on her grandmother. After the turbulence of recent events, Stella felt even more grateful for her friend's presence in her life.

'Right, are we about ready?' Stella said to Rick, whose job was to keep the groom company.

'Uhuh,' Rick said. 'Loads of good stuff in the fridge guys, help yourselves. Gerta, be good and go to bed when Grazja tells you, okay?'

'Okay, Daddy,' Gerta said. 'Just one more sleep till the wedding!'

'That's right. Don't you think too much about it though, or you won't sleep and you'll be tired tomorrow. Flower girls have to be as fresh as daisies.'

'Because daisies are flowers!' Gerta cried. 'And I'm a flower girl.'

Grazja's phone chirruped. She took it out. 'It's Elliot,' she said, then frowned. 'He wants me to call him. Says he's made 'big boo-boo'? Hope it not about Gina's dress.' I'll give him a call.

Before Stella could respond, her own phone went off. George's name flashed on screen.

'Hi George, we're just setting off,' Stella told him.

'It's Gina,' George cried. 'She says the wedding's off. She's locked herself in her house and I can't get in.'

Stella's heart sank. She'd been half expecting something like this given Gina's proclivity for creating drama. 'Hang on George, we'll be right around. You know what she's like. She's just having a last minute wobble. It'll be fine.'

'Trouble?' Rick asked. 'You said it was going too smoothly.'

'Gina's called the wedding off,' Stella rolled her eyes. 'It's fine; it'll just be a last minute bid for attention, I'm sure.'

Grazja, who'd gone into the garden to talk to Elliot, returned, looking worried.

'Bad news,' she said. 'Elliot told Gina about the Lawton house. She knows you're moving.'

'What?' Stella gasped. 'How did he know? Did you tell him?'

'Course not,' Grazja said. 'He knows estate agent – Janette? She told him.'

'That's Janette fired,' Rick snarled.

'Elliot thought Gina knew. Realised when she hung up on him that he did wrong thing. He very sorry. He hope it not cause trouble.'

Stella felt sick. 'Too late,' she said. 'George called. Gina's locked herself in her house and called off the wedding.' She covered her face with her hands. 'Oh God,' she groaned. 'Gina will be devastated. She'll see it as a double betrayal, not just me moving but me not telling her too.'

'We must get round there,' Grazja said. 'I come with you.'

Stella nodded. 'Good. Rick, you stay here with Frank and Gerta. We'll call if we need you.'

'Actually,' Grazja said. 'Maybe Frank come. We may need to kick in door if she won't let us in.'

'Jesus,' Rick said. 'Let's not make a drama out of a crisis.'

'Daddy,' Gerta piped up, voice breaking. 'Is Grandma Gina not going to have the wedding? Won't I get to be a flower girl?'

Stella gripped Rick's elbow. 'You stay with Gerta,' she said in a low voice. 'I'd rather she was with you. I'll call you if I need you.'

They took Stella's car for speed, although they'd normally walk.

'I still don't understand why a move to Lawton is such a big deal?' Frank said from the back seat.

'Gina has abandonment issues,' Grazja said. 'I tell you.'

'Yes, but...'

'There's stuff in Gina's past even I don't know,' Stella said, steering white knuckled. 'But I've seen the damage it's done to her. Trust us when we say this is serious.'

Frank fell silent.

George was hovering in the cul-de-sac, hurrying over when Stella pulled up outside Gina's house.

He'd been joined by Pam, who'd heard him calling Gina through the letterbox, and gone out to see what the commotion was.

She looked as anxious as he did.

'She won't answer,' George told Stella. 'She called me to tell me the wedding was off. She was so calm, not like herself at all. Now she won't answer her phone or the door. I've tried the spare keys but she's deadlocked the doors, front and back. I'm that worried it's set me angina off.'

Stella took him gently by the shoulders. 'It'll be fine George. You let me and Grazja sort this out. You know what Gina's like. Loves a bit of drama. Pam'll take you in and make you a cup of tea, won't you Pam?'

Pam stepped forward, taking George by the elbow. 'Of course I will. C'mon love. They know what they're doing.'

'Pam,' Grazja said. 'Make sure George takes his spray for his angina.'

George was prescribed glyceryl trinitrate spray to treat his angina attacks.

'You know where your spray is George?' Grazja asked him.

George nodded.

'Good, tell Pam where it is and make sure you calm down. No good getting Gina back on track if you end up in hospital.'

George nodded again, and winced as pain struck him.

Pam, looking terrified he was about to keel over, guided him slowly towards his bungalow.

Stella ran up the path to Gina's door and bent to the letterbox.

'Gina, it's Stella. I need you to let me in so we can talk.'

Nothing stirred in the house but silence.

Stella pressed on the doorbell. God Save the Queen chimed out. She knocked and kept knocking.

'I'm not going anywhere,' she called. 'So you might as well open up.'

Again, nothing.

This scared Stella more than any amount of screaming and shouting could. Gina was usually very vocal with her rage. The lack of any response from her was eerie.

'Maybe she gone out the back,' Grazja suggested. 'Not even in house.'

But Stella was sure Gina was in there. Somehow she felt it.

They went round the back anyway. The kitchen was empty, and the curtains had been drawn closed in Gina's bedroom. Stella stood outside the window, pressing her ear to the pane. Again, she could hear no sound, and she began to feel an ominous sense of foreboding.

She knocked on the glass. 'Gina,' she called. 'C'mon now. You've got me worried. We need to talk about this. I know what Elliot told you.'

No sign of life came back.

Frank, in the meantime, had quietly tried the back door and found it locked. 'How do we know she's in there?' he said. 'Did George actually see her?'

'She is,' Stella said.

'Let me try,' Grazja said. She tapped on the glass of Gina's window. 'Gina, it me, Grazja. If you not want to talk to Stella, talk to me. I your friend. I care about you. Please Gina. George is so worried.'

This had no more effect than Stella's plea.

'I don't like this silence,' Grazja said quietly. 'Not Gina's style.'

'I know,' Stella said. All sorts of mad images formed in her mind. Gina had knocked her head and was dead. Gina had taken pills. She'd made a noose... Horrible, idiotic thoughts.

If only Gina would scream and shout, smash a window or two, be abusive – they would know she was alive and all right.

'Frank,' Stella said. 'Do you think you could kick in the door?'

'Really?' Frank said, looking doubtful.

Both Stella and Grazja nodded.

'I'm not sure I'm that strong, but I'll give it a go.'

'I've always thought it's too flimsy a door,' Stella said. It took Frank three mighty kicks, but then the bottom panel of the door broke and Stella was able to squeeze through and unlock it from the inside to let the other two in.

If anything should have roused Gina it would have been the crash of her back door being smashed, but still nothing moved.

Heart in her mouth, Stella rushed through the bungalow to Gina's bedroom, opened the door and saw a shape, lying very still, curled almost into a foetal ball under the duvet.

'Gina!' Stella sprang to the bed. Trembling she sat beside the shape and gingerly drew back the covers.

Gina's eyes were closed. Stella shook her gently.

Gina said, very quietly. 'Go away, Stella. I got nothing to say to yer.'

Stella let out a quivering sigh. 'I thought you'd died,' she breathed.

'Wouldn't matter if I had,' Gina murmured. 'Better for you.'

Stella almost smacked her round the head. Instead she kicked off her shoes, pulled back the duvet and slid into bed, curling around Gina's curved back. Groping for her grandmother's hand, she whispered: 'You daft bogger,' and began to cry.

Reluctantly, Gina's fingers tightened around hers. Soon she started to cry too, small hurt whimpers that swelled into bone-shaking sobs that she couldn't hold back.

Stella held her.

'Why didn't you tell me you were leaving me again?' Gina eventually blurted out.

'I'm not leaving you,' Stella said. 'We're thinking about moving to Lawton, that's all. Hardly any distance at all. It's not London, or another country, not even another county! I was waiting to tell you until after your wedding.'

'I'm not getting married,' Gina said. 'This decided me. It'll never stop happening so there's no point. I were stupid to think I could.'

'But why?' Stella asked. 'George loves you.'

'Don't matter,' Gina said. 'He can love me today but won't mean he won't leave me tomorrow. You're supposed to love me. Won't stop you leaving. Won't stop no one leaving. All me life, anyone I loved just up and left, or didn't want to know me anymore. Me mam and dad didn't even love me to begin with. Did yer know that me dad weren't even me real dad? He didn't want me neither it seemed.'

'Oh Gina,' Stella sighed, closing her eyes against the pain. 'You never told me. I'm so sorry. But I'm not leaving you. It's not like before; you'll always be a major part of my life. I love you. I need you too. Gerta needs you. She loves her Grandma Gina. And George loves you more than anything.'

Gina sniffled. 'He does, don't he?'

'He does.'

'Dunno why,' Gina said.

There was a knock on the door, and Grazja poked her head round.

'Ready for a cup of tea, ladies?' she asked, nudging into the room bearing a tray with three mugs and some biscuits.

'Bloody hell,' Gina said. 'It's like déjà vu. D'you remember? We've done this before when you first came to Mapton. It were Stella's fault then too, getting me all upset.'

Grazja handed them each a mug and taking one herself sat on the other side of Gina on the bed and held out her mug for a toast. They all clinked, careful not to slosh hot tea on themselves and the duvet.

'To us three,' Grazja declared. 'May we ever be together when Gina goes nuclear.'

'To friendship and family and us,' Stella said.

'To daft boggers,' Gina said. She sipped her tea and looked at Stella. 'You should have told me, duck.'

'I know,' Stella said. 'But I really didn't want to upset you before your wedding. I thought once you were married you'd feel more secure. I know what you're like. You overreact.'

She expected Gina to argue, but for once Gina looked thoughtful. 'I think it were the harvest festival that really set me on,' she said. 'I mean, I'd got me heart set on this perfect wedding, but it were the festival brought back a lot of old feelings. Insecurities you could say.'

'But that was funny in end,' Grazja said. 'The way the flour bag burst and all.'

'Not that bit,' Gina said. She told them about the harvest festivals of her childhood, and the one that changed her life. It made them all a bit weepy again.

'It's being humiliated 'n all,' Gina explained. 'It weren't just you moving Stella, it were the humiliation of other people knowing before me, like I'm not important enough to tell.'

'I understand,' Stella said. 'I'm sorry.'

'I thought, the wedding's just a sham, like the harvest basket. It'll get snatched away and leave me looking stupid.'

'But it won't,' Grazja said. 'Everything is ready. And it isn't about you, and what you look like to the outside world. It's about you and George. Do you love George, Gina?'

'Of course I do,' Gina snapped.

'Then you need to tell him wedding is on before he die of heart attack. Pam's had to give him his spray cuz you set his angina on.'

Gina sat up, thrusting her empty mug at Grazja.

'Oh my God, George,' she said, pushing out of bed. 'Is he all right?'

'He will be, I think, once you tell him you sorry for nearly killing him. Tell him wedding is on!'

Gina ran for the door. As she grasped the handle, she turned back with a sudden guilty look.

'I was so mad earlier,' she said. 'I wanted to cut my wedding dress up.'

'But you didn't?' Stella asked.

'I couldn't do it,' Gina admitted. 'So I cut up your Matron of Honour dress instead.'

And then she was gone.

Gina's Wedding

Gina stood beneath the arched entrance to the church. Grazja, Pam, and Pauline waited in the porch behind her, while just in front of her Gerta bobbed impatiently with her basket of flower petals, barely holding back.

The day had dawned with a sunrise as beautiful and blushingly pink as the rosebuds laced into the bridal bouquet she clutched before her. It had felt like a blessing following a storm.

The only major obstacle to be faced that morning was that the Matron of Honour had no dress to match the other bridesmaids, and nothing in her wardrobe that might suffice. The wedding wasn't until two which gave them a small window of time to find an alternative.

It was Elliot who came up with the solution, and in doing so added an extra element that made the day more special. It was a generous gesture by himself and his husband Tim, as it was Tim's white groom's suit from their own nuptials that Stella wore, with quick adjustments by Elliot (very eager after his slip-up to make amends).

The suit might have looked odd if Stella had retained her role as Matron of Honour, but Elliot suggested that she be made 'father of the bride' as Gina had elected no-one to take her down the aisle.

During all the preparations Gina insisted she needed no 'giving away'. 'I never had a father help me through anything,' she said. 'I'll go up the aisle on me own as Gina Pontin and George to walk me back as Mrs Wentworth.'

In the bright morning, hugging Stella close, she said: 'It should be you duck. It's perfect.'

So it was, Stella sleek and elegant in her white morning suit with embroidered waistcoat, offered her arm to Gina, magnificent in her Judy wedding dress, and enormous hat.

Fred Spring struck up the wedding march on the organ.

The moment seemed to tremble with emotion; Stella ducked under the hat to give Gina a quick kiss on the cheek and whispered: 'Ready?'

'Ready,' Gina said, squeezing Stella's arm.

'Now, Gerta,' Stella instructed her daughter.

Gerta began to dance down the nave like a fairy in her frothy white dress, enthusiastically flinging petals hither and thither. Gina and Stella followed her rather more sedately down the aisle, trailed by Grazja (bearing Gina's parasol), Pam and Pauline. Pauline looked rapturous, smiling and nodding at every turned head in the packed church to watch them.

'You might've thought it was her getting married,' one town gossip later said. 'She looked that proud of herself in her bridesmaid dress. Mind you, it was nice to see her looking less like a pudding than she normally does.'

'I didn't notice nothing but Gina's dress and hat,' her companion said. 'Ridiculous on a woman that age. What was she thinking?'

Gina, as she finally walked up the aisle, wasn't actually thinking about her dress (which was perfect and she knew it), she was thinking how fine George looked as he waited next to Rick (his best man). He might not have all his own teeth but he still had a good head of hair for a man his age – any age really, given how many men lost their hair early – and Gina felt lucky. He was a handsome old devil, and his smile told her that in his eyes at least, she was beautiful.

Fortunately, George's angina had settled due to the spray and to Gina's return. He'd insisted they sleep in their own bed together, eve of the wedding or not. Who knew how long they had left to enjoy each other – why waste a single night by being apart?

Gina Pontin had caught herself a good 'un.

Stella, laughed along with the congregation as her daughter, upon reaching the altar way ahead of the bridal procession, started to scoop petals back into her basket so she could run back and start afresh. Her eyes caught Rick's, who grinned at her, and she too thought how lucky she was to have this handsome man, looking gorgeous in his sharp suit.

Off to the left, the Reverend Rivers hovered, ready to step forward and perform the wedding service. Stella had been dreading this moment; she, Rick and the reverend all in close proximity. It wasn't supposed to happen this way. George had chosen an old friend, Ken Toton, as his best man, but at the last moment Ken had been forced to drop out due to ill-health, and Rick stepped up to do best man duties.

The vicar was as startlingly good-looking as ever but glancing at him now, she saw his features as bland in their perfection, with none of Rick's character or humour. She felt none of the fever that had consumed her before. With relief, she felt as though she had shaken off a sickness that had held her in thrall and come back to health.

Stella glanced gladly back to Rick, but he had turned away, mouth set in a line, mind on the job in hand, as she and Gina arrived at the altar.

Rick was not happy. Despite the brief moment of shared amusement over Gerta's antics, he'd been tense standing so near to Reverend effing Rivers. It had been the first time he'd seen the man up close since Easter. Oh yeah, he knew his wife had almost thrown herself into an affair with the man. For so long he'd managed to convince himself that it had been the result of her hormonal imbalance, as she claimed, but seeing the guy today he had to face it - he wasn't so sure.

He knew he'd feel uncomfortable meeting him, but George needed a stand-in best man, and Christ, didn't George have enough to deal with? The man was a saint for marrying Gina.

So Rick knew he'd feel weird, standing near the vicar, but he hadn't expected to want to punch the man in the face the moment he set eyes on him.

He hadn't of course. Mapton didn't need more juicy scandal to tattle over, and decking a vicar at a wedding lacked class, not to mention Gina would eviscerate him if he ruined her big day.

Yet, God, had he wanted to wipe that pious bastard's smug smile off his face when he came up to greet them and run them through the order of play.

'If you ever go near my wife again,' Rick had wanted to snarl, 'I will tear your balls off and make you eat them in hot batter.'

Instead, he'd smiled tightly, nodded, and otherwise kept his mouth shut and his fists loose at his sides.

Rick could disguise his feelings when he wanted to. It took all his control to keep a grip on them when Stella, a split moment after smiling at him, turned her gaze to the vicar. Jealousy rose like gorge. He forced it down, focused on giving the ring to George, whispered 'Good luck, buddy,' and stepped away swiftly as the vicar came forward, taking his seat on the front pew where Stella and Gerta joined him.

'Sit here between me and mummy,' he instructed Gerta.

'Sit on your knee, Daddy?'

'No honey, sit between us, there's a good flower girl.'

George and Gina were blissfully unaware of any currents of tension. Their moment was finally here and they only had eyes and ears and hearts for each other.

George's daughters watched, the sisters exchanging looks of resignation and muffled horror, as their father married the woman they'd privately nicknamed the 'red-haired monster'. As neither of them visited their father as often as they knew they should, they supposed they could live with it.

Frank, admiring Grazja in her bridesmaid dress, wondered if she would ever consider getting married again. Technically, he supposed, having been married she shouldn't be a bridesmaid, but she looked as fresh and maidenly to him as any young slip of a girl.

Pam, in her seat next to Pauline and Grazja, was enjoying her flower displays. The grace and beauty of the blooms seemed to glow, as though radiating joy into the sanctity of the church.

Pam leant forward to catch the eye of Laura Rivers, tucked quietly into a space beside a pillar. The two women smiled at each other. Laura nodded towards a floral display. 'Perfect,' she mouthed. Pam beamed.

Pam was still pinching herself that she was involved in Gina Pontin's wedding at all. It was beyond belief; not that she was responsible for the flowers, including Gina's bouquet, but that she was here as a bridesmaid. Adding to her delight was the knowledge that beneath her modest bridesmaid dress, Pam was wearing her laciest, frilliest, babydoll knickers, and only Ray knew it. No wonder he had given her such a saucy wink as she passed him.

Elliot squeezed Tim's hand as they watched the ceremony. It had taken too many years until he and Tim had been able to get legally married. Once attending weddings had felt like a special torture – look but don't touch; this isn't meant for the likes of you.

He felt the warm strength in his quiet, gentle husband's grip, and swiped a tear off his cheek.

'Look at Gina,' he murmured. 'That dress is a triumph. Utterly over the top. I don't think Glinda could look more camp.'

'I can't believe Stella Distry is wearing my wedding suit,' Tim whispered back. 'I'm going to frame it and hang it on the wall.'

After Gina and George had exchanged their vows the congregation stood to sing George's favourite hymn, All Things Bright and Beautiful, then as the bride and groom signed the register, Dusty Velour sang 'Someone to Watch Over Me'.

Dusty, was a renowned cabaret singer in the area, booked for Christmas events, weddings, and special appearances throughout the year. Gina had been determined to get her, offering to pay twice her usual rate if she'd cancel the wedding booking she already had to sing at Gina's instead. Dusty, a woman of integrity, had turned Gina down, but then the wedding she was originally booked for was cancelled anyway.

'See,' Gina had said. 'This wedding is just meant to be.'

Dusty was booked for the reception too.

'She don't lip-synch,' Gina had informed Elliot tartly. 'She's the real thing. She's so good she could sing on a cruise ship.'

'I know,' Elliot had said. 'Dusty is a wonderful singer. We go way back on the cabaret circuit.'

'You telling me she isn't a lady?' Gina had asked.

'Dusty is most definitely a lady,' Elliot had said. 'And a wonderful woman.'

Dusty's rendition of 'Someone to Watch Over Me' set a few folk sniffling.

Gina's choice of exit song made everyone laugh. As Mr and Mrs Wentworth travelled back down the aisle proudly beaming, Dusty burst into Judy Garland's 'Get Happy'.

Outside in the glorious hot sunshine, where Gina announced she was sweating like a cheese after posing for a variety of wedding photos, a young woman approached Gina who was standing with George and the vicar.

As she approached the vicar said: I see my wife needs a word with me,' and hastened away.

The young woman's eyes followed him, then she looked at Gina. 'That was a beautiful wedding,' she said. 'It was supposed to be mine.'

'Yer what?' Gina said. She didn't know this woman but had assumed she'd come with a guest when she spotted her loitering around.

'We'd booked this wedding slot,' the woman explained. 'We had it confirmed a year ago last April. Then we got a call just after Christmas to say it had been double booked and ours had to be rearranged. My fiancé was spitting.'

'I don't know nothing about that,' Gina said, defensively. 'Our's was booked long before April last year, weren't it George?'

George looked vaguely away.

'Oh, it doesn't matter,' the woman said. 'Actually, I changed my mind, you see, after the date was cancelled. Already had my doubts but was too scared to admit them. The double-booking was like a sign I couldn't ignore, so I broke the engagement off.'

Gina stared at her. 'Why d'yer come to my wedding? Bit odd, ain't it?'

'Everyone said I'd regret it,' the woman sighed. 'I thought if I came to yours, same time, same day, same place mine should've been I'd know if I did.'

'And?' Gina asked.

'Not one twinge of regret. Your wedding was beautiful,' she said. 'It felt just right. Mine would have felt so wrong. It was meant to be yours,' she smiled at them both. 'I just wanted to say congratulations.'

Potential trouble dispelled, Gina said impulsively. 'Stay for the reception. It'll be a great knees up.'

The woman laughed. 'Thanks,' she said. 'But I'm going to enjoy my entirely free afternoon.'

'Suit yerself,' Gina shrugged. 'Glad it worked out for yer. It's got to be the right one or not at all.'

She and George watched the young woman walk away. 'Well, I never,' Gina declared. 'The vicar's a cheeky bogger, giving us someone else's wedding slot.'

'You put a lot of pressure on him for a June wedding, love.'

'I got loads more people going to his church, like I said I would. He knows which side his bread is buttered on.'

#

The reception was held in the Mapton Community Hall, a seventies one-storey brick building that was used for everything from town meetings to elections to ballroom dances and slimming clubs. It had a stage, toilets, a rudimentary bar, and a kitchen with a serving hatch, but best of all, the hall could hold a large number of people so was regularly booked for weddings and wakes, or the sort of parties where kids could run around insanely without reprisal.

Gina had opted for a buffet. 'I can't be doin' wi' a big sit down dinner,' she'd said. 'I always like a nice buffet meself. Folk can grab what they want and mingle.'

The other convention Gina had nixed was the speeches. Once George had asked his old pal Ken to be his best man, Gina swiftly decided a best man's speech was a waste of time. 'He's a boring old fart,' she'd confided to Stella. 'Got one of them voices could send a chronic insomniac to sleep. Takes so long to tell a story I can feel me hair growin'.'

Before the wedding party reached the hall there was a jolly excursion to the boating lake where a white swan pedalo had been tied to the back of a little motorboat.

This was an extra surprise for Gina, arranged by George. The swan was wreathed in streamers, while a 'Just Married' sign hung from its neck and Babycham bottles trailed in the water behind it.

Gina clapped when she saw it. There was a tricky moment when she clambered in with her hooped, ruffled skirts but nothing disastrous occurred. George climbed in beside her. The swan was a pedalo, but neither George nor Gina had the knees to take on that challenge, so Frank took captaincy of the motorboat to tug them gently round the lake.

Gina waved queen-like to all the bemused tourists and day-trippers, while her entourage laughed and whooped from the sides. Soon, a number of over-dressed people in entirely the wrong footwear had hired boats and swans and were getting themselves sweaty, and in some instances wet, messing around on the water.

By the time they got to the hall, where a number of people were already milling around, wondering when the wedding reception would begin, various guests had sodden shoes, or lost their fascinator, or had a child who needed to be taken home and changed into dry clothing.

Gina somehow managed to keep herself immaculate. She had enjoyed the opportunity to 'swan' around beneath her fancy parasol, hat perfectly balanced, and enjoy the attention her bridal procession drew.

George had got it right again.

The hall, usually a bit dark and dingy, looked glorious festooned with bright bunting, strings of white lights, and Pam's floristry. Two giant, neon letters linked by an ampersand - G&G – glowed in the centre of the stage.

Two thrones had been set up for the meet and greet. It was another surprise organised by Stella and Grazja. Gina shrieked her delight when she saw them and immediately assumed her regal seat. George sank gratefully onto his. Stella and Grazja exchanged a knowing look. They'd been concerned that standing too long for the meet and greet, following on from the wedding ceremony and boating lake, would be too tiring for George, but they also know he was such an old-fashioned gentleman he'd insist on standing to welcome the guests. The thrones (provided by Elliot) worked beautifully; they appealed to Gina's vanity and allowed George to sit without losing face.

Before the guests started to file past, Dan Joules brought in Bing Crosby, holding him tight on a leash, or he'd be across the room and on the buffet table in a flash. Ginger Rogers waddled along demurely on Dan's left.

'Where's his little waistcoat?' Gina demanded, looking at Bing. 'He's supposed to match George.'

Dan shook his head grimly. 'Was never going to happen,' he said. 'Wouldn't let me put it on.'

'Yer little bogger,' Gina said fondly, giving Bing a chuck under his whiskery muzzle. 'Just like me, aren't yer? Pig headed.'

Bing wagged his tail and licked her, but his mind was on the delicious smell of sausages emanating from the other side of the hall. He was just waiting for an opportunity.

Ginger, a fat little corgi wearing a bow made from the same ruffles adorning Gina's dress, could smell the food too, but she preferred her treats to be fed to her and was sure they'd come, especially from George, who was a soft touch.

Bing was remarkably well behaved as the guests filed past, merely sniffing their ankles as they offered congratulations, cards and presents, which Stella and Grazja took, adding them to a pile growing on a side table. Only when Peter Moss, looking uncomfortable in a suit that was fraying at the cuffs, came forward did Bing stiffen and begin to growl.

Peter stepped back quick-smart.

Gina eyed him sharply. 'You ain't got that ferret in yer pocket, have yer?'

'No,' Peter protested. Bing had a history with Wilson, Peter's ferret.

'Must be able to smell it on yer,' Gina said.

Bing snarled at him.

'You ought to put a muzzle on that dog,' he said.

'Someone oughta put a muzzle on you,' Gina snapped back. 'Move along, Pete, you're holding up the queue.'

Peter moved along, muttering under his breath as he made his way to his seat.

'Did we invite him?' Gina asked Stella.

Stella shrugged. 'I can't remember. Probably.'

Long trestle tables had been set up in horseshoe shape in the centre of the hall, while the buffet table, groaning under its load, ran along the wall beneath the windows with their lowered blinds.

After the meet and greet, Gina and George's thrones were moved to their table and Gina declared the buffet open after a champagne toast.

'Babycham's on the house, and squash for the kiddies,' she shouted. 'The rest you have to pay for yerself at the bar. Now, go grab your grub!'

There was a stampede for the buffet. Gina and George had pre-filled plates that Stella fetched from the kitchen to save them having to join the fight for the food.

There were a lot more drinkers of Babycham that afternoon and evening than was usual, and many a child who wanted a fizzy pop was told to have squash. Some regretted being quite so free with the Babycham, underestimating its potency. Others discovered a taste for it, including Sam 'Wolf' Hodson, Mapton's resident tattooist and hell-for-leather biker, who drank Babycham for years afterwards. It became his secret home tipple, and he ordered it online to avoid the indignity of being spotted buying those pretty little Bambi bottles and the teasing that might ensue.

Laughter and high spirits filled the room, people eating and drinking, exchanging gossip, swapping places around tables to talk to friends, neighbours and relatives. Gerta ran around with a gaggle of her pre-school friends once Stella and Rick had managed to get her to eat.

At one point Gina noticed Elliot's partner Tim had been missing for a while.

'Tim gone home?' she asked. 'Yer had a row or summat?'

'Oh no,' Elliot laughed. 'He's just gone to check on Princess Alys. She hates being left alone too long. He'll be coming back.'

'You should have brought her,' Gina said. 'It's a daft long way to go and come back just to check on her.'

'It's fine,' Elliot said airily, waving her away. 'Go and mingle. I'm having a lovely conversation with Beryl Finch. I can't take my eyes off her blue-rinse. She's just popped to the loo. Oh, here she comes…'

Gina moved between tables, enjoying the attention lavished on herself and her dress.

'Don't knock me hat off,' she said, as Andy Timmis went to kiss her cheek.

'Isn't it time you took that off,' Andy backed away. 'Isn't it bad luck to wear a hat indoors?'

'Dunno,' Gina said. 'Don't care. You look nice in that royal blue, Carole.'

Carole, who was Andy's girlfriend, looked doubtful. 'You don't think it's too much?'

'No duck, makes you look less pasty than usual.'

Gina swept on, bantering with her guests, accepting their congratulations, doling out her back-handed compliments, and occasionally rapping sticky-fingers away from her dress with her furled parasol. A few fingers and feelings felt a little stung, but no one really minded, as this was Gina's day, and she could do what she liked.

The eating and drinking and chattering period went on for quite some time, before the lights were dimmed and Dusty Velour took to the stage which signalled it was almost time for the first dance.

Gina, looking round, realised she hadn't seen Stella for a while, and actually, Rick was missing too.

'Have you seen Stella and Rick?' she asked Grazja, who along with Frank, was chatting to George and his daughters.

Grazja nodded. 'They thought they had left iron on. Went back to house to check. Asked me to keep eye on Gerta.'

'What, it needed both of them to go?' Gina said.

Grazja's eyes twinkled. 'I think iron too hot for one to handle,' she said.

Gina frowned at her uncomprehendingly.

'It's almost time for the first dance,' Gina said. 'They better be back for that.'

Grazja looked past her and smiled. 'Ah, here they are.'

Stella and Rick came into the hall, each looking a touch dishevelled. Rick gave Stella a peck on the cheek, and headed off in the direction of the buffet table, while Stella weaved her way through the tables to Gina and Grazja.

Gina surveyed her, noting Stella's rather flushed cheeks, and the button missing off her waistcoat.

'You dirty boggers,' she said. 'You better find that button. That's Tim's waistcoat, remember?'

Stella flushed even more, but despite her embarrassment she looked absurdly pleased with herself.

Grazja grabbed her hand. 'Toilets, now,' she said. 'I want to know details.'

'Not *now*' Gina snapped. 'It's time for me 'n' George's first dance.'

Space had been left for a dance floor in front of the stage where Dusty's mic was set up alongside her accompanying keyboardist's synthesiser and DJ equipment. The evening entertainment was to be part cabaret, part discotheque with a mix of old-fashioned classics and dancefloor pop but 'none of them modern hump and bump rude songs' according to Gina, 'and none of that raving.'

'As Mapton's never musically moved beyond 1986, I don't think you have to worry,' Stella said.

It was actually George who chose the song for their first dance. Louis Armstrong's version of Only You was one of his favourites, and encapsulated his feelings for Gina perfectly. George had been unusually crafty in his bid to win the first dance choice. Initially he'd suggested You Spin Me Round (Like a Record) by Dead or Alive. This he'd once sung to Gina at karaoke in the hope of wooing her, and he knew she'd reject it. She wanted 'Zing! Went the Strings of my Heart', another Judy number, but George argued that no one would know it, and counter-offered with his real contender, Only You. Gina liked it too (preferring Sinatra's version) and having already knocked George back once, she felt satisfied that he wasn't getting his own way too easily .

Dusty did the song exactly as George wanted it sung. He'd played her the Armstrong version, and as well as arranging the tempo, she gave her voice a wonderful slight gravelly quality without doing a parody.

The guests clapped and cheered as George, despite being unable to exert himself for too long, swung Gina around the floor in a fluid foxtrot. They'd both been good dancers in their youth and practised their dance for weeks.

Gina twirled around the floor in her dream dress, face shining as happily as a little girl in a tutu, believing herself to be a ballerina.

Everyone applauded as George spun Gina to an elegant finish.

'Didn't expect that, did you?' Gina shouted breathlessly, making them laugh. 'Right, you lot, time to get this party started. The next one's for all of you.'

She nodded to Dusty who grinned, and her synth player hit the opening bars of You Spin Me Round before Dusty launched in with the lyrics.

George's mouth was a startled 'o' of astonishment. As friends and family filled the dancefloor around them, Gina grabbed him, shouting in his ear. 'You're not the only one who can arrange surprises, duck.'

George laughed, hugging her. 'I love it,' he said. 'But I think my old ticker needs a sit down before we do another dance.'

'C'mon then,' Gina said, leading him off the floor. 'Let's get you sat down, you old codger. We'll have a slow one later.'

Rick surveyed the scene as he dispatched four vol-au-vents and a slice of lemon cheesecake. The unexpected 'intermission' he'd shared with Stella had left him ravenous. Who knew Stella would find his jealous side so arousing? She'd never seen it before, and until recently he'd never felt it.

That moment in the church when her gaze had slid to the vicar, ignited a green flame he could barely tamp down through the rest of the wedding and following celebrations. He'd been 'off' with Stella, tense and terse, watching her for any signs she was thinking of Michael Rivers, but turning away when she turned to him.

Finally, Stella had dragged him into the hall kitchen to demand: 'What's going on? Have I done something wrong?'

Rick snorted. 'I saw the way you looked at the fucking vicar,' he said.

'When?' Stella looked bewildered.

'In the church,' Rick snapped. 'Don't pretend you're over him.

'It was never about him,' Stella protested. 'We've talked about this…'

'Yeah, I know. It was all your hormones. Well, maybe I wanted to believe it, but when I saw you and him in the church… C'mon Stella, I saw it. He looks like a movie star. I saw it on your face.'

'You imagined it,' Stella said. She had a strange, wild look in her eyes.'

Rick assumed it was the effort of lying and it made him even angrier.

'If he shows his face at this party I'll crack his fucking jaw for him,' he said. 'I don't want you near him ever again.'

'Don't you?' Stella stared at him, her breathing a bit ragged.

'I don't,' Rick growled. 'You're my wife.'

'I am,' Stella said. 'I am Rick. I don't want him, I want you. I want you right now. I've never wanted you more!'

Her face was flushed, her eyes locked into his. He grabbed her, crushing her in a possessive kiss, her body responding in a way she hadn't for months.

(It was all very Mills & Boon, Stella told Grazja later.)

'We can't do it here,' Stella panted. 'But I can't wait.'

'Home,' Rick grunted.

'I'll ask Grazja to look after Gerta,' Stella said.

That done, they practically ran out of the hall.

Fortunately for them, Jeff, Mapton's one taxi driver, had just dropped a late guest off, and they were able to jump in his car and order him to take them home.

'Hardly worth the fare for you,' he said, as he dropped them off after the two minute drive, and Rick dug around for his wallet. 'Don't know why you didn't walk.'

'Left the iron on,' Stella said, frantically exiting.

In the end they didn't even make it to the bedroom before tearing their clothes off and coming together in an intense, explosive encounter the likes of which they'd never had before.

'Actually, I was looking at the vicar,' Stella told Rick afterwards, as they held each other close. 'But it was the opposite of what you thought. I was thinking how bland his looks are, and how much I prefer you. I was thinking how much I love you. I do,' she lifted her head off his chest. 'I love you so much.'

'I love you,' he replied. He felt a rush of happiness; not just a release of sexual tension, but of hurt and anger long held, and gladly let go of.

He had his wife back; he knew it for sure.

'Oh God, we'd better get back before we're missed,' Stella groaned.

'Hope there's some food left, I'm starving,' Rick said.

Rick spotted Peter Moss loitering at the other end of the long buffet table, casting him hang-dog glances.

Rick hadn't seen Peter in the diner since he'd kicked him out. He'd heard Peter had started frequenting a number of the seafront cafes in Mapton, but most were seasonal and only did take-aways and outdoor seating. No-one else was willing to put up with Peter's tendency to nurse one coffee while he took up space for hours.

Rick walked over to him. 'Hi Pete,' he said. 'How's it going?'

Peter cleared his throat nervously. 'Um, er, ha! Yes. Erm, I want to apologise Rick. What I said back at Easter about Stella. I was out of order. It was very bad of me. I didn't mean it.'

Rick nodded. 'I appreciate that Pete,' he said. 'Let's put it behind us. How's that ferret of yours?'

Gratefully, Peter launched into a list of Wilson's exploits, and soon Rick wasn't listening, simply nodding occasionally, and enjoying the sight of his wife dancing with his daughter and Gina.

Frank came over to rescue him.

'Peter,' he said. 'I hear Andy Timmis is thinking of getting a ferret. Perhaps you can give him some advice.'

'Thanks,' Rick laughed, as Peter headed towards Andy. 'What's Andy ever done to you?'

'I've just been listening to his daft conspiracy theories. It's payback for twenty minutes of wasted life.'

'Hard to believe you were once a man of the cloth,' Rick said.

'Talking of men of the cloth,' Frank nodded towards the door. 'Look who's just come in.'

Rick followed his gaze. Reverend Rivers had entered, no longer smocked and dog-collared. He scanned the room, looking for someone, as various Maptonites drifted towards his magnetic pull.

Stella and Grazja were heading his way, but as Rick watched, Stella didn't even notice the vicar until he moved to say hello. They looked up briefly at his greeting, acknowledged him with polite smiles, but then continued past, immediately wrapped back up in their own conversation, as though he were no more than a neighbour you waved to dutifully but didn't want to get to know.

The vicar spotted Rick and Frank, and wove his way over to them. 'Hello gentlemen,' he said. 'I'm looking for my wife. Have you seen her?'

Rick smiled, shark-like. 'I generally don't pay much attention to other men's wives,' he said. 'I'm afraid I can't help you.'

The vicar's smile faltered slightly.

'I think I saw her heading towards the Ladies,' Frank stepped in smoothly.

'Ah, thank you,' the vicar said, retreating.

When he'd gone, Frank looked at Rick. 'You okay?'

'I'm great,' Rick nodded. 'Never better.' He meant it. 'Now, I think I want to dance with my daughter,'

Heading into the fray, he went to boogie with Gerta.

Stella and Grazja were outside, enjoying a bit of fresh air. They'd found a bench around the side of the hall, away from the smokers who were milling around the front door. Stella had just finished telling Grazja about her and Rick (though not the intimate details) when Laura Rivers appeared.

'Oh,' she said, coming over. 'I was just looking for a hidden spot for a sneaky cigarette.'

'I didn't know you smoke,' Stella said.

'I don't – just sometimes,' Laura admitted. 'Social events and booze make me crave one for old time's sake. I thought it wouldn't do for the vicar's wife to be seen puffing on a fag.'

'We won't tell,' Grazja said, patting the bench seat next to her.

'Do you mind?' Laura asked, waving an unlit cigarette.

They both said no.

'You both look glowing,' Laura said, after taking a deep drag which she blew out away from them with a sigh of satisfaction.

Stella and Grazja exchanged naughty grins.

'Do you mind if I ask you a personal question?' Stella asked, giddy from sex and Babycham.

Laura eyed her. 'Okay,' she said warily.

'After what we, er, talked about … with your husband…' Stella paused. 'Why did you come back to him?'

Laura looked taken aback. 'Because I love him,' she said.

'Yes, but…' Stella trailed off. Laura had told her about the vicar's lack of libido in confidence. She shouldn't have brought it up in front of Grazja but sex was on her mind right now.

Laura regarded her, calmly puffing away on her cigarette as she decided how to answer. She looked at Grazja, weighing up. 'My husband doesn't have much of a sex drive,' she said.

Grazja shrugged. 'Not everyone does,' she said. 'Everyone is different. Nothing wrong with that.'

Laura looked at Stella. 'Do you remember I said that only one woman had truly fallen in love with him – not a crush that faded?'

Stella nodded. That was a conversation she had etched on her memory.

'Well, that was me,' Laura smiled. 'I'm the one who didn't get away. Because it was real, and Michael felt the same way about me. He loved me. He still does. When Frank found me, I'd already started wanting to come back to Michael if he'd have me. I didn't regret leaving. I fell in lust with the man I ran away with but I didn't stay with him for long. If I'm honest – and this really does have to stay between the three of us...' (She paused while Stella and Grazja assured her it would.) 'I had lots of lovers while I was away. In fact if I never have a sex life again, I've had more than enough sex to last me. What I have with Michael is a truly deep love – it's not platonic for either of us –it's genuine, intimate and romantic. That's all I can really say. Nothing in life is simple; it's always more complicated than we expect because people are.'

'That's beautiful,' Stella almost sobbed. Grazja agreed.

Then Stella said: 'Never mention any of this to Gina. She can't even say 'sex'. She can only say 'intercourse'.

They were still laughing when the woman herself appeared, as though conjured by the words.

'What you doing out here?' Gina called, flouncing up. 'Stella, every time I look around today, you've disappeared. We're going to cut the cake.'

They met Elliot on their way in. He was coming out of the front door.

'I've been talking to the vicar,' he blurted excitedly. 'Oh my God, he is hot! I swear he was flirting with me.'

'He wasn't,' a chorus came back at him, making him blink.

'There's plenty of gay vicars,' he said, defensively.

Stella grinned. 'It's not that,' she said. 'But trust us on this. I'll explain tomorrow. This is the vicar's wife, by the way,' she said, hitching her thumb at Laura. 'Elliot, meet Laura.'

'Oh God, sorry,' Elliot blushed. 'Major faux pas.'

'It's fine,' Laura laughed. 'Lovely to meet you. Gina's dress is amazing. I heard you made it?'

Elliot was about to answer, but Gina interrupted. 'Chit chat later,' she snapped. 'I want to cut me cake.'

She ushered them all in, but Elliot slid past her. 'I'll be in in a sec,' he said. 'Here's Tim.'

Tim was turning in to the car park in his sleek silver Audi.

Elliot shot a look back at Stella as she disappeared inside, and she gave him a wink.

The cutting of the cake was going to be the last official act before the wedding reception slid into an evening of discarded shoes, undone ties, bad dancing, over-tired kids, and general inebriation.

'Is she alright? Is she ready?' Elliot said to Tim as he climbed out of the car.

'She's fine. Had a bit of a sulk when we first left, according to Sandi, but settled down. I fed her, took her out to do her business and gave her a bit of honey for her throat.'

Elliot opened the back door to find Princess Alys sitting up on her velvet cushion, yawning after a nap.

'Hello lovely,' Elliot cooed. 'Let's get you ready for your big turn.'

Gina and George had opted for a traditional three tier wedding cake, but instead of 'musty tasting' fruit cake, they'd gone for butter cream filled Madeira sponge, covered in smooth white royal icing over apricot jam. It was very simple and elegant by Gina's standards, but the figures on top made it much more fun. Stella had crafted caricatures of Gina and George from Fimo clay, complete with Gina's orange hair and Judy garland dress. Bing Crosby flanked Gina, along with a string of pink sausages hanging from his mouth, while Ginger Rogers sat at George's feet gazing at a miniature plate of biscuits.

The only minor mishap of the wedding day thus far occurred when Gina and George fed each the first forkful of cake. Gina, withdrawing her fork from George's mouth, almost hooked out his dentures. George quickly pretended to wipe his mouth, pushing them back into place, but not before keen-eyed Peter Moss shouted 'You almost had his chompers out there, Gina.'

Gina retorted, good-naturedly for her: 'I'll set George's chompers on *you*, Peter, if you don't pipe down.'

When everyone who wanted a slice of wedding cake had lined up to receive one, and most people were seated again, munching and chatting, or buying drinks, or nipping out for cigarettes, or taking kids to the loo, and all the other business of a wedding reception, Dusty took to the stage again for another set.

'Ladies and gentlemen,' she announced. 'To honour our bride and groom, Gina and George, we have a special treat planned. I'm going to sing a duet with a very talented singer. Please put your hands together for Princess Alys.'

Gina clapped a hand to her mouth. George looked bewildered.

The guests applauded, although at first they couldn't see any other performer join Dusty on stage. Then Elliot appeared from behind a screen that had been set up at the side of the stage, photos of Gina and George displayed on it, and at his side he guided a tiny dog wearing a white tutu and a double string of pearls up the stairs.

Princess Alys pranced up the steps, poised as a prima ballerina, nose high, born to be on stage.

Dusty slid off the stool she had been perched on, and Elliot scooped the Dachshuahua up, placing her neatly on the vacated seat.

As one the guests let out an 'ah', and waited, breathless, to see what the little dog would do.

Dusty opened her mouth and the first words of Over the Rainbow sighed melodiously out, building beautifully as her accompanist picked out the tune on his keyboard. She looked down at Princess Alys as she sang, but Alys only looked up at her, and then over to Elliot who had moved to the wings.

Elliot nodded encouragement to her. Tim had joined him, and holding hands they began to sing softly too.

Then, just as the audience felt the dog would do nothing but provide cuteness, Princess Alys, threw back her head and began to sing like the diva she was.

People began to clap. Gina was on her feet, laughing and clapping, singing along, hugging George in absolute joy at the sheer spectacle of it.

She understood this had been arranged for her. Stella ran over and threw her arm around her grandmother, and they swayed together, with George, singing.

Everyone was singing, and cutting through it all, Princess Alys's high-pitched operatics soared above their choir, until it was matched by two more canine voices. Bing Crosby and Ginger Rogers had added theirs – Ginger's a yowl, and Bing's a howl – until it seemed the roof of the hall might blast off, so great was the pressure of that cacophony.

'We practised for a week,' Stella told Gina when it was over, and they'd sunk into their seats, weak with emotion.

Princess Aly's performance was the peak of the celebrations. Dusty was done for the evening, and her accompanist donned his DJ cap and exchanged his keyboard for his decks.

Princess Alys was a star; Elliot and Tim spent much of the evening having to fluctuate between displaying her as proud 'daddies' and playing bodyguard to protect her from too many eager hands.

Dusty sat with them, accepting only a fraction of the praise she normally got, as Alys stole her limelight. She didn't mind this once. It wasn't the first time she'd sung with Alys; Dusty was an old friend of Elliot and Tim. It was the first time she and Alys had sung together in public. Dusty rather hoped it would be the last. She didn't want to be regularly upstaged by a sausage-shaped dog in a tutu.

The evening wound down gradually.

Laura and the reverend took Pauline home. Like an exhausted child, she had fallen asleep by nine 'o'clock, her face pink and flushed, bridesmaid dress wrinkled, clutching Gina's bridal bouquet to her breast. She'd been exhilarated when she'd caught it, although that had really been because Pam, towards whom the bouquet had flown, quickly knocked it into the path of Pauline's eager hands, knowing the pleasure it would bring her friend.

Eventually, as people bade their goodbyes and drifted off, only a core few were left, slow dancing to the DJ's choice of end-of night songs, his signal that the party was over.

Stella and Rick rocked gently, with Gerta nodding off in Rick's arms between them, smiling into each other's eyes and at their child.

Grazja was dancing with Frank, and Elliot with Tim. Pam and Ray said their goodbyes to Gina and George, Pam kissing Gina on the cheek.'

Dan had long since departed with Bing, after Bing had started making amorous advances to Princess Alys.

Alys was snoozing on her cushion, which she had deigned to share with Ginger Rogers, much to Tim and Elliot's amazement.

'We'll have to have Ginger round some time,' Elliot told Gina. 'It'll be nice for Alys to have a friend.'

'Last dance folks,' the DJ announced.

George made a smart bow to Gina, opening his arms to her. 'May I have the honour of this dance, Mrs Wentworth,' he said.

Gina stepped into his embrace, sighing.

'Happy my love?' George asked.

'Never thought I'd be this happy,' Gina said. 'It's been a perfect day.'

THE END *

* If you want to know more about the events of Christmas Eve that are rather mysteriously referred to in this book, you can read about them in the short story **Merry Xmas Mapton** (which I wrote some time before Mapton Wedding Daze).

Review Request

Thank you for reading Mapton Wedding Daze. If you enjoyed this book (or even if you didn't) please visit the site where you purchased it and write a brief review. Your feedback is important to me and will help other readers decide whether to read the book too.

About the Author

Sam Maxfield is an author who writes about the funny things people do and say. She thinks fiction should be able to make you laugh and cry - sometimes at the same time.

Before writing the comic Mapton-on-Sea series, Sam taught English literature for many years. If teaching in FE doesn't make you see the funny side of life, little will. The novel Mapton on Sea (originally published as The Last Resort) was longlisted for Mslexia's Best Women's Fiction prize and led to Sam's life being taken over by the slightly insane fictional characters of Mapton. There is another Mapton novel currently underway and a number of stories brewing.

You can find all the Mapton stories, and other books by Sam at https://www.amazon.com/author/sammaxfield

Printed in Great Britain
by Amazon